The Envoy

A civilization of aliens called Homakuwa exists under the seas and has now chosen to reveal itself to the surface world. The world is in an era of unprecedented peace partially due to a single government, the Unified World Government (UWG). In addition, a new Prophet has appeared who brings a message of tolerance and non-judgment. Rather than conflict with existing religions, he has absorbed them into Faithism.

Not everyone is ready to embrace this new religion or the UWG, and plots against them turn into active conflict. The alien civilization, actually native to Earth, is caught in the middle, condemned and feared for their ability to genetically manipulate and create life as the surface civilization engineers and builds tools and machines.

The alien civilization creates beings adaptable to the environment of outer space enabling expansion to a number of habitats orbiting the Earth, as well as on the moon. In the midst of the conflicts on Earth, an asteroid hurtles into the Solar System breaking up and heading toward Earth. Under the threat of total destruction Homakuwa dispatches one of its citizens to intercept the incoming meteoroids to divert them. The surface world follows up with additional interceptors. But only the largest and most dangerous objects can be diverted.

A number of smaller meteorites strike the Earth resulting in Impact Winter, almost destroying civilization. The Collective mind of Homakuwa, the remaining surface world survivors and the Prophet struggle to rebuild, while Homakuwa begins to expand their society. As they do so, they evolve into a new species.

The Envoy continues the fast-paced character-driven and realistic future portrayed in Clayton's first book, *Sea Species.* This theme seemed familiar, and then I realized it is Noah's ark and the coming of Christ combined in a secularized version. This future also illustrates that just as the dinosaurs and millions of other species were doomed by catastrophic events on Earth, so could be humankind. *The Envoy* is thought provoking and not to be missed. What evolutionary step will the third book cover?
Robyn Lester, Author and Editor

I just finished *The Envoy*. Great book! In this character driven story, the portrayal of politicians shows how those in charge use the system to seek any advantage and stay in power. The catastrophe that befalls Earth is both believable and disheartening. Being a product of our times, I keep looking for someone within Homakuwa to say "ENOUGH!" and take over the world and save the humans. As is rightly shown, that would lead to rebellion and more chaos than is already in our lives.
Robert Koerner

R. L. Clayton astounds us yet again with another view of the future in *The Envoy*. In his first volume of The Evolution River Series, *Sea Species,* he took us through the birth of a new species on Earth and the interaction with humans. Two generations later in *The Envoy*, humankind is now the species left behind, and the new species, Homakuwa, evolves again to do what is necessary to survive. This is

truly an epic journey through evolution with a unique slant couched in reality and metaphysics. The teaser for the third volume has me on the edge of my seat.
T. Vonn

"_**The Envoy**_ by R.L. Clayton, the second installment in the _**Evolution River Series**_ trilogy, takes readers on an unexpected journey. The non-human civilization called Homakuwa rejoins humanity after 80 years of separation. During this time, Homakuwa developed a synergistic living environment and continued to genetically alter their citizens to create thriving cities throughout the oceans of the world. They re-emerge to rejoin the human race where a Unified World Government (UWG) oversees the citizens of the surface world, and many of the world's beliefs have been absorbed into a single world religion. Faithism creates a sense of peace and tolerance among the once warring nations of the world. But some seek to control or destroy Faithism, the scientific advances Homakuwa has achieved, and the UWG using technology and economics to win their war of domination. Get ready for a surprise ending as a twist of fate threatens to destroy all of Earth's civilization, and Homakuwa evolves into a new species. What will happen next and where will this evolutionary path take this new species as they continue their journey into the universe? It leaves me eagerly awaiting the third volume."

Katharine Nelson, Author and Arizona Community Connection Magazine, Publisher

ACKNOWLEDGEMENTS

Terry Vonn, you've stuck with me through both of these volumes and more. I know it has been hard work for you. In your intensely busy life, it takes away from your own time to write. Thank you, and I'm ready to work on your writing. Your continued support keeps me going.

Katharine Nelson has continued to work with me on top of her own work load and family. You input continues to be invaluable, making me a better writer. Thank you Katharine.

Alexis Powers, you continue to make my writing better, Thank you

Thanks to Steve Linebaugh (artist_stevel@tx.rr.com) for the cover art, the help with the web site, evolutionriver.com and the artwork on it. Good job and great patience with me! Volume 3 awaits, and I have some others in the works

THE ENVOY

Why rewrite The Envoy? I've learned so much since I first wrote this in large part due to those I've met in the writing community. Thank you. Though the story is the same, it's better now.

This book contains an excerpt from the forthcoming Volume 3 of the Evolution River Saga by R. L. Clayton. This excerpt has been set for this edition only and may not reflect the final content of the forthcoming edition

THE ENVOY

Second Volume in the Evolution River Series,

The Future History of Man's Evolution

By R. L. Clayton

Prologue

Kent Ronald Carson–known as Kit–fought the wheel as the Davidson 45 crested the twenty-five foot wave, and the mainsail caught the full force of the wind. They had stopped at Pitcairn Island to resupply and spend a little time on dry land before the one-thousand-two-hundred mile trip to Easter Island. From there they would stop at Sala Y Gomez Island before the crossing to Chile. Two days ago their satellite weather report had shown the large storm coming up out of the south. It looked like they could bear slightly northward to skirt the edge. Once past the storm, they would head southeast for Valparaiso, Chile. Yesterday their radar had shown a change in the storm's path, and now they were bearing due north trying to avoid being caught directly in its path.

The boat heeled sharply in the stiff wind causing Kit to slightly ease the mainsail. They had already reduced the sail by taking one reef. As he contemplated taking another, from the mast his wife, Susan sent him a questioning look. She had the same thought. Catching his nod, she yelled below for Dave to come up to help. Kit headed into the wind and eased the main, and Dave and Susan hauled it down to the next reefing point to secure it. If the wind continued to build, they would have to change to a storm sail. As they came back to the cockpit, Kit nodded his thanks, and Dave headed below to continue his rest period. He and his wife, Jackie, would begin their shift in two hours, and with this storm, their rest would be needed.

Kit and Susan hadn't been getting along since the start of the election campaign over a year ago. This trip was supposed to give them a chance to patch things together. Although it had helped, neither Kit nor Susan was sure that their marriage would last past the voyage. The four sailors had picked the boat up in Auckland after two weeks of seeing the wonders of the North and South Islands. The boat was Kit's acknowledgement of success, and it would be his escape before he began his second term as the junior senator from Idaho. The plan was to sail from New Zealand to Chile and then up the South American coast and through the Panama Canal. From there they would hug the eastern coast of Central America and Mexico until reaching Texas and then across the Gulf Coast to travel up the East Coast to the Potomac and finally to Washington DC. It was a trip liberally sprinkled with touristy things to do and see.

Kit gripped the wheel tightly as they crested another huge wave, and the strong gust caught the mainsail, causing the boat to heel sharply again despite the second reef. As he looked ahead, he could see the mountainous waves. The howling wind was blowing the tops off into mares' tails and mist. The sea was a dull gray-green, but ahead the water appeared to change to a bright green. The quick glimpse disappeared as they slid down the face of the wave into the trough. 'Did I really see that?' he thought. As the next wave lifted them, he anxiously looked forward, fascinated, as the sharp line of color seemed to glide over the face of the waves. Kit looked up hoping to see a hole in the leaden clouds letting a sunbeam peek through. No such luck. If anything, they were darker, seeming to press down on the small craft, as if trying to push it below the roiling water.

Could it be seaweed, broken off by the storm this far out to sea? Kit changed course to avoid it, but as they crested the next wave, it appeared in every direction but the one they came from. "Get the seaweed pole," he yelled to Susan. Her eyes widened as she saw the huge mass dead ahead. They were going to plow right into it. Quickly, she retrieved the pole and moved to the windward side, attaching her lifeline while hanging on to keep from sliding down the sharply tilting wet deck. It was important that she clear the entangling mass from the keel and the rudder to keep the boat controllable. No sooner did she have the pole over the side than the boat slowed as if it hit a mud wall. The motion threw her forward, and the boat yawed to one side. As the next wave lifted them, the wind caught them full abeam. The boat would normally heel to spill the wind, but the seaweed held it vertical, and the full force strained the mainsail and mast. Kit tried to release the mainsheet to spill the wind, but before he could reach the cleat, he heard the sharp twang as one of the stays let go. By this time, they were in the trough of the next wave and somewhat protected from the full force of the wind. Things would happen quickly when the wind caught them again.

Frantic, he yelled for Dave and Jackie to get on deck. As they came through the hatch, the boat tilted and rose on the next wave. The boat had slued about so that the wind was behind them, and this time the wind caught the mainsail on the lee side, snapping it across the deck. Susan looked up from the kelp pole in time to see the boom a second before it smacked her like a steam locomotive. The sickening sound was louder than the howling wind. Her limp form disappeared over the side.

Dave raced to the taut lifeline but the swinging boom prevented him from doing anything but ducking. With the wind behind the boat it rose again and nosed over the wave crest being driven down the face of the wave like a screaming jet. As the stern came out of the water Kit realized that they might flip end over end–pitch-pole–or submerge the nose in the trough. They were riding the face of the wave, and when Dave again tried to retrieve Susan's lifeline, it came up freely in his hands–broken. Stricken, he looked over the side and saw Susan's inert form, buoyed by the life jacket but face down with the boat swiftly moving away. Without hesitation, Dave went over the side to rescue Susan.

The boat raced down the face of the wave nosing into the trough. As water burst over the bow and flooded the deck, the forward hatch came undogged and opened. Jackie tried to close it, but it was too late. Seawater poured through and flooded the cabin. The boat became heavier, and as it rose on the next wave, the wind caught it again and it slued, trying to heel, but it was prevented by the seaweed mass and the water-filled cabin. The boat was low in the water as the sea flooded across the gunnels. With a twang, another stay let go, and the mast folded up over the side. Jackie screamed as she slid overboard. Kit looked up at the next wave as it roared toward him. When it hit, the boat rolled, and he flew overboard. Terrified, he watched as the overturning boat blotted out the sky in slow motion coming down toward him. When he put his hands up to stop it, something pulled him down into the water. Everything turned seawater green before blackness took over.

PART 1

OCEALLA RESCUE AND REUNION

Chapter 1

Kit struggled up from the depths of darkness. Gradually his awareness of himself grew. He had legs, arms, eyes. He opened his eyes, but then blinked hard to be sure they were open. A dim green light was apparent, but it was like looking into a soft fog–impossible to get any perception. When he tried to move his arms and legs, they were trapped in honey, hardly moving at all. With effort, he turned his head, but was not sure that it had moved. Something pushed against his legs, and he fought against it, but it was like pushing against a water-bed, it just gave and pushed back. He felt liquid surrounding his face as if he were drowning, but blackness came up and swallowed him before he could do or think anything more.

Unaware of how much time had passed, Kit gradually awoke. This time his awareness came more quickly. Again Kit opened his eyes. The amorphous green glow was there, but something moved, and an object came into his field of vision.

As his eyes slowly focused, the object became a face, a pretty dark face with striking green eyes peering at him with concern. "Don't try to talk. Just blink your eyes if you understand."

Kit tried to speak, but his mouth was full of goo, and he couldn't make a sound. He blinked.

"I'm Leticia Gardner, and you're in a medical facility. You had a close call, but we were able to get to you in time. Your friends are here too, though not in as good shape as you. Do you understand?"

Kit could not speak around the thick liquid in his mouth and then gave up and blinked again.

"You've been in one of our medical repair cells for more than a week. It will take care of you until we can talk again. You relax and let it take over." Kit felt pressure against his arms and legs, and then darkness again surrounded him.

Leticia looked carefully at Kit. Another few days in the cell, and he would be ready to start moving around on his own. The thick bubbly liquid in the softly rounded tank rose and submerged him. The currents in the cell moved his body in an intricate exercise routine, and she watched his chest move as he breathed in the super-oxygenated solution. She turned and walked out of the dimly lit room, a worried crease on her brow. She wasn't worried about his healing. The med cell did that. She was worried about what to do with him afterward. He would emerge into a world that had been hidden from the surface world–one that was unknown and needed to remain so. What would they do with him and his companions? How would they answer his questions about where he was and who they were?

As she moved toward the glowing wall, an opening formed, allowing her to enter a room with several people. In the dim light, it was difficult to make out the forms sitting on softly molded chairs. Around their necks, each wore a collar, like a neck pillow. This room was like a flattened bubble. The unusual flooring was like a thick carpet–solid but not easy to walk on. In the center of the room was a raised platform containing a pool of water. In the pool were several figures: one a dolphin, another looked like the Creature from the Black Lagoon, and a third resembled a thick bodied squid with odd arms. All wore a similar collar.

Leticia walked toward the inert figure of a seemingly asleep tall honey-blonde woman. Her eyes opened and focused on Leticia as she neared. "He seems to be healing nicely. The med cells are working as well on our old brothers as they do on us. Why did you want me to awaken that one?"

Katharine Levey shook her head. She resembled Lauren Bacall, except her eyes radiated a depth of wisdom. "I sense something special. We can keep the others under until we figure out what to do with them."

Leticia nodded and watched Katharine's eyes defocus as she again moved into the realm of the Collective group sharing the control of their home. Behind Leticia, the floor rose to form a rounded stool. As she sat, it cocooned around her. She put one of the collars around her neck. The collar was warm, and the room disappeared as she entered the Collective and the organism that was their home. Everyone who lived here took their turn in the Collective and helped with the control and care of their habitat.

Looking out into the sea, Leticia was aware of all directions. Around her were hundreds of swimming creatures shaped like those in the pool. As a squid-like creature swam toward her, Leticia focused on the habitat skin creating an opening, and it swam through into a water-filled chamber. She formed a hole in the top with a wall extending up into an air-filled chamber above. Her eyes focused on the room with a new pool and creature inside. The other figures in the room were also looking at the newcomer. The squid put on a collar and words began to form in her mind, though no sound was made.

[Ship completely broken. Are other saved creatures humans?]

Leticia spoke silently. [Yes, they are humans and are healing well in our medical repair cells. One was already dead, so we can do nothing but harvest.]

[What now?] posed the creature as it looked at each of them. It was a sensation they had grown accustomed to, where they saw themselves through the creature's eyes and also their own, like looking into opposing mirrors and seeing repeated images. Though they couldn't actually read minds, they were able to receive transmitted thoughts and visuals, but the sender had to actively open those aspects of themselves to be shared within the Collective. There was still privacy for the individual, which they valued.

[We'll have to see. Perhaps it's time we joined the surface world,] thought Katharine.

[We should watch the surface world closely for a while and find out more,] said the Dahlfin. They all nodded. The Dahlfin looked like a normal dolphin with a slightly larger head, though it was anything but normal. Having been genetically modified, they were as intelligent as humans, equal citizens in this undersea world, and a partner in their society.

Chapter 2

Former President of the United States of America and the first former President of the United World Government, Ron Carson was mystified by the data scrolling down the screen in front of him. Asked to investigate problems showing up with the United World Government Education Division, he noted a discrepancy. The original programming in the educational curriculum for the Mideast school computers was different from what was showing up now. How could somebody get into the system to do that, and why had they made the changes?

A knock at the door by his housekeeper took him away from the computer. "Sir, Vice Admiral Brentwood and Dr. Ngami are here to see you."

"Please show them in, Jessica," he said, wondering what in the hell they were doing here.

Ron rose as they entered, motioning them to chairs facing his desk. "What can I do for you, gentlemen?" Ron asked.

"Sir," said Admiral Brentwood, "I'm afraid we have some bad news regarding your great-grandson, Kit. His boat is missing along with all hands. We've dispatched Search and Rescue, but the cyclone is making the search very difficult."

The stab of pain in his heart nearly caused it to stop. Ron Carson grabbed his chest in reaction. Dr. Ngami looked at him in alarm, rose quickly, and came around the desk. A stethoscope magically appeared on his chest. The beat was strong. Ron waved him away. "Kit lost at sea. How could this happen He is such a good sailor. Has the search turned up anything?"

"No sir. We've got everything in the air we can under the conditions but it is pretty bad. We've deployed several ships from the Pacific Fleet to the area to aid in the mission. The closest carrier group is steaming in that direction, and we're using air refueling to keep the search going around the clock. So far there's been no sign. No wreckage, no emergency beacons, they've completely disappeared," said Vice Admiral Brentwood.

"Thanks, Jess, I appreciate the efforts. I couldn't ask for better support. Have you contacted his father?"

"Yes sir. He and his wife arrive here today."

Ron sat up. His spirit had flown. The anomalies in the backup record of the Government Computer System were forgotten. His mind was numb.

"I'm okay," he said to them, waving them back. "There's nothing you can do for me. I just need to be alone for a while."

Shakily, he rose and headed for the enclosed solar patio. The sun glinted in a blinding glare off the snow-covered land outside. The glass room was slightly chilly. He watched as the Admiral and his doctor drove down the lane toward the country road. Dismayed, he sat in his favorite chair, feeling it begin to heat under his weight. Beyond the glass, he looked out to the endless horizon, the crystal blue sky sharply meeting the white land.

Jessica appeared at the door. "Would you like some tea, sir?"

"Please." She turned. How could he have let Kit take that trip? They all knew the danger, but Kit had been so convincing; it was what he and Susan needed, and he could handle it. Kit worked hard to minimize the risk and Ron had let himself be convinced. He sat staring as his brain shut down. The yawning chasm in his heart opened, and he seemed to fall in. A prayer formed in his mind that his great-grandson would be found. He didn't even notice Jessica as she put the steaming cup next to him. When he finally reached for it, it had grown cold, and the sky was dark.

***

Consciousness flowed back into Kit quickly. The room came into focus despite the disorienting featureless walls. Hearing a sound to his side, he turned his head slowly, roiling the viscous liquid he floated in. The pretty dark woman appeared, moving toward him as the liquid was sucked away. "Are you feeling better?" she asked.

He coughed up the goo.

"That's it, cough it out."

He nodded, coughed again, and then spoke in a high voice. "I'm much better," surprised that it was easy to speak, but the high timber of his voice wasn't his.

"It's the atmosphere," said Leticia. "It distorts your voice. We have to do that to adjust to the pressure."

"Who are you?" Kit asked, again coughing.

"I'm Leticia Gardner. You're in a medical facility. Your boat sank in the storm, and we were able to rescue you and your crewmates. Do you remember any of it?"

Kit closed his eyes, and the scene replayed itself. "Is my wife all right?" he asked.

Shaking her head, Leticia answered, "One of the women was dead when we got to her. There was nothing we could do. Her head was crushed."

He felt a pain in his chest, knowing at once it was Susan. "What about my friends?"

"They are healing nicely," Leticia said simply. "Want to sit up?"

Kit took stock of himself for a minute. "Yes."

"Just think about it," said Leticia. He did, and the vat slowly changed shape until he was sitting in a lounge chair. The liquid didn't drain, but seemed to be absorbed. His eyes opened wide in amazement–not understanding what had happened or where he was.

"The healing cell senses you and your thoughts and accommodates your needs," she said. He looked down and saw that the chair had created a band across his lap to keep his modesty intact. He hadn't even consciously thought about it.

"We have a lot here that you will find unfamiliar. This is a special place–different from your world–and it will seem strange to you."

Her use of the word 'world' struck a note within him. Had he been whisked away by aliens?

"Would you like to see more?"

The stunned Kit nodded. The chair moved beneath him toward the smooth wall. As they approached, an opening formed and the chair flowed through. Leticia followed. The room they entered had several people sitting or lying on raised parts of the floor. In the center of the room was a pool holding a dolphin and some other creatures. Kit blinked, his eyes not used to the dim lighting. The dolphin spoke in a high squeaky voice, clearly understandable. "I am Blue Streak. We understand you are healing nicely. We were concerned."

If Kit hadn't been sitting, he'd have fallen. Had he tumbled down the rabbit hole with Alice? Almost as soon as the shock jolted him, he felt his mind calm. Drugs? The talking dolphin didn't seem so strange after all. "I'm doing well," he said, realizing he meant it. "I'm not sure what to think about this," he said gesturing with his hand. "Where exactly am I? Am I on Earth?"

A stunningly beautiful blond clad in a long white robe rose, removed something from around her neck and walked toward him. "I'm Katharine

Levey," she said, holding out her hand. "Welcome to Ocealla."

Kit clasped her cool hand and looked into her eyes. He guessed her age to be about forty, but as her pale blue eyes held his, he wondered how someone so young could hold such wisdom in her eyes?

"Where is Ocealla?"

"We are on Earth–in the central southern Pacific about two-hundred feet below the surface."

Kit felt momentarily anxious, then, again, calmer. "Is this some sort of submarine?"

"Yes, though not like any you've ever seen. This is not a ship as you think of one; it is our home, but it is more than that. It's an organism we are all part of. Rather than try to explain further, let us show you. This," she said gesturing around the room, "is what you would call the control room. We control our habitat with direct interaction."

Looking around the room, Kit could see no gauges, no meters, nothing that looked like it could control anything.

Katharine watched him attempt to absorb it before speaking again. "The collars we wear integrate us into a community mind–the Collective–where we act as the brain controlling our habitat. We don't have to be physically in the same room, but there are times when we want to talk outside of the connection. Our control is like your control over your body. In fact you could think of us as one organism. Let me show you more."

Again, she moved toward a wall, and it opened into another room. Kit's chair followed along with Leticia. This room was featureless, and as they moved toward the opposite wall, it changed from the typical opaque surface to a clear bubble. Looking out, Kit could see into the dark sea. Around the window were shadowy shapes. He saw the greenish silvery glow of the surface of the ocean high above them.

"We'll enhance the visual by modifying other senses for optical input." The sea brightened, and the indistinct shapes resolved into creatures like those in the pool. The window now showed a crystalline seascape around them. Visibility extended for a mile, and the sea was alive. "We're converting thermal, sonar, and other sensory input into a visual picture for you. This is our habitat. If you look up you can see the green of our sunlight collector bed. Your boat entered it and was ensnared. We harvest sunlight with plants—the same basis as life on the surface. That bed produces the food for our farms and oxygen to be used here in the habitat for us air breathers. As Kit looked up he could see the green layer, and just at the limit of his vision was the edge where the green gave way to a bright silvery mirror.

"How big is that?" he asked pointing up.

"We have more than ten square miles." Leticia added from behind him.

Mentally, Kit pictured the area. "How many of you are there?"

"With the Altereds, the Dahlfins and the Cons, about two-thousand of us live here." Katharine said. "We have about an equal split, though the Cons are growing in numbers. The Cons are the squid-like creatures, while the Dahlfins are the dolphins, and the aquatic manlike creatures are the Altereds."

"Where do you come from?" asked Kit slowly, staring out and then turning toward them.

Leticia looked at Katharine, then at Kit. "We come from here. We're native to Earth."

"That's impossible!" exclaimed Kit. "We would have known about you."

"Creatures like the Dahlfins and the Altereds are modifications of Earth's natural species. We tweaked dolphins by adding cognitive brain function, modifying their bodies to accommodate the changes. The Altereds were humans we modified to live in the sea. They have extra layers of fat to insulate them, webbed hands and feet, and gills, though they maintain lungs, so they can live outside of the water for short periods of time. Their eyes have been modified for better light gathering and to see a wider spectrum of light. They are amphibians.

"The Constructs are fully designed by us. We started with a squid shape and added arms, both typical and modified. We increased their sensory capability by adding infrared, large lenses and multiple eyes. They have 360 by 360 vision, sonar capacity, and the scent senses of a shark. Their whole body is a sensory organ. They are the most advanced of our citizens, fully designed for life under the sea."

"You did know about us once," added Leticia. "Have you ever heard of Kahchk Kihhim?"

"My great-grandfather told me a story about it when I was small," said Kit.

"Who is your great-grandfather?" asked Katharine.

"He's the former President of the United States, Ronald Carson."

Katharine stared at Leticia with wide eyes. Both of their mouths gaped open. After a moment, Leticia asked, "What did he tell you?"

Kit paused to collect his thoughts. "He told me what's in the history books. Kahchk Kihhim was a small group of rogue scientists who built a floating laboratory. They were experimenting with genetics in areas forbidden by international law. Some of their human experiments were quite grotesque, and during some nuclear experiments, they blew themselves up. Nothing was left." He looked at them.

"We are the residents of Kahchk Kihhim," said Katharine, "and that version of our history isn't quite correct."

"I'm certain that is the story released to the historians," said Leticia.

"We were a small community in Southern Arizona," continued Katharine. "When we were forced to leave the United States, we formed our own nation at sea, Kahchk Kihhim. Yes, we did genetic work forbidden by international law. We adapted ourselves to be a truly aquatic nation, becoming an integrated part of the sea. There was unrest and intrigue between Earth's nations then, and we were caught up in it."

"Our technology represented a threat to the international community," said Leticia. "Nations wanting to use us as a weapon for conquest tried to gain control. And we were feared by those recognizing the potential for us to usurp mankind as the dominant species on Earth."

Kit glanced from Leticia to Katharine, astounded by this story, this fairy tale.

"To protect ourselves," continued Leticia, "we threatened the existence of the human race, thus giving credence to their fears. Whether we would have carried out the threat didn't matter because it was a valid danger. We could not be allowed to exist, so our floating country was destroyed by nuclear missiles. As you can see," Leticia smiled, "we escaped."

"That can't be true!" exclaimed Kit. "My great-grandfather was there. He knew first hand!"

"We were there, too," said Leticia, "and we knew Ron Carson."

"That's impossible! My great-grandfather is well over a hundred years old. You're both not even forty."

"What's the average age of people now?" asked Leticia.

Kit thought for a minute. "About eighty-five."

"Your great-grandfather is much older than that, isn't he?" asked Leticia.

"He is," conceded Kit.

Katharine looked at him intently. "He visited us several times. The last time he asked us to assist him in his election campaign. Because he had aided us a lot over the years, we gave him the help he sought. Before the end, we gave him his longevity."

"It was during his second term, was the attempt to destroy us." Leticia's eyes were hard.

"You make it sound as if he knew of this," responded Kit. Katharine and Leticia said nothing. "Can we call him?" Kit asked.

"We can," said Leticia, "but we'll wait. By remaining unknown here, we've been safe and secure. We're not sure we want to join the surface world and its woes yet. Revealing our existence could jeopardize our safety and way of life."

Kit stared at her as the realization dawned that they were prisoners in this underwater world!

"You must understand our position," said Katharine. "The surface world tried to exterminate us.

"They would try again, if they knew about us," snapped Leticia.

"I don't accept that the United States tried to destroy you! Why would they?" cried Kit.

"They feared us," said Leticia.

"We need to learn a lot more about the surface world before we can decide whether to come out," said Katharine.

"What would it take to convince you?"

"I think we should start by talking with your great-grandfather," said Katharine.

Chapter 3

Stunned, Ronald Carson sat in his study, his body trembling, staring at the email he'd received. Anyone looking at him would think he was fifty years old. Usually he felt middle-aged, but he was three times that, and now he felt every year. He looked around the rich wood-paneled room, completely lost for a few seconds. Gradually, the shelves of books, the large desk, and bright sunlight from outside became familiar again.

He stared out of the window across the well-kept lawn of his home near Boise. The message was obviously some kind of hoax, somebody's idea of a sick joke. The address of the sender was his great-grandson's, but the name of the sender was someone else. It was impossible! She'd been dead for decades. He'd given the order to terminate her and her people. Everyday her face haunted him.

He closed his eyes and pictured Katharine Levey. She was a very beautiful woman, the leader of a race of mutants. She had frightening power. He shivered inside. With her civilization, she had extorted protection from the United States, while they established a floating nation in the Pacific Ocean.

They had used their abilities to manipulate life on the genetic level creating intelligent sea creatures and modifying themselves to live at sea. They were also capable of extending life by renewing DNA to youthful status. The body would then renew itself. That secret capability itself made them the greatest prize on Earth. These changes had ostracized them from the human race. They were aliens, not from outer space but home-grown.

Ron shook his head remembering that period of his presidency. The true magnitude of the threat they represented to the human race became apparent when he'd asked them for help to avoid a world war. They had applied their genetic skills to create viruses capable of killing or changing specific targets–biological guided missiles. These viruses had silently killed their enemies and changed the leadership of a world power to avert a nuclear war. Good deeds, but the potential for evil inherent in this power was terrifying and could doom the human race.

The decision to destroy them had been the hardest decision he had ever made. Only he and the Chinese Premier had understood the true threat to the human race. Together they had agreed to eliminate the geneticists. Neither could allow the other to possess the technology. They made the destruction look like an accident caused by the scientists at Kahchk Kihhim. Ron wiped a tear from his eyes. Murdering those people because of what they were capable of, not what they'd done tore at his soul.

With the death of the Chinese Premier, Ron was the only living person who knew the full story. The threat was gone, and the memory had faded, but the guilt continued to agonize him. It was the one act in his illustrious career that would condemn him to hell.

Again, he looked at the message before him.

Have good news for you regarding your great-grandson, Kit. Would like to come talk with you in person. I should be there by 8:30 a.m. today, Katharine Levey.

The loss of Kit had been devastating. For weeks he'd hounded the search agencies, but nothing was found. He and the boy had been so close. With Ron's coaching, he'd been elected the junior senator from Idaho.

Both he and Kit's father, Hal, had objected to Kit's idea of sailing from New Zealand, but Kit was as stubborn as both his father and Ron. Kit's future looked so bright in the US Senate, and Ron took great pride in watching him develop into a representative of the people. Kit's troubled marriage was a political problem in addition to being a personal problem. The plan to work it out during the voyage had been the only reason Ron and Hal had finally relented.

Nothing had been heard from Kit or the others in his crew since their ship had been lost despite an extensive search over thousands of square miles of ocean. The Carsons maintained a vigil until the search was called off. Ron had broken down during the memorial service, and had only recently managed to pull himself out of the depression that followed.

Now the misery came crashing back. There was a soft knock at his door. Jessica put her head through and said, "I'm sorry for the early hour, sir. There's a young lady, a Miss Katharine Levey, to see you. Should I show her in?" A stiff nod was all he could manage. The door swung open wide, and the image in his memory walked in. She hadn't changed a bit in all of these years. Standing before him in a simple cream-colored dress was the exact image he had carried in his mind for decades.

Awkwardly, he said, "That'll be all, Jessica. Thank you." He and Katharine stared at each other silently as the door closed behind her. Neither moved.

At last Katharine spoke. "May I sit down?" she asked.

"By all means," said the former president, recovering as he gestured to a large leather chair in front of his desk.

He wasn't ready to give up the protection offered by his desk yet, thought Katharine, reading in his face the shock from the message. Deliberately, she sent it from the taxi so he would not have time to think. He was obviously having trouble accepting the situation.

"It's been a long time," she started. Ron's mouth opened, but nothing came out. "We're fine, thank you. How have you been?" asked Katharine.

"I...I'm sorry," stammered Ron.

"Mr. President, we understood at the time what had to happen, and you did us two great favors. Your call alerted us, which gave us a way to disappear so we could survive. We thank you," said Katharine.

"It's just Ron now," he said. "I'm not sure I intended to do you favors at the time, and I've had to live with the knowledge that I'd murdered friends ever since."

"But you didn't," said Katharine, smiling. "I think you and I are more alike than you know, or perhaps leaders have to think along the same paths. We knew the Kahchk Kihhim civilization represented a threat to humankind in some people's eyes, and even though only you knew the secret extent of our abilities, it would have to come out eventually. When it did, our fate would be out of your hands. We would either be taken over and used, or we would be destroyed. Your action truly did save us."

"Thank you, Katharine, at least for trying to ease my pain," the former president said, rising from his chair. "Let's move over to the couch. This desk seems so formal." In the genteel gesture to assist her in standing, he held out his hand. She accepted it, rose and turned toward the leather-covered couch. She was well aware of Ron's eyes on her as she sat down. He sat a comfortable distance away. A pregnant moment of silence grew until Katharine spoke.

"Mr. Pres... Ron, we were able to rescue Kit and his friends from their sinking boat."

"Oh thank God, thank God!" he said, holding his heads in his hands. When he looked up, tears glistened in his eyes.

"Unfortunately, we arrived too late for his wife. Kit seems to be taking it very hard. I think he blames himself."

"When can I see him?"

"Ron, we have a problem. We're not sure… We don't know if…"

Ron's eyes narrowed. "You can just let them go! They're capable of keeping a secret. I can make sure of that." Ron leaned toward her to emphasize his words.

She held up her hand. "Perhaps it's past time to keep secrets. You've had a couple of generations to accustom people to the existence of other intelligent species. Would we be accepted now?"

"If you were just a new species, you'd be welcomed. But a species that builds lifeforms like we build different models of cars is another thing. Humans are still tool builders, mechanical tools and electronic tools. Life as a tool is only now becoming accepted. You will be hailed as evolutionary heroes by most, and damned as devils by a few," said the former president.

"Our safety has been in our anonymity. We have no defenses but that," said Katharine.

"We now have the United World Government. As a member, your safety could be assured."

"Can you give me some history? We didn't keep up at Ocealla. Ocealla is the name of our habitat."

"The nuclear war you helped prevent didn't happen, although another took place about a decade after you..." Ron grimaced, "disappeared. It was very limited because the rest of the world stepped in. The threat to the world community gave rise to a strong coalition of nations."

"Stronger than the United Nations?" asked Katharine.

"A truce was forced upon the combatants by the world. That was the start of the United World Government as a force to maintain peace." He smiled. "At the beginning, there were nations who refused to join. They were left alone until an issue came before the United World Government. They were forced to bring the issue before the World Court and abide by the decision. Before long, all nations were members."

"How does that work with the different forms of government?"

The United World Government doesn't dictate the form of government required, but it does guarantee basic human rights. The World Court enforces its decisions through the United World Peacekeeping Forces. The Court's decisions are not always in favor of those originating the complaints, and issues are extensively investigated."

"How do you keep political influence out of the decisions?" asked Katharine. She watched Ron's body language. He truly believed in this.

"Part of the rulings issued from the World Court come from artificial intelligence computers. They look at facts, instead of being swayed by bribes and underhanded trading. If the ruling government of a country suppresses its people and violates their human rights, the judgment may be in favor of the uprising, and they will be allowed to form a new government."

And what happens to to old government? wondered Katharine.

"This era of world peace has been unprecedented in mankind's history. In most parts of the world, citizens are much better off than they were in the past. My Presidency was instrumental in starting the United World Government, and I take great pride in the accomplishments. I felt honored when elected as the first President, and I served a full six year term during which I tried to keep mankind from being its own worst enemy."

Let's cut to the chase, thought Katharine. "Would we be allowed to join? How does that take place? What do we have to agree to?"

"There are a number of agreements signed by the members. Most of those have to do with non-aggression, human rights, weapons, those kinds of things. I don't think any of those would be a problem for you." He looked at her, his eyebrows up awaiting a reaction.

Katharine stared at him. "For us there are different issues. Could they redefine 'Human' to include us? What are the agreements regarding genetic development?" Had the human race matured enough to accept another native intelligent species on Earth?

Ron's brow furrowed. She could tell he was wrestling with the old questions along with new ones. "Genetic engineering has continued since I last saw you. There are areas regarding human genetic development that are banned, mostly out of fear. All of them have been violated in the decades since they were drawn up."

"What happens to the violators?"

"Complete human constructs and clones for replacement parts are forbidden. Enhanced genetic constructs are still banned. In your case, I think we can get them waived. The definition of 'Human' has been liberalized and is now more of a figure of speech. Presently, we are struggling with artificial intelligence. Where do those beings fall under the definition of human and what rights do they have? I believe you would be accepted," he said.

"The real concern is how to find out without risking our existence. Is there a way to put our toe in the water? Do we have to reveal ourselves first and risk our survival? Would you do that with the human race, Mr. President?" asked Katharine, purposely using the honorific. A troubled look crossed her face.

Ron looked down. "No. No, I couldn't take the risk. We'll have to find a way." He looked saddened and then looked intently into her eyes. "Is there a way I could see my great-grandson?"

"Right now you're the only human being who could visit him. How soon can you make arrangements to leave?"

"I need to change my schedule, so I could leave and not be missed. Even former presidents have some on-going duties." His face brightened. "Have you eaten breakfast?"

"Yes, but it was quite a while ago."

"I could take you out for an early lunch. Have you seen much of our world since you left? Where are you staying?" He stopped to gaze at her. Tears formed in his eyes.

"You don't know how wonderful it is to see you." The tears ran freely. "All my friends, my wife, they died decades ago. I had to watch them go, one after another. A long life without those you love, those you know, and even those you hate can be hell. It's a different kind of loneliness—one that seems unending."

Katharine watched his shoulders sag. She leaned over to put her arm around him. "We've had some who chose not to continue with an extended lifespan. I watched them struggle with the decision, and though it was theirs, and I had to agree with it, I miss them. That includes Robert McWilliams, my husband. Yes, he and I did marry and were happy for decades. I can't imagine losing everyone in my generation. Come visit us, reunite with your great-grandson. There are others there you'll know." Feeling his shoulders shake, she held him tighter.

Chapter 4

It took them only minutes to move Katharine's carry-bag into a guest bedroom. Ron had insisted, and it suited her too. She begged for an hour to freshen up, and as she lay on the bed with a collar around her neck, she closed her eyes and felt herself move into the Collective of Ocealla. The Collective mind was strong enough to draw her in regardless of the distance. Rich Lewis had voiced the opinion that the Collective operated in a different dimension. No one had been able to prove otherwise. As she played the scenes back for them, she could feel their agreement. They were as eager as she to learn more of the surface world from firsthand observation.

When she again opened her eyes, Ocealla saw what she did. The guest room was decorated in western style with Saltillo flooring and the walls painted a light tan. On one wall hung a Navajo blanket, similar to a small tapestry. On another wall was a Georgia O'Keeffe painting of the New Mexico countryside. A deep blue sky with some brilliant white clouds rose above two rounded hills. The view portrayed the tapering valley between the hills. At the narrow end, some sagebrush grew, hiding the end of the small canyon. It was hypnotic, soothing, and erotic. There was a soft tap at the door.

"Yes?" she said.

"Would you still like to go to lunch?" Ron asked from the other side of the door.

"I'll be out in a few minutes," Katharine said, carefully touching the soft collar which changed into a necklace of woven strands of ivory beads. In the walk-in closet, she stood before the full-length mirror. Her dress became a soft white sheath hanging loosely on her. When she touched it in several places, the living fabric responded to the image in her mind. At places it pulled in, shrinking smoothly until she had the fit she wanted, hugging her body without being tight. The shoulders were wide and loose, but it narrowed at her waist. The front was designed so that she did not need to wear a bra. Not happy with the result, she pulled the neckline down, and it turned into a vee neck.

The dress fit perfectly showing off her figure, revealing nothing. At the last minute, she changed the color to rose.

Many years ago they had developed this fabric. The fibers were spun of living strands, and it was woven into a cloth which responded to the wearer's thoughts and changed to fit the shape desired. Not only could the fabric be thick or thin, shear or opaque, it would catch the light and change color or seem to glow with a light of its own. In addition, the fabric was very tough, difficult to cut or penetrate. The fabric lived on the products of the body and skin: dead cells, moisture, oils etc., and thus cleaned the body. While worn, it was a part of the body, contributing to health.

Katharine ran her fingers through her hair pushing it into shape as it hung to her shoulders. She sat on the bed and slid her feet into the white shoes. They were a modification of the same fabric, but thicker. They molded themselves to fit. She changed them to pink. Before leaving, she took one last look in the mirror to make sure, grabbed her carry-bag, and was out the door.

As she entered the living room, Ron rose from his chair. She walked toward him watching his face.

Ron couldn't believe his eyes. There was something strange about her dress. One moment it seemed tight, revealing her shape beneath, the next it seemed to move apart from her, then become a part of her again–most enchanting. She held out her hand; he took it, and they turned toward the door as Jessica held it for them.

Outside waited a car with the doors open. Ron helped her in and walked around to get in. As the door closed, Ron said, "Airport, general aviation terminal." Without a driver, the car smoothly accelerated away from the house. "I could actually put an airstrip at the house, but all of the instrumentation for bad weather exists at the airport, along with the maintenance facility. There's this exquisite restaurant in Tahoe. Don't worry. We'll be sitting down to eat in about an hour. I hope that's soon enough. You're not too hungry are you?"

She looked a little stunned. "I'm just not used to thinking of distance in those terms. Our pace is much slower."

"I'm sorry if this bothers you. We can go somewhere closer or even eat at the house. I've become a pretty good cook. It's just that I have all of these nifty toys I hardly ever get to play with anymore. You're my chance to show them off."

"I'm in your hands," said Katharine, as he turned to look at the passing countryside. It was a gorgeous Spring day, with green hills accented by a cloudless blue sky. The traffic moved swiftly until they approached the city. As they neared the outskirts, the car entered a tunnel.

"This is the new highway system," said Ron. "The surface roads are for local access. We built this system for rapid travel around the city. The mining companies were contracted to do the tunneling, and we built the highway system with limited access. It reduces the danger of travel through populated areas, gives us more room above ground for development, and greatly speeds the flow of traffic."

Katharine watched the wide well-lit tunnel pass by. There were exit and entrance ramps angling upward out of sight. Traffic merged smoothly and moved swiftly. After what seemed like a short time, their car rose up an exit ramp into the sunlight, and the airport was in front of them. They bypassed the large commercial terminal and went to the smaller general aviation.

"This is one of the few advantages I get as an ex-official and consultant. I have my own plane," Ron said. The car slowed as it entered a hanger. Inside was a small sleek airplane with an American flag on the nose. Behind was another flag showing the Earth. As she looked, the globe appeared to rotate.

When the car stopped, the doors opened and Ron got out. He came to her door and held it. She took his hand and stepped out, smiling at the courtesy. In front of them, stairs slowly descended from the plane. On the nose was a name 'UW Gov 1.' When the stairs clicked into place, Ron gestured for her to go up into the cabin.

The plane had seating for eight in addition to the pilot and copilot seats. "Let's sit up front," said Ron. "It's just us for this trip." As they sat down, he showed her how to use the safety harness. The plane's door clicked shut behind them, and a woman's voice spoke.

"Welcome aboard Mr. President. What is our destination this morning?"

"Take us to Tahoe Regional Airport."

"Thank you, Mr. President. Flight time will be thirty eight minutes. Please confirm."

"Proceed," said Ron. The engines started, and a heads up display appeared on the windshield. For the first time, Katharine realized there were neither gauges nor any of the standard controls she had seen in airplane cockpits in the past. Ron put his hands into a pair of silvery gloves and then rested them on the arms of his chair. He noticed her look of puzzlement. "These controls are never needed but just in case."

The plane taxied out onto the apron and turned toward the end of the runway. There were two other private jets ahead of them, and as they waited, the roar from the departing planes shook the cockpit. Ron hadn't moved his hands from the armrests.

Suddenly, the craft accelerated, pressing her back into the soft seat. As the objects outside became a blur, the nose lifted, and the vibration of the wheels ceased. There was a thump as the landing gear retracted, a roar from the engines, and the plane accelerated, pointing almost straight up and leaving her stomach behind.

After only a few minutes the nose leveled, giving a view of something beside the clear blue sky. Far below was the brown and green of the western US as it transitioned from winter to spring. On the horizon to the west, snow-covered peaks poked up through the clouds. There was a slight bump and the noise of the engines ceased. "We just passed the speed of sound," Ron explained. "It'll be quiet until we start our descent. I wanted to re-introduce you to our civilization in Tahoe since it's been protected from the ravages of growth and is still a nice place."

The jet streaked through the morning sky with a quiet hiss as Katharine spoke, "Since we left the surface world, we've had no contact and not much monitoring. Fill me in on what the world of humans is like today."

Chapter 5

Ron took a deep breath. "The bio and cyber-attacks on the United States nearly destroyed us. We lost more than half of our population, much of our infrastructure and our position in the world. We pulled our country together."

"Ocealla knew of the attacks and counter attacks. It strengthened our resolve to remain hidden."

Ron nodded. "We had serious philosophical differences within our government, but the realization that these differences, rather than right and wrong, represented the strength of democracy. That led to a resurgence of tolerance. Tolerance took the venom away, and we've been able to make positive progress in uniting our people again."

"Tolerance was in short supply when we left," said Katharine.

"Make no mistake, the attacks changed the face of America as well as the entire civilized world.

Moving from complacent attitudes so prominent at the turn of the century, we reawakened to the work and attention that must accompany democracy to ensure a free society. This task became everyone's responsibility, not just a few and not delegated to someone else. At that point, terrorism and crime began to lose the grasp on society they held."

Ron felt Katharine's gaze. He hurried on.

"We had to minimize the threat from terrorism, so our efforts could go into bettering our lives and re-establishing the rights and freedoms given up or lost in the name of homeland security."

Katharine looked out the window at the land below. Through her collar, Homakuwa was listening and learning about the surface world. "How did you minimize that threat?"

"Terrorist organizations exist because weak societies have no other weapon to use against oppression by the strong. Wars can never be won with terrorism, but governments can fall. The frustration of futile resistance to overpowering influence is what gave rise to this unrest. The United States was a major source of this influence. So we started a long-term multi-phase program to re-establish the United States as a more self-reliant world power.

"Before the attacks, we were a nation in decline. The roots of our creation were lost in the glare of our success. It was the strength of our resource development, our innovation, our export of products and technology, and most of all, the individuality of our people which had put us in place as a world power. But we let that foundation crumble when we became a nation of importers and consumers. We depended on the resources of the rest of the world rather than maintaining an environment where individual citizens could create, build, and realize gain from their efforts. We exported technology, but that is something which can be copied. It's not a consumable, and it builds on itself."

"Technology was always a strong point with the US," agreed Katharine.

"Countries using technology became technological," continued Ron. "We needed to be in a position of a global exporter. What does any technological economy need? Energy! We needed to change the balance of trade. We needed to stop pouring money into unstable areas of the world, places where our enemies were born. Most of all, we needed a positive national focus. We had to exploit space and space technology where we would eventually have to go to grow."

"I would have thought that after the devastation within the United States space would be far down the list of priorities," noted Katharine.

"I had to make decisions. The nation needed a focus beyond ourselves. We were in the unique position of having extensive knowledge about space, plus the resources to develop space, but if we continued to decline, that window would pass, and our resources would go into merely sustaining ourselves. The Space Program of the 1960's showed what could happen when government moved into positive programs. I decided that was the type of program we needed again.

"I began the Orbiting Power System program. A string of geosynchronous satellites collects solar energy, converts it to microwaves, and beams the focused microwaves through lasers to collectors on Earth. The power density is about the same as you would receive standing in front of a backyard spotlight. It's not harmful to anything passing through it. It's also a very narrow and specific frequency, because the photovoltaic cells are very efficient in that same frequency range."

"You wanted to make the US energy self-sufficient."

"It started that way," said Ron. "We offer these energy cells to home owners to use on their roofs at a modest price. The lasers are all computer controlled and target those houses on the program. Each house collects more than three times the power the household needs, with excess feeding back into the grid. Each house becomes a generator. They pay us for all the power received and get a credit for what they don't use. We charge the distribution companies for power entering the grid for resale. We offered ownership shares in the plan, so it didn't take long for the electric power industry to realize they didn't want to compete against this project to provide energy."

"I see," said Katharine. "The money required to upgrade the older technology generating plants would be wasted when this clean energy was available.

"Right. "In North America, seventy percent of the electricity users are on this system, with the remote and undeveloped areas of Mexico and Canada having the highest percentage of users. Once electricity becomes available, they're not nearly as undeveloped as they once were."

"How could you pay for this?" asked Katharine.

"The US Government was in the position of owner/builder/operator. It was the type of investment that can only come from government. We began the program by selling bonds–like war bonds–that represented an investment in America. The response was overwhelming. People wanted to believe in a program for America, and they were eager to invest. Here was the offer of an investment, secured by the government, with a guaranteed return. That money was enough to get the program moving.

"The power generated is more than competitive with the old ways of generating power when the liabilities of pollution and carbon penalties are included. The OPS is a long-term project, and we are now providing domestic power and selling the excess overseas. No other nation had the knowledge, capital, and interest to start a program of this scope. Once established, it's difficult for them to initiate a similar program. Even the European Space Authority chooses to pay us to expand our system rather than initiate their own program. China has the wherewithal but has chosen expansion into other areas instead. Their space program is directed more at military uses."

"When we left the United States," said Katharine, "we saw a nation heading into the downward spiral of increasing dependency on government."

Ron sighed. "There's nothing harder than trying to pull entitlements away from those who believe they deserve them. Our debt was spiraling astronomically, and the size of government to manage all of the expenditures ballooned. The grand experiment of democracy was about to sink itself, and Congress was squabbling, like two birds fighting over a seed while the cat approaches."

"But then the attacks occurred," noted Katharine.

"Yeah, we had to start almost from scratch. The new members of Congress had a mandate and changed the elitist position past Congresses voted for themselves. Members of Congress now have the same Social Security program as everybody else, the same health care program. They are no longer a privileged class. Gone are the exorbitant retirement programs, along with the automatic pay raises. Campaign financing is completely transparent, and

PAC contributions are public record. Congress answers to the people again."

"I'm sorry such destruction is what it took for the change,"

"The needed change wasn't happening at the ballot box. Whether we ever got a single kilowatt of power or not, the program was a success in what it did to energize the country. We pulled together for a positive goal; we pushed people into education and productivity. But we did get kilowatts of power, clean power, and now it's more than we need. We have power to sell to a power starving world, enough to reverse the decades-old trade deficit. This new program put government resources into science, technology development, and education. We now allow heroes who are builders and thinkers. Our success puts us back into the position of exporter to the world."

"What about transportation and petroleum," asked Katharine.

"In North America, we moved to a hydrogen fuel based transportation energy system. That started when you gave us the hydrogen producing algae, but we moved ahead. Three things happened that pushed us forward and away from dependence on petroleum." Ron held up three fingers. He dropped one. "We found a catalyst that vastly improved the electrolysis of water to make the hydrogen." He dropped another finger. "We got the price of fuel cells into the affordable range." The last finger dropped. "We were able to use adsorption to safely and efficiently store hydrogen. Those three things moved the transportation industry from petroleum fuels."

"I bet you had quite a fight with the petroleum industry over that."

"Only by letting them operate the hydrogen system were we able to move ahead. We had to give some pretty healthy tax credits to get people to change, but it's been worth it. The oil industry lobbied mightily to stop us, but in the end, they joined us, seeing this as the secure future for themselves. Those political battles almost did me in. Gradually, these industries are taking over ownership and operation of the hydrogen algaculture. The government's been in the black for a number of years due to the income from energy sales and stock purchases."

"What about the terrorist war?" asked Katharine.

"Two things happened. As international banking became more transparent, the terrorist money started to dry up. More importantly, the United States is no longer seen as the Great Satan trying to influence politics in the region to protect petroleum interests. We are much less of a target. The frequency and magnitude of the attacks has fallen tremendously."

The nose of the plane dipped, signaling the beginning of the landing sequence. Ron again put his hands into the control gloves. He instinctively did this for safety, trusting himself as a pilot. Katharine looked out of the windows and watched the snow dotted countryside rise up to meet them. Below she could see hundreds of bubbles covering the landscape. "What are those?" she asked.

"Greenhouses. I'll tell you about them after I land."

He pointed out the window. "There's Reno."

Katharine looked, and below was a city. "Reno? How big is it?" she asked.

"The population is now about four million," said Ron.

"It doesn't seem that large."

"Another thing we've done is build more underground. We always knew it was more energy efficient, but Kihhim showed the housing development industry that it could also be attractive."

"Ron Emerald became one of the wealthiest men in the world by promoting underground developments as efficient, safe, and attractive. He's responsible for whole underground cities. Environmentally, there's much less strain, and areas that were covered by concrete and asphalt are again growing things."

Ron turned his attention to the airplane when a number of clicks and thumps sounded. The runway rushed to meet them. There was a solid thud, and the sound of the wheels on the tarmac. The plane steered itself toward a small hanger. The engine noise dropped and fell silent. He turned to her. "Welcome to Tahoe." He got up, opened the cockpit door, and lowered the steps. Katharine rose and took his offered hand, and they descended to the concrete floor.

A small car waited for them, and as they approached, a driver got out and held the door open for them. "Good morning, Mr. President. It's good to see you in Tahoe again."

"Good morning, Jack. It's nice to be back." Ron turned toward Katharine. "I'd like to introduce Ms. Katharine Levey." Katharine stepped forward and held out her hand. "This is Jack Laurer. He's watched out for me for a long time. When I retired to Boise, Jack decided to retire in Tahoe, and when I come here, he takes care of me again."

"Are you a friend of President Carson's?" asked Jack.

"Remember that it's Ron now, Jack. She's a friend from my first term as President of the US."

Jack's eyebrows rose. "That was way before my time. I didn't think I remembered you. You must have been a baby then," he said peering closely at her.

"We were all a lot younger then," said Katharine.

"It's been a long time since she's been in the US, so I thought I'd take her out to brunch and show her around. Where's good to go this time of day?"

"Well sir, do you want to eat light, or do you want something more substantial?"

Ron looked at Katharine. "I'm not used to eating much, so light is better."

"Climb in. I know just the place," smiled Jack.

Within a few minutes they were speeding along the road away from the airport. The little car was almost silent, with only the rush of air, the low whine of the tires, and a quiet hum from the electric motor. Jack was quite talkative, pointing out sites of interest along the way. The sky was crystal clear, the countryside was thickly forested, and the parking lot was invisible until they turned into it. There were only a few cars and a small building at the forest edge. The trees surrounded them completely.

Jack held the door for them as they got out. The air was crisp, almost cool. They walked toward the small building on a path through the trees. "Would you like to see the view first?" asked Ron.

"Sure," responded Katharine. Jack started down a branch off the path, and Katharine and Ron followed. Quite suddenly they came upon a small view point looking out over the sapphire deep blue of Lake Tahoe. The vista was on a high bluff that plunged straight down, and the view was breathtaking. The soaring peaks were snow-capped, and the emerald-green forest went right to the water's edge. She leaned over the rail and looked down.

Below them was a wooden railing surrounding a dining porch with umbrella-covered tables. Only two were occupied. "It's called the Aerie Restaurant," said Jack. "Best view in Tahoe."

"It's magnificent," said Katharine, realizing it had been a long time since she'd been able to view scenery like this. Only now did she miss it.

"Let's go get our table," said Ron. Katharine took a last look before turning to follow Jack back up the path. At the building, the elevator waited. They entered, the glass doors closed, and it descended into the darkness. Suddenly, before them was a cavern, with tastefully lit tables and a glass wall looking out at the lake. When the elevator door opened, a well-dressed gentleman waited.

"Good morning, Mr. President, Jack. Welcome back to The Aerie. Would you like to sit inside or outside?"

"Outside," said Ron.

"Inside," said Jack, at the same time. "I'm sorry. Habit. Outside will be fine, Albert."

Albert guided them through the glass doors to one of the umbrella-shaded tables. As they sat, a waitress approached with the menus. "Drinks?" she asked, looking at Katharine.

"Latte," Katharine said, looking at Ron. "It's been a long time since I've had one of those."

"I'll have the same," said Ron.

"Coffee black," said Jack.

"I guess you don't get much of that," said Ron. Katharine looked sharply at him, not comfortable revealing her background to others yet. Ron glanced at Jack, who seemed oblivious, looking at the view. Ron gave a quiet nod. Instead of saying anything, they looked silently at the lake, where a small sailboat silently danced across the water. Its white sail was in stark contrast to the deep blue of the lake but matched the reflection of the snow-capped peaks behind.

Ron got up. "I'm going to wash my hands," he said. Jack made to rise and follow, but Ron signaled for him to sit. He walked into the cavern, leaving Jack alone with Katharine.

"Are you any relation to the Katharine Levey of Kihhim and Kahchk Kihhim?" he asked. Katharine started. "Of course I'm tied into the central data bank. All agents have the implants," he said by way of explanation and letting her know he took his job seriously.

"I am," Katharine said simply. Jack waited for more, but Katharine remained mute.

Appraising her, looking for a threat, he brusquely inquired, "Perhaps you'd care to tell me why you have no id implant."

"Katharine didn't respond.   Jack's eyes narrowed as he continued to access the central bank. As he started to say something, the president returned.

"Are you grilling her, Jack?"

"Just doing my job, sir.

"Of course you are. All you need to know is that I vouch for her completely, and I want no further investigation of her."

"Sir…" Jack stammered.

"Period," said the president. Jack shrugged assent, but they all knew it wouldn't happen. Someone somewhere was already trying to find out who she was, as the data banks had everybody in them from the day they were born. As soon as they left the restaurant, her DNA would be collected and that avenue pursued.

"Now I'm glad that's decided," said Katharine, trying to lighten up. "Let's have a pleasant lunch."

Ron smiled at her. "The salmon salad is delicious which is what I usually have. The spinach omelet is also quite good. Everything's fresh and locally grown." The waitress returned with their drinks.

"Ready to order?" she asked. Katharine and Ron ordered the salmon salad. Jack had the omelet

"During the landing, we saw all of these greenhouses. What's happened with agriculture in the US?" inquired Katharine.

"Much of our agriculture is now in greenhouses. The technology developed in Kihhim has grown substantially. Once *genengineered* food was accepted, it became the agricultural norm. Kihhim had quite an influence on today, even though it existed for only a short time."

"What happened to DEM, the company that bought the rights to our technology?"

"When they became too powerful and too successful, the government stepped in to dissolve them. Over several years, China purchased many of the pieces. Within fifteen years of the purchase, they became the world's major food exporter and the number one superpower. They remain so today. If we hadn't taken steps to become the world's major supplier of energy, we'd have been left in the dust.

"Most of those farms you saw as we were landing are Chinese owned. Other agricultural conglomerates took over the technologies as soon as the patents ran out, but China continues to make advances in *genengineered* food production that keeps them ahead of everyone else."

"In other words, the day of the small family owned farm is gone," Katharine said sadly.

"They were gone long before Kihhim was sold. The quality of food available now is much better, and we no longer need the pesticides with controlled environment agriculture. Water use is also much more efficient," said Ron.

"What about the position of the United States as a world power?"

"Since we now supply much of the world's power, we are in a very strong position. The world powers now reside in blocs. The strongest blocs are China and the Asian Bloc, the European Bloc, the North American Bloc, the South American Bloc, and the Russian Bloc. These blocs represent the major economic powers and control the United World Government. The African Bloc and the Australian Bloc do not represent an economic power. And the Mideast Bloc lost much of its power when the world began to switch to clean energy."

"Are there still wars?"

"Conflicts are settled in World Court and enforced by the United World Government Police Forces. Pre-emptive strikes are a major tool. Peace between nations has now existed for decades, and democracy in various degrees is the dominant form of government throughout the world."

"What about the environment?"

"A series of international agreements were signed limiting production of greenhouse gases. These and controls of water and air quality are strictly enforced by the United World Government. Agricultural and forested nations produce excess oxygen, and they are paid by industrial nations who use it and have carbon debts. Businesses producing pollution pay by the ton. The rates are set by the amount and type they produce, linked to the cost to treat it. Businesses treating pollution are well paid. The economics have caused an explosion in the waste treatment industry. It's all monitored by the United World Government."

"That all sounds good. Does it work well?"

"Generally it does, but as with any large system, there are problems here and there. We have to stay vigilant."

Katharine felt Ocealla digesting all of this. There would surely be more questions later.

"To a bright new future for us," Ron offered as a toast.

They all touched mugs, each seeing different depths in the simple toast. Katharine first sniffed the latte. It was rich and full, and she hadn't tasted anything like it in a long time. She didn't really swallow it as much as let it coat her throat. Memories came back–things she hadn't thought about in years. Tears formed in her eyes, tears of things lost, people gone, loves she held in her memory. She turned away from the table looking at the view, so they couldn't see her eyes. She didn't dare speak, as her voice would betray her.

Thankfully, their food arrived, and they ate in silence. When they finished Ron asked "Where would you like to go? What would you like to do? I've been able to open my schedule for a day or two."

Katharine looked at him. "Could we go to Tucson?"

"We'll leave after lunch. Jack, would you arrange to accompany us?"

"I'll need to make a few calls," said Jack, rising and walking away.

"Jack could have accessed directly, but left us alone so we could talk. He really is a good guy, and he watches out for me. If he didn't go with us, someone else would be there–someone I may not trust as much. It's one of the prices I pay for my past, so I make things easy for them, and everybody stays a lot happier."

"I just want to have a look, to see some of the past, a sentimental and nostalgic journey," said Katharine. "I'd also like to be able to pass some of this on to those of us in Ocealla who have no familiarity with that history."

"We can pick up a camera, if you like."

"We won't need one," she responded.

Ron peered at her, puzzlement on his face.

Jack came back. "I've arranged to travel with you."

"Thanks, Jack," said Ron. He looked at Katharine. "Whenever you're ready."

As they walked through the restaurant to the elevator, Katharine took a last look through the glass wall at the scenery. The elevator door opened, and they entered. When the door opened again, they were at the parking lot.

Within thirty minutes, they were at the airport awaiting instructions for takeoff. As soon as Ron got the "Go Ahead" from the tower, the sleek little craft rolled forward, seeming to leap into the air. As they rose, Katharine watched the mountains drop away, and they turned south.

Chapter 6

Rhualla Hussein showed his ID to the guard who commented, "Mr. Hussein, you're the only one here this weekend. It is a holiday, and everybody else is celebrating. If I didn't have to work, I would be too."

At the secure gate he leaned forward so his iris could be scanned. The door clicked, and he entered–his entry being recorded. He had made a habit of working at the UWG computer security office on weekends knowing his presence would raise no alarms. At his office door, he entered a code to allow entry.

Seated at his workstation, he logged in to begin the arduous task of moving through the firewalls and passwords to gain access. At last the system opened. He inserted a flash drive, and it began doing the security checks that were his job. Confident the system was running well, he stood.

The records would show he spent four hours grinding through his normal workload.

Quietly he opened the door and peeked out. The hallway was still empty. Down the hall, he stopped in front of another secure door. One last look down the hall–it was still deserted. He entered another code, and this door opened. Later he would edit the record to show no entry here and no exit from his office. At his manager's workstation he logged on, knowing he would change that record later too.

Once he entered the system, he created the backdoor to allow him entry from a remote station. This done, he opened the pathways to access all levels of security when the time came, but he did not install any of the viruses now, afraid the monitor system might stumble across one. The chances were remote, but why take a chance, he thought.

Rhualla opened the Education section and followed the pathways to the Mideast Education section. As firewalls appeared before him, he entered the passwords painstakingly worked out over the last year. The basic history program opened before him. Placing his fingers on the keyboard, he smiled to himself and began to rewrite history.

Only minor changes were made. Subtlety must be my guide, he reminded himself. The change of a few words altered the tone and the context, painting the struggle of the Imams as heroic, while the control of the UWG as oppressive. Rhualla looked at the clock. Though it seemed only a few minutes had passed, he had been in the system for several hours. No wonder he was exhausted.

Carefully Rhualla backed out, covering his tracks, erasing the log-on for the computer and the door entries and exits.

Back at his workstation, he pulled out the flash drive and logged out.

Chapter 7

Awed by their beauty, Katharine watched the Rocky Mountains fall away as Ron spoke the destination to the flight computer and finished his checklist. With a roar, the plane slanted upward and headed southeast. When Katharine closed her eyes to doze off, Ron studied her for the first time since she had showed up at the ranch.

Amazingly, she hadn't aged at all. If anything, she seemed younger. When their paths crossed many years before, he had been attracted to her; and he felt she was to him. At the time, their positions eliminated any possibility anything would come of the attraction, but they had respected each other deeply. They understood the total loyalty and dedication each felt toward their respective countries.

In some ways, Ron had envied the challenge and adventure that building the nation of Kahchk Kihhim from nothing presented. When he had reviewed the record, as they utilized every avenue to maintain their independence, he held a grudging respect. That they were able to force the United

States of America to become their ally and protector was a monumental feat.

Kahchk Kihhim held many of the values which had been the basis that created the United States. Ron was saddened to admit that in comparison, so many of those values had been lost as the US grew. The balance between independence and self-reliance and caring for the citizens had swung too far toward government reliance and too far away from the self-reliant individual. Vivacity dragged into indolence, and in the end the country suffered, tilting into decline.

It had ripped his soul apart to realize the world couldn't accept Kahchk Kihhim. He thought he could, but this small nation represented a threat to humankind even more dire than the nuclear threat of the Cold War. Their existence could inevitably destroy humankind. In the end he had been the one to destroy it, along with a part of himself. Had humanity changed enough in the subsequent decades, so they could now coexist? Was the world big enough for both of them? The old doubts came back. Could two intelligent species live in this world together? The uncertainties he felt about his own species arose. Was he betraying mankind for his great-grandson?

His unseeing eyes looked out of the cockpit as the clouds flew by.

From the back seat, Jack watched Katharine. He was in direct contact with the Secret Service via electronic implants. They were still trying to identify Katharine Levey. She had to be a descendant of the Katharine Levey from Kihhim. That she had no identifying chip implanted was troubling. Every hospital implanted one at a baby's birth. Only those not born in a hospital were without. The chips gave everyone access to the data banks, to communications, to their accounts. It took the place of the old system based on Social Security Numbers, so holding a job without one was difficult. How did she survive without those? Perplexed, he called up history on Kihhim.

His direct link displayed a picture on the glasses he wore. The impersonal voice in his link narrated. "This is a video of two political prisoners who were detained to recover sensitive data about a rogue community called Kihhim. Kihhim had experimented in human genetic engineering, and just as the government was closing in, they disappeared. Only John Vance and Katharine Levey were captured. Four years later Kihhim reappeared as a floating nation declaring independence. John Vance and Katharine Levey were allowed to return to their friends on Kahchk Kihhim.

"The United States formed a pact to protect Kahchk Kihhim, but their relationship became strained when suspicions of bio-weapon use surfaced, and accusations of human bio-engineering were leveled. Ron Carson was the United States President who held the world at bay during the clamor for investigations and sanctions. In the end, Kahchk Kihhim blew up in a nuclear holocaust caused by its own experimentation with nuclear weapons."

Jack broke the connection and mused: Why did the United States form this pact with Kahchk Kihhim? How did a whole community escape arrest?

Katharine Levey was far from napping on the plane. The contact with Ocealla was strong. They had been able to establish a link with the collar—now appearing as a necklace. Those at Ocealla had enjoyed their virtual tour of the surface world, some for the first time. They had also been able to help her focus on those around her, and though she couldn't read minds, they all were quite aware of Jack's intentions. They would have to arrange for Katharine and Ron Carson's departure soon.

Sensing Ron watching her, Katharine felt his fear, realizing she would have to find a way to reassure him, convincing him humanity encompassed more than human beings. After that would come the monumental task of convincing the world her civilization represented no threat. They could live in harmony. If she were unable to persuade Ron, they stood no chance with the rest of the world. She relaxed and drew her attention inside herself, feeling she was back in Ocealla with her friends around her.

As the companionship of being part of a conscious whole again overtook her, a sense of warmth and security surrounded her. The skin of Ocealla moved as the water of the sea pressed in. It was her skin, and it was her senses forming the images both inside and outside as she merged smoothly into the Collective and questions started forming.

[Soon?]

[From Tucson we'll go to Puerto Peñasco. One day?] Katharine formed the words and her last memory of the small Mexican city on the Sea of Cortez. Even though their conscious minds were joined, she had to form and project ideas into images for the others to sense them. They could only get what was projected.

[Yes. We anticipated this short timeframe and have moved the necessary personnel into the area.] was the response. The image of Jack formed in her mind.

[I don't think he suspects we intend to leave so quickly. He may suspect we intend harm or kidnapping, but one step at a time. First, we must get to Mexico.] Quietly she settled in with the others. Ron's voice brought her back to the cabin of the small plane.

"We'll be landing at Ryan Field in a few minutes, and Jack's arranged for a car. Are you sure you want to go to Kihhim? It's not what you remember."

"I need to see it." What it is now will tell me a lot, she thought to herself. "Can we see it from the air before we land?"

Nodding, Ron spoke into his headset. The plane changed course and headed toward Kitt Peak, losing altitude as the mountain neared. There was another slight course change, and they were flying parallel to the Baboquivari Mountains. The plane slowed, and in a small valley ahead was a sharp reflection.

Her heart stopped for a second, and she projected everything she was experiencing, sharing it with Ocealla. Kihhim hadn't changed much–at least as she could see it. The glass-covered hillsides that were the greenhouses rose up out of unspoiled desert. The plane circled, and she could see figures moving inside, tending to the crops that supported the underground community.

As the shadow of the plane moved across one of the greenhouses, faces turned toward her, and some of them waved. Slowly returning the waves, she remembered doing this hundreds of times in her mind during the many years she'd been away. This was where it had all started. This is where they were born. Feeling like an adult returning to a childhood home, it pleased her that it hadn't changed much.

The plane circled again, and more faces looked up and more hands waved. The plane turned north toward Ryan Field. Within minutes, they were on the ground. Ryan Field was a general aviation field on the western edge of Tucson. The city had grown around it, but many of the buildings were underground. Ventilation and light gathering towers marked the large complexes, but the ground was desert with a grid-work of roads.

Ron taxied toward some hangers, and a figure stepped out into the light. Jack pointed and Ron taxied toward the open door. The brilliant sunlight was gone in an instant, and they parked in a space indicated by the man. Jack opened the door and lowered the stairway as Ron completed his shut down list. Always a gentleman, he took Katharine's arm to help her down the stairs and toward the white car, where Jack was holding the back door open for them.

It was an older model car, without the autopilot. Once she and Ron were in, Jack got behind the wheel, driving into the bright sunlight. In seconds, the car windows polarized to block out the glare. The access gate to Ryan Field passed behind them, and they were on the Ajo highway heading west toward Three Points.

Katharine watched the barren desert countryside flow past, bringing back memories. There was an ache of nostalgia as her mind drifted back, with visions of her life appearing. They were pleasant times: when she grew up, went to school, and lived with her father at Kihhim. These were things she hadn't thought of for a long time. Enjoying the memories, she felt some of the tension released.

The car turned off the highway and headed toward the mountains. The prominent granite dome of Baboquivari Peak towered in front of them. The Tohono O'Odham legends held that The People emerged from the Earth through this peak to inhabit the world which was their version of creation. This road that had been dirt when she lived here was now paved, but the countryside seemed much the same, unspoiled Sonoran desert. They rounded a corner, and the gatehouse appeared before them. Filled with emotion, she half expected to see Rico step out.

Instead, the gate opened automatically, and Jack drove through and toward the garage opening carved in the side of the low hill. Again, the brilliant sunlight disappeared suddenly. Once their eyes and the car windows adjusted, a pretty dark-haired woman directed them to a parking place. She walked over to the car as Jack jumped out to open the doors for them.

"Hi. I'm Maritza Lopez. Welcome to Kihhim," she said, holding out her hand.

"Katharine Levey," said Katharine. Maritza gave her a puzzled look and then turned as Ron and Jack introduced themselves. "Please follow me." She turned and headed through a door. As they entered the underground community, the roar of a waterfall could be heard.

"Please sign the visitor register," Maritza said, indicating the book on a desk. While Katharine signed, she continued, "I'm sort of the historian here, and your name is familiar. There was a Katharine Levey who was a resident here a long time ago," a question in her voice.

"We're related," said Katharine.

Maritza's eyes opened wide again, when Ron Carson signed the register. "We're honored to have you visit us, Mr. President," she said. She watched Jack sign but didn't recognize his name. "The visit request didn't give any names. Is this your first visit here?" she asked. Ron and Jack nodded. Katharine said nothing, as Maritza turned to lead them into the reception area.

A waterfall dominated the huge atrium. Sunlight streamed through the glass ceiling high overhead. Lush plants grew down the walls and from the balcony two floors above them. Cool air, pushed by the falling water caressed their faces.

"This is part of our air conditioning and water treatment system," Maritza said. "It's also quite pleasant to sit and watch." There were several people seated around the large room. Some of the people watched them—curiosity on their faces. Others ignored them.

Maritza spoke again. "Perhaps you'd like to join us for lunch in our cafeteria. Afterward I'll show you the greenhouses."

"We had brunch not long ago, but perhaps a little something to drink," said Katharine. She turned and started through a door before Maritza could even indicate which way to go.

"How did you know which door to use?" she asked.

Katharine shrugged. "I just guessed."

Maritza looked at her again, and Katharine stepped aside so she could lead the way. They walked down a short hallway, and Maritza held a double door open for them. The delicious odor of food wafted out to greet them. "Our food is all grown here," said Maritza, indicating the steaming trays. If you have any questions, please ask."

Katharine took a tray and started down the line. Most of the dishes were vegetables, but there were a few fish. The salads and fruit looked great, though she wasn't able to recognize some of the fruit. She chose a cup of vegetable soup, along with a glass of iced tea. Maritza nodded toward a table occupied by a woman.

As they placed their trays on the table, Maritza introduced them. "Barbara, I'd like you to meet our visitors. This is Katharine Levey, Ron Carson, and Jack Laurer. This is Barbara Boyer." They shook hands before taking their seats.

"Are you just visiting or looking to move in?" asked Barbara.

"We're just visiting," said Katharine.

Barbara turned to Ron Carson. "You look very familiar to me. Are you related to former President Ron Carson?"

"I'm him," said Ron.

Barbara sucked in her breath. "Oh my!" she said quietly. "I was just a child when you were elected to the World Government. You look so young!"

Ron smiled at her. He had heard that phrase much too often to feel anything. "Thank you. Good genes." They started eating, cutting off more conversation. Barbara ate slowly, watching the guests, obviously awed.

Katharine leaned close to Ron's ear. "How soon will you be able to arrange to leave to see Kit?" whispered Katharine.

"It should be possible in a few days. I'll know more by tomorrow," whispered Ron. "Jack trusts me, and I can get away from him if I have to, but he'll get fired if he loses me. I'd like to figure something out, but my great-grandson comes first."

The others at the table rose to bus the trays. "In a way, I find this depressing," said Katharine, looking about, "but also gratifying. It's depressing in that we're not here, but it's gratifying that much of what we created still continues for the betterment of mankind. The synergy with nature is still here, though to me it seems overpopulated but I sometimes think the world is overpopulated. It's certainly better than what was happening when we started this."

"With what I know of you and the people of Kahchk Kihhim, I can see how this was your birthplace," said Ron. "It was our nature not to trust you then, but we feel differently now."

Katharine looked at him for a long moment, saying nothing.

"Can we go to Puerto Peñasco?" she asked. "I'd like to swim in the ocean there again."

Chapter 8

World Purchase of Mideast Oil Falls Again, Hits Historic Low

The production of oil in the Mideast has hit record lows as the demand for petroleum has fallen off. The use of power from the Orbiting Power System (OPS) and the increased use of electric power for transportation have displaced the need for oil. With the loss of demand, the price has fallen to levels not seen since 1978. When oil prices are valued using the US dollar standard, the picture is indeed bleak, as the dollar has strengthened tremendously with world energy sales from the OPS.

Today, China is the largest consumer of oil, purchasing sixty percent of world production. China remains on the fossil fuel based energy system, refusing to participate in the emission reduction programs agreed to by most of the world.

The loss of oil revenue from those nations mainly dependent on petroleum production has greatly reduced their standard of living. This petroleum recession has given rise to high unemployment and unrest. The United World Government continues to monitor those regions. Global Petroleum News

Mideast Report

Summation: Report to the UWG on the status of the Mideast

The Western Nations' support of the democratic uprisings early in the century in the Mideast known as "The Arab Spring" continues to have disquieting consequences. The elected governments that replaced the brutal dictatorial regimes are increasingly becoming fundamental Islamic. In the elections held after the revolts, the most organized groups were Muslims, and they dominated those elections. Today, those moderate governments are being replaced by radical Islamic sects. The old tyranny is being replaced by a new one of fundamentalist Islam. Tribalism is again rising, and battles between the sects are becoming increasingly vicious. The United World Government is carefully monitoring the situation. Through the United World Government human rights have been maintained. In many cases, these rights are in conflict with conservative Muslim law.

As a nuclear power, Iran is of great concern. Now the dominant military power in the Mideast, they have been careful to export their influence through religion and thus avoid a confrontation with the UWG. Even with the blanket of protection the UWG maintains over Israel, there is still concern. The territories given back to the Arabs in that agreement are quite peaceful, but increasing infiltration, particularly in Palestine, has established a hostile presence. Israel's previous policy of pre-emptive strikes and land

*buffers are no longer allowed with the UWG troops
maintaining the borders and security.*

Imam Abayat Hussein led the normal prayers,
while silently praying for Allah to give them
strength for the upcoming battle. The new struggle
for power lay with the spread of Islam, and the
battlefronts would be those countries with growing
Muslim populations. The governments of countries
like Pakistan and Indonesia had long been in
Muslim control as was much of Africa. Europe was
a bigger challenge, because those Christian
governments were not accepting the growing
Muslim influence.

The battle was firmly for the souls of the
people. The UWG was supposed to be neutral, but
it had stolen their children from the path of Islam
with the forced education and exposure to Western
ways. Imams and followers tried and convicted
under local laws served prison sentences when they
carried out Islamic law. These actions further
isolated Muslims from the locals and built deep
animosity. When called upon, these followers
would rise up, but another factor had intruded.

A new Prophet had appeared who turned their
world upside down. At first the true believers had

fought this infidel, but one-by-one they converted, thus changing the faith. Strict adherence to Islamic teaching was waning. The mosques were filled with new believers, who were tolerant of other religions and non-believers. The time for a resurgence of true Islam was running out. They needed to move before their numbers shrank further. Now was the time for the meeting with the Ayatollah and the Foundation.

***

Ayatollah Aiassi Komini carefully observed the others in the lecture hall as they watched the recording of the meeting between the false Prophet and the Foundation's most loyal Imam. He had seen it enough times that it was etched into his brain. The odd mix had united to fight this scourge known as the Prophet, for they had all suffered losses.

The Ayatollah spoke. "I stood before the false Prophet once, and I know the power of his mind. Only by fleeing his presence was I able to escape falling under his enchantment." He shuddered when he remembered. "At first I felt a warm glow enveloping me. The devil spoke to me, inviting me to join him. It would have been so easy to stay and fall under that spell. Alas, as you can see, all of my brothers did," he said, pointing to the video. "They proclaim his way leads to peace and life in heaven. But I saw this path leading to subjugation and eternal hell. I ran in terror.

"I know it has been the same for you. The Prophet steals our priests and followers to build his own religion called the Faithists. They fall under his spell and no longer listen to us. Whatever gospel we use, the Koran, the Bible, the Torah, or the others given to us as the rules of our beliefs, the Prophet convinces our followers to talk to God directly. He uses the power of his mind to delude them into believing they don't need us to guide them."

He looked at the gathering of religious leaders for the old faiths.

"We must build our forces to resist this Prophet. Our recruiting was easy at first, but it is becoming harder as the number of our followers shrinks until we now know each and every one. Unless we can regain worshippers, we will die out. Without the internet, we would not have found each other, and our struggle as individual religions cannot survive. We must unite.

"We have a unique group representing the remaining major religions of the world: Christian,

Protestant, Catholic, Jewish, Hindu, Buddhism, and Islam. All of us are resisting the spell of this devil Prophet. Only by keeping the goal of defeating this menace in sight and setting our different beliefs aside, will we be able to regain our power. Make no mistake. That is what this is about, the power of our leadership over our followers.

"It is we who civilized the world, bringing law and order. Without our organizations, the people will be lost and us with them. We will all become interesting topics in history books of failed religions and old gods.

"We have been able to overcome our differences and conflicts by keeping our goal in sight. It is critical we do nothing to cast light on this alliance. We must stay underground and plan how to fight the menace." The heads of the other leaders nodded in agreement.

"A number of times we have seen our followers kill the Prophet, and yet another appears. He has been poisoned, shot, and blown up. We have tried stabbing and strangling, but when our agents get close, they are unable to proceed, and give up their secrets. Still, there have not been retaliations. Instead more Prophets show up at our centers of worship, and those followers are lost.

"Once lost, we can have no further contact, or like a plague, they spread the change. The question we so often pose to ourselves: 'Where in the world can we go that will allow us to practice our religions in the old ways, those of the Koran, the Bible, the Torah, and the other teachings?' The United World Government now dictates what we must teach our children and how we live. We all face the same annihilation."

He looked out over the representatives of the Foundation: priests, imams, lamas, pastors, and rabbis, those who read and interpreted the holy scriptures of their religion and taught and directed their followers. Without that hierarchy, each organization would fall into disorder and the religion lost. A religion with only one follower isn't a religion, but merely a belief.

"The tactic used by the Prophet is the same with all of us. He enters our place of worship as just another believer. Slowly at first there is a mere tickle in the minds of the people, but it grows until his presence fills the room. The clergy are equally susceptible, and all fall under his spell. Prayers change, sermons change, interpretations of the scriptures change. Thus the followers take the new path, leaving the old ways behind.

"The religious scholars still read their scriptures, but from a different perspective. The followers are encouraged to read them also, but the interpretations are from the Prophet, who is in their mind. Gradually the people drop from the congregation and worship on their own. The people gain faith, but the religions lose their power. Church leaders preach to themselves.

"We have argued for days, first among ourselves, then all of our groups together about how to attack this hideous abomination. Killing the Prophet only results in stronger belief in him when he reappears. It is a disastrous situation, like trying to fight a fog.

"WE NEED CHAOS! If the people have chaos in their lives, they will flee to the old sanctuaries and come back to the old religions. It is our last hope.

"We cannot simply resort to the terrorism of the past. That tactic may disrupt people's belief in their government to protect them, but it does not offer an alternative. A disruption in the main basis of UWG is what we have to bring about. Only without the oversight can we reestablish control over the people. I await your thoughts on this."

A lively discussion followed. Several offered interesting comments about other members–non religious–who were not fully satisfied with the policies and control of the UWG. Many of the old world leaders wanted to regain their power, but there was no unifying organization.

Aiassi smiled to himself. What an unholy alliance had been created with the world religions and the leaders of nations such as China and Korea, not to mention much of Africa. Could they ever agree to anything more than the ousting of the UWG? Or was that enough? How large would the coalition have to be to initiate a movement and attract other dissidents? How large an organized uprising would stand a chance of being successful?

This wasn't the first time he had asked himself these questions. The Foundation had already begun inquiries seeking to form an alliance of resistance. This uprising would be different, because in order to attract the number of followers needed for success, they would not be able to use religious fervor as a tool. This had to be founded on a purely political stage. He didn't feel good about their chances, because without the force of government to enlist followers, they would have to rely on other factors.

"As we have spoken, it is clear we must create economic strife and undermine the system of justice. We must create outrage at the failure of the system. The first part of the plan has been formulated and begun with a concentrated effort to hack into the computer system. The goal is not to crash it but to subtly corrupt it." He glanced at Rhualla.

"A succession of small changes are occurring, each of which on its own will not attract attention but as a whole will move the UWG away from control." The Ayatollah smiled at them. "It is much more satisfying to trick your opponent into giving you what you want than beat them up for it. It is also much more permanent.

"Our first efforts to gain access were directed toward the education computer system. Though there is a centralized computer system, the lessons are localized. That is where we have been successful. Very small changes have appeared in the lessons. The basics of math have not changed, but history has been altered. Social study lessons also have changed. Doing all of this without leaving any tracks has been a daunting task, and the Chinese have been of great assistance." The Chinese representative nodded acknowledgement.

Abayat motioned to his brother, Rhualla, that he was finished. As his few followers left in twos and threes, no words were spoken. They had studied the great UWG monitor system enough to know there were levels of oversight. The lowest was audio only, and key words and phrases triggered visual monitoring. Tracking systems would follow those who showed suspicious behavior. He had been diligent to remain invisible whenever he was with any of his brothers and sisters, not wanting to bring attention to them. He gave Rhualla a data cube to take to a courier, who would travel with it to the Imams. In a strange twist, the courier was a fundamentalist Christian.

Christianity was another religion sworn to defeat the UWG, who had stolen their children, and the Prophet who had stolen their religion. For now the alliance of the established religions was necessary. Of course, after the overthrow, the non believers must be destroyed.

***

France Institutes More Restrictions on Muslims

Despite the objections of Muslim leaders, the government of France has enacted a number of laws directly opposing Muslim law. These include a ban of the wearing of the burka in schools and public places.

Government identification cards for women must have photos taken without the veil in direct violation of Muslim law. Also enacted are laws requiring girls to attend public schools and forbidding the reading of the Koran in public. Demonstrations have resulted in violent clashes between protesters and police. Cars have been overturned, and shops set on fire as Muslim leaders decry these laws. Troops have been placed on alert after a government press release stating, "These actions will not be tolerated. Those responsible will be prosecuted to the full extent of the law." French police are detaining thousands of protesters in the soccer arena awaiting trial. A declaration of martial law is expected tonight. AP

***

Rhualla showed Abayat the headline he had printed out from the online news service. As Abayat read the article, he shook his head. France was only one of a number of countries enacting laws against Islam. It was the same old story, one he had lived with all his life, going back for generations.

He closed his eyes and remembered the stories his grandfather had told him. His great-great-grandfather had been attacked by the lackeys of the cursed Jews, and he and his family forced to flee the Golan. When he was murdered by the Mossad in a rocket attack, his wife and youngest son were also killed.

"Never forget Abayat," his grandfather has said, "you must swear revenge, and as long as one of your family is alive, you must fight the infidel." Abayat had struck at the infidels whenever he could, admonishing his followers to stay strong, though in the last decades the fight had needed to become covert.

He was the third generation raised in secret, trained from the cradle, and given only one purpose in life–to destroy the invaders. To break out into the open would ensure destruction at the hands of the UWG, so they stayed small, plotting in secret. They infiltrated and gathered information for the day they would rise up to regain independence and power to attain their true position in the world.

Abayat, home born and raised in a refugee camp, was able to avoid the insertion of the electronic spying device that would defile his body. He could move undetected in the world, though he needed help from his brothers for support–buying things and sending messages. Unmonitored persons were unable to get jobs with the government and could only work for cash, for the chip was required for a bank account.

Periodically, his group was monitored. They needed people in the government, and it had taken a generation to infiltrate into the high levels needed to make a difference, but they were close, very close.

The oil market now was a buyer's market with the loss of the Western oil consumption. The increased competition for buyers drove the price down until they were no longer a rich region. World power no longer lay in oil. A strike against the Orbiting Power System would change that.

PART 2

REVELATION AND REUNION

Chapter 9

Not quite a part of the United States, Puerto Peñasco was in a special tourist zone requiring no tourist visa, but it was still a foreign country. Jack voiced his discomfort with the trip to Mexico as he drove back to Ryan Field. Ron insisted, adding that the trip would be kept totally quiet and casual. No officials were to be alerted of his short visit. The only time his name would appear would be upon his return when he presented his passport to immigration guards at the border.

Jack handled the official requirements for the trip, using his name and "guests." The one hour flight took them over some of the most desolate country imaginable. Only volcanic peaks–some so new as to be still barren of vegetation–interrupted the desert. The rocky ground gave way to sand dunes, and the sky on the horizon became a dark blue. A few dilapidated buildings appeared, and they could see high-rise complexes as they circled the small but modern airport with a number of private aircraft tied down. "Let's take a quick look at the beach," said Ron. The plane headed toward the town.

The wide bay opened up below them with a white beach littered with tall buildings. The blue water stretched to the horizon, where the mountains of Baja, Mexico were visible. They descended to five hundred feet and flew down the beach. Few people were out, but some waved. They continued along the coast, over the town and past the gated community of Las Conchas. More condos populated the beach until they flew over a large estuary. Beyond rose a multistory complex of hotel and ultra-plush condos. In an area where all fresh water was either harvested from the sea or piped long distance from inland aquifers, the multiple swimming pools represented a great luxury. Ron turned the plane back toward the airport. They circled once and made final approach. Customs was perfunctory; the sleepy official's eyes were glued to Katharine. He barely glanced at the passports, not recognizing Ron.

Jack had arranged a rental car while at Ryan field. With only the single tote for Katharine and the light travel pack that Ron kept in the plane for both himself and Jack, they were on the road into town within minutes.

The city of Puerto Peñasco had begun as a small fishing village with Arizona residents maintaining a presence for recreation. With no source of fresh water, growth was limited to what water they trucked in. The construction of a pipeline from wells inland changed that, and the town exploded into a city of high-rise beachfront condos and hotels. The beach was spectacular, but just over the dunes was parched desert, dry sand, and miles of nothing but cholla cactus.

They drove into the heart of the city, past the docks and shipbuilding facilities until they were on the Malecón. This crowded street held the tourist shops in addition to fish markets. A young man frantically waved them to a vacant lot where Jack parked the car, and they walked along the street mixing in with the hundreds of other tourists.

"Let's go to Señor Froggy's for a margarita," said Katharine. Ron nodded his agreement.

Their table overlooked the bay, and the afternoon was warm and peaceful. As Katharine and Ron ordered margaritas, they enjoyed the scene with a cool breeze wafting off the bay. Boats moved across the water, some with purpose, others just cruising. Gulls frequented the rocks below them hoping for a handout. Music from a Mexican trio completed the aura.

The waiter brought their margaritas and Jack his cola, before placing a basket of real tortilla chips–actually made from tortillas–on the table along with a bowl of salsa. They ordered seafood cocktails and sat back. Ron raised his glass in a toast.

"To a few days away from the world," he said. They clinked glasses and took a sip. The feeling of serenity was palpable.

The short stroll down the Malecón was a pleasant diversion. On the right were the seafood markets, with the vendors holding up filets of fish and shrimp. The other side of the car-choked street was filled with small shops gaily decorated with brightly colored curios for sale to the touristas.

Driving out of town, they turned south on the road to Caborca. The road paralleled railroad tracks with the dunes and condos on their right and desert on their left. Their hotel, the Mayan Palace, was south of Puerto Peñasco on the large secluded estuary they had flown over. The resort was spectacular, even more awesome from the ground than from the air. The walk-in entrance passed through a domed space which seemed to pick up every sound and focus it. An almost subsonic roar was an undertone, giving a mystical feeling to the place.

The entry opened into a large reception area of stone and dark polished wood. Restaurants and shops lined the perimeter, but a two-story tall glass wall looking out onto the crystal white beach and turquoise sea dominated the room. Immediately behind the window, a laminar pool overflowed in a cascade to a winding canal below. Beyond the canal they saw a series of swimming pools with walkways crossing over them. Only the beach bar separated the pool from the umbrella dotted beach. The hotel was magnificent.

The rooms were well furnished in the vividly colored Mexican tradition, with heavy rough-hewn wooden furniture, Saltillo tile floors, thick adobe walls, and a patio overlooking the beach. The tide was going out when they arrived, and the waves gently broke on flat sand in the distance.

"Let's go for a walk on the beach," said Katharine.

Ron looked at Jack, and he shrugged. He had arranged for a satellite overhead enabling him to monitor them without leaving the patio. There was no need for him to be with them, and the beach was not crowded. Ron was aware of this. As Jack watched them walk across the sand toward the surf, he reconnected with his data base.

"The DNA sample of Katharine Levey from Kihhim matches the one taken from the restaurant. She is a clone." That is completely against every international law, Jack thought. He would have to bring her in for interrogation. First, he would have to get her away from Ron Carson, and Ron was obviously enchanted by her. That issue would need to wait until they were back in the United States.

***

A gentle breeze, laden with the smells of the sea, cooled them from the scalding interior desert only a few hundred meters over the dunes. This was a peaceful world, where the sea life struggled to survive oblivious to man.

With most of the beach to themselves, they walked until the hotel tower was barely visible. As the sun lowered in the western sky, they turned back. Vee formations of pelicans skimmed the shallows looking for a last meal on their way to the nesting site, and the wispy clouds turned the sky various shades of pink, orange and red. Nearing the hotel, the glow in the sky faded, and stars began to appear. A fat orange moon rose above the horizon making a wavering line of light on the water. Katharine sighed. "It's so nice here, just as I remember. Sunsets were always my favorite time of day."

***

Jack was waiting for them when they got back. "Do you want to eat dinner here or go back to town?

"Let's go to El Capitán," said Katharine.

Jack looked at Ron, and they both shrugged. Neither was familiar with it.

"It's above the town, atop the mountain. There's a fantastic view," explained Katharine.

They got in the car to make the twenty-five minute drive back to Puerto Peñasco. After winding up a steep track that climbed the mountain above the town, they entered a concrete parking area and were met by the parking security team. They parked the car and went into the restaurant. The hostess asked them where they wanted to sit. "Outside on the corner," said Katharine. The lights of the city spread out below them, while the full moon lit the sea. The bay curved to the west, and the hotel lights on the beach sparkled across the water. Out in the sea of Cortez, the lights of fishing boats were independent specks on the dark sea. The setting was quiet and idyllic adding to the magnificent view. Ron ordered margaritas for them, but Jack chose coke. The satellite had shown him the restaurant was isolated, and he had it watched, ready for any alert.

For dinner, Ron ordered shrimp tacos, Katharine the seafood enchiladas, and Jack the blackened sea bass. The waitress left, and they looked out at the darkness, sipping drinks while enjoying the sense of peace. Music drifted up to them from a tourist boat crossing the bay. Fireworks erupted from the beach hotels, streaking into the sky and bursting into colored glitter spreading across the star-filled night.

Ron and Katharine held each other's gaze enchanted by the magic moment until the waitress arrived with their food and more margaritas. The food was delicious.

When they got back to the Mayan Palace, Ron and Katharine went for another walk on the beach. Jack stayed to continue surveillance of the area.

The stars and the moon were enough to light the beach with the pollution free sky over the Sea of Cortez. Ron and Katharine took off their shoes to wade in the warm water. As the tide receded, it seemed to race across the flats. Ron felt a tranquility he hadn't experienced for years. His memories and worries seemed far away, and watching Katharine engrossed him. She was so beautiful, looking decades younger than her age, and he felt a stirring of his emotions he'd missed and thought lost.

Could she really take him to his great-grandson? What would she want from him? Why was she here? He pushed these thoughts aside to enjoy watching her walk ahead seemingly without a care. She was like a girl, but he knew that she was so much more.

The lights of Puerto Peñasco glowed to the north, and to the south only a few specks of light glittered. The water, almost bath warm, splashed their feet and left glowing trails. Algae, fluorescing when disturbed, and the small waves created a line of light along the shore for them.

As they drew even with the hotel, they climbed the sandy rise from the beach flats. Jack was no longer on the patio that joined the three rooms. A pitcher of cold margaritas was there (thanks, Jack) and Ron poured for Katharine and himself. They said nothing as they sipped the icy drinks.

At last, Katharine broke the silence. "Do you want to snorkel tomorrow?"

"I haven't done that in years,"` said Ron. "Sure."

She rose, and he did the same, not certain what to do. She moved to him and put her hands on his arms. "Thank you for bringing me here. I hope you don't regret it."

"It's been a true pleasure for me," he said. She leaned toward him and kissed his cheek, her hands keeping him from embracing her as he wanted. He felt a tremble in them, and then she turned away toward her room. A promise hung in the air.

Chapter 10

In the morning Katharine called Ron's room to have him meet her for breakfast. Jack joined them, and they sat on the patio under an umbrella. Huevos rancheros with fresh warm tortillas were served with a side dish of chorizo. Katharine relished each sip of the dark rich coffee. She caught Ron watching her. "I've really missed this," she said by way of explanation.

"You don't have coffee?" asked Jack.

"Not like this," said Katharine. She pointedly didn't explain further. She broke the silence. "Ron and I thought we'd like to snorkel. Would you care to join us?" she looked at Jack.

He declined, knowing he could observe them much better from shore where he had all the tools at hand. They checked out the gear: flippers, masks, snorkels, an inner-tube float with a small anchor, a diver's flag, and a net for any treasures they might find. As they waded out into the slight surf, they turned and waved at Jack on the patio. He used his binoculars to keep an eye on them as they moved away from the beach.

With the tide coming in, the water was only waist deep fifty yards off shore, and few other swimmers were in the water. They put on their flippers and swam out until they were 150 yards from the beach. Here the water was only fifteen feet deep and the bottom sandy. There was not really much to see, but they were away and alone. Through the binoculars, Jack envied Ron.

Obviously, he liked Katharine, and she liked him. Acknowledging to himself that she was beautiful, Jack saw how good she looked in her classic one-piece black bathing suit with the white trim. By the end of the day, he'd have more information about her. The archives were being researched for any information, which would be transferred to him as soon as available. The former president deserved to meet someone like her so he hoped she was no threat. A pod of dolphins swam near Ron and Katharine, seeming to surround them. They breathed in and out several times and dove under the surface. Shadows moved under the water and then away as the dolphins continued up the coast feeding.

Ron and Katharine hung on to the inner-tube float looking down through their masks at the bottom. Through the clear water, they could see the outline of an occasional stingray. Ron felt wonderful for the first time in years. Below them a sudden flurry of activity drew his attention, and then large dark shapes swam by. At first, Ron was startled, but he calmed as he saw they were dolphins.

The dolphins surrounded them, and one brushed against his legs. He jerked back. "It's all right," laughed Katharine. "They're just checking us out. Let's dive down with them." She took several deep breaths, held the last one and dove beneath the surface. Ron hesitated, but then did the same.

Once underwater, the dolphins came up to them and seemed to beg to be petted. Katharine reached out and stroked the flank of one. It rubbed against her, pushing her in the water. Ron felt one against his side, and he stroked it. They both surfaced. "This is wonderful," said Ron. "I didn't know they were so friendly in the wild."

"They've obviously been around people," said Katharine. "Let's go back down." They breathed deeply and dove. The dolphins surrounded them again. Katharine reached out and grabbed the dorsal fin of one, and it swan off giving her a ride. Ron did the same, and they moved quickly through the water, towed by the dolphins.

Realizing he needed air, he let go of the fin and started to rise toward the surface. He felt a tug on his leg and looked down. Below him, Katharine pointed downward. On the sandy bottom were two sets of SCUBA tanks. She pulled him toward them. What if they were empty? Ron needed air now! He struggled to break free, but Katharine would not let go.

She forced the mouthpiece into his mouth, and he tentatively breathed in. Air! He took several deep breaths before giving Katharine a questioning glance. She held up her set of tanks, pointing to the back. Ron looked closely. The initials KRC leaped at him. These were the tanks Ron had given to Kit before he left for New Zealand! Katharine put the tanks on and signaled for Ron to help her buckle in after which she assisted him. How did these get here? Confused, he looked at her, his eyes wide open inside the mask. Above them, the dolphins circled. She pointed behind him, and he turned to see more dolphins appear. Again, they grabbed onto the fins, and this time they tore through the water.

***

At the hotel, Jack waited for them to surface as he scanned the water. Nothing. He called up the satellite image, and the overhead view on his glasses showed only clear water. Changing to infrared, nothing showed. The sea was empty. He moved the view to the pod of dolphins but they were gone. Frantic, he immediately called for help, explaining what had happened. He needed more eyes on this. Now! A helicopter was dispatched from Yuma, getting permission to enter Mexico as it crossed the border. While Jack gave hurried explanations, his panic increased.

In his soul, he knew Ron was gone, but he couldn't believe it. They had total monitor of the area. Nothing could move in or out without their observing it. The inner-tube float bobbed alone in the sea, its anchor rope descending through the clear water to the deserted sandy bottom. Jack widened the scope, but nothing showed except the dolphins heading west. Ron and Katharine had disappeared!

***

For quite a while, Ron and Katharine moved underwater, while dolphins switched off in a relay to return to the surface to breathe. When Ron's arms seemed about to fall off, they slowed and went deeper. In the dim light ahead, a gargantuan form hung in the water before them.

Something as large as a whale appeared. When they got close, they let go of the dolphins and swan toward it. Katharine held his hand, leading the way. The large shape was inert, unmoving. It was the size of a bus, Ron thought as they swam alongside. They rounded the end, and Ron was relieved to see no gaping mouth waiting to take them in. Instead he saw a hemispherical indentation like a small room. Katharine swam into it. Ron hesitated, but she pulled–motioning him to join her.

As they pressed themselves against the huge animal, a transparent film formed and enclosed them in a bubble. Only Katharine's hand on his arm kept him from trying to get out, his heart pounding. Gradually, the water level in the sphere dropped until it was below their chins. Katharine removed her mask and mouthpiece. Ron did the same. Stunned by what had happened, he tried to speak but no words came out. He didn't know what to ask first and just pointed at the SCUBA gear.

"We're going to see Kit," said Katharine, "and this is our transport. We call them Travelers."

Shocked into silence, Ron looked around. The floor and back were smooth and soft, while the bubble surrounding them remained transparent. The last of the water disappeared, and the room was dry. Slowly, he removed the diving gear, placing it to one side. Katharine put on a white robe and handed one to him.

"I'd suggest you sit down," said Katharine. "The motion can be a little unsettling until you adjust." The Traveler rose slowly until it was at the surface. From somewhere inside her suit she withdrew a phone. "You should probably call Jack."

Ron punched in Jack's number which was picked up on the first ring. "You better have a goddamn good explanation as to what happened!"

"Jack, Katharine and I are taking a little trip. I wanted to let you know so you won't worry. And you can call off the search. You won't be able to find us. Mark it down to youthful indiscretion. Seriously, Jack, we're fine, and I'll be in touch later."

"Goddamnit! You can't do this to me. At least tell me where you're going!"

"I don't know yet, but I'm not concerned, and neither should you be. We're going to see Kit." Ron hung up.

Chapter 11

Ron looked behind him, noticing that the back of the room had formed into a shape resembling a lounge chair. Katharine reclined. He slowly did the same. The chair was soft and formed to his body, somewhat like the old water-beds but was warm and comfortable. As soon as he was down, he felt the whole room move, and the huge fish started to swim. Its tail made large sweeping arcs as they slid through the water

Outside, the dolphins kept pace, breaking away when they needed to return to the surface for air. The only sound was the slight swoosh of water rushing by. The rhythmic motion was smooth. Through the clear bubble, the water was featureless with little sea life in this part of the Sea of Cortez, but as they continued south, that changed.

A land mass appeared underwater, and as they swam past, Ron realized they were moving fast! The island disappeared in no time. Ron looked up at the mirrored surface far above, and glimpsed schools of fish, but they moved much too quickly for him to see any detail. Glancing at Katharine, he saw her reclined in the chair, her eyes closed. She sensed him looking and opened her eyes, a smile reassuring him. "Are you doing all right?" she asked.

Ron was still overcome. He nodded. Katharine reached to one side and held something up. It looked like a thick white sausage but soft and pliable. "This is what we use to communicate with those around us." The white trim of her bathing suit had formed into a collar around her neck, and she settled back into the chair, looking at him. "You're welcome to try it," she said.

Ron looked to one side of the chair and picked up a similar shape. The collar was warm but not heavy. He put it around his neck like a neck pillow and lay back, not knowing what to expect. Nothing happened. He looked at Katharine.

"Close your eyes and relax." He did and heard her voice. "Try to make your mind a blank." He seemed to melt into the soft warmth of the chair, and the motion relaxed him. Although he knew what Katharine said, he had not heard her words with his ears. [Think of this as a headset.] The words had formed in his mind! [Now, just sit back and let go. Enjoy the ride.] An image of the room formed in his mind, and he saw himself reclined on the couch. Katharine lay beside him, her eyes closed as if asleep.

In an effort to figure out what was going on, he turned to look through the bubble. The sea was bright, and he could see much farther. [You're seeing through the senses of the Traveler,] Katharine said. [The image is not only light, but infrared, sonar, all the senses combined.] The view was as if he were looking out of his airplane. The sea floor stretched out before him, and far above, the surface was an undulating mirror. Now he could see the schools of fish. He could feel the water rush by, and it seemed to be touching his skin!

Katharine's comforting presence reminded him of walking by an unseen infrared heater and suddenly feeling the warmth. She seemed to be so close–almost a part of him. He sensed her soothing him, as if she spoke things to calm and reassure him. The words weren't there, but the feeling behind them was. His discomfort eased. As if in a dream, his mind flew through space, but he was not alone. He opened his eyes. Katharine was still beside him, but when he looked out, it was as if he were almost blind. He could barely see. He closed his eyes again and everything opened up once more as the senses of the Traveler became his..

[This is wonderful!] he thought.

[It is, isn't it!] Katharine answered. [When you formulate and project your thoughts, I'm able to pick them up. Let me show you where we're going.] An image formed in Ron's mind. A layer of bubbles hung in the water. At first he had no perspective, but as the image cleared, he saw many figures swimming around the cluster. The bubbles were huge. Startled, he realized he was looking at a city hanging in the water, a huge city! The bubble structure seemed to have no end.

The vision drew near, and he could see into the bubbles where figures moved. They passed through the wall of the bubble and were inside. Before him was Kit! He looked up and smiled. [Hey, GreaPa.] That was the name he had called Ron from when he was too young to say great-grandpa. Ron's chest tightened, then a rush of relief flowed through him. There was no doubt he was seeing his great-grandson.

The words formed in his mind. [GreaPa, we'll be together in a few days. Enjoy the trip with Katharine. We have a lot to talk about.]

[I miss you,] Ron formed the words in his mind.

[I miss you, too,] Kit said.

Ron opened his eyes, and again the spherical chamber appeared around him with the sea rushing by. Katharine looked over at him and saw the tears on his cheeks. "We'll be at Ocealla in a few days," she said. He closed his eyes, but the vision of Kit was gone. Exhausted, he drifted into a dreamless sleep.

When he awoke, he looked over to Katharine's chair but instead of the seat was a partition. "Katharine!" he called.

An answer came from beyond the wall. "I'm here. Give me a few minutes." He looked out at the sea, and it was dark. Must be night, he thought. A noise brought his attention back to the wall, which was melting, into the floor. Katharine stood in a white robe.

"I needed to freshen up," she said. "You can do the same if you wear the collar and visualize yourself in a small bathroom. Think about a shower."

Ron put the collar on, and as he pictured a bathroom, a wall–like a curtain–rose from the floor giving him privacy. He thought about a toilet, and one formed. He used it, and then thought about a shower. Before he could remove his robe, warm water sprayed from the wall. He yelped and started removing the robe, but it was already soaked so he took it off, letting it fall to the floor. Soap appeared on a shelf on the wall. When he finished washing, the water stopped, and a towel appeared where the shower-head had been. He toweled himself dry. Before he could hang it back, it changed into a clean dry robe! Ron visualized being back in the small spherical room with Katharine, and the wall melted into the floor where Katharine waited. Flabbergasted, Ron said, "That's really amazing. What senses my thoughts and changes everything?"

"The Traveler can shape parts of itself to accommodate your thoughts, like it shaped itself to form this cabin we're in. Just as the collar allows you to see through the Traveler, it senses your thoughts. The basic shape of the Traveler is the giant fish-like configuration, but certain membranes inside are pliable and reform. Your direct connection into the Traveler's brain is the collar. Without the connection, it's similar to a pet, an animal with survival instincts but little cognitive abilities. We supply those and become a part of it."

"How far away is Kit?" Ron asked.

"A few days. We'll need to exchange our Traveler for a fresh one. Without stopping to feed, this one will become exhausted, so we're going to another city to rest for the night. We'll resume our journey tomorrow. The stop will give you a chance to meet some of our citizens and see one of our habitats first hand."

"How many habitats do you have?" asked Ron.

"Several," said Katharine. "Not nearly as many as there are cities in the United States, but we are every bit a civilization–just as you are–only living in another part of the Earth," said Katharine.

"How could you be that large and still remain unknown to us?" asked Ron, clearly disturbed by the idea.

"The world beneath the sea surface is foreign to you and your civilization. Staying out of your way isn't hard. When you're underwater, you're almost blind, and your only concern is either food fish or other men in manmade vessels. You really don't look for organic structures in remote places," she said. "The seas are vast when compared to the habitable land area. That's a big part of why we want to talk with you about joining the surface civilization and the community of man on earth. Is humankind ready to meet and accept us?"

This was the crux of the matter. Humans always believed they owned the Earth, even though most of it was uninhabitable to them. They were the strongest species–sure to triumph in any battle for survival–yet Kahchk Kihhim had delivered a lesson few knew about. Human life was tenuous and could be wiped out by numerous calamities.

Were humans capable of existing alongside another intelligent species? Could humankind accept another species without viewing them as a threat? Could there be equals in Earth's civilization?

"Humanity has come a long way in the last half century. We've accepted the idea of alien life elsewhere in the universe, and some of them are surely more advanced than and superior to humans. A residual fear remains, but there's been no contact–ever."

"You still fear the unknown," Katharine said.

"Humanity has matured, in part because we are aware of existence and balance. The old tales of swashbuckling and plundering spacefarers, raiding from the skies has proven wrong so far. Most feel that to travel the vastness of space takes a measure of maturity and a level of technical ability far beyond that needed to survive."

"We always thought the greatest threat to humankind's survival was man himself."

"That was brought under control by the United World Government," said Ron.

"Perhaps you're ready to meet the long-anticipated aliens," noted Katharine. "If these aliens aren't from other stars, will make a difference?"

"You'd be accepted. We've grown up and are no longer the frightened and insecure species ready to destroy any perceived threat."

"What taught you this tolerance?" asked Katharine.

"Two things happened. First, we accept and trust the United World Government. Initially, there was great fear about the loss of identity, of culture, and of control with a world governing body. The charter of the United World Government is very restrictive in the areas which come under its control. The UWG doesn't restrict local governments, except for basic human rights and the preclusion of war. All areas have access to The World Court and the United World Government guarantees an education to all citizens."

"Education!" exclaimed Katharine. "How does that fall under the United World Government?"

"Through the education of the children, attitudes change, and the control of education is paramount to true awareness of the world. All children attend school from age three through age fourteen," Ron said. "The schools are operated locally but overseen by the UWG. They are taught fundamentals such as reading, math, science, history, human rights, and current events."

"How can schools be set up to do this? Where do the teachers come from?" asked Katharine.

"Central areas are used for the schools, and the teaching is all done by machine and computer. Students progress at their own pace and receive individual attention at their own workstation. The curriculum is fact-based and meant to give the basics of education, not social influence. Cultural and social issues are the responsibility of the local government. These are taught in separate schools. The children are the key," said Ron.

"You said two things happened. What was the other?" asked Katharine.

"A new faith arose, one encompassing all other religions. People had grown weary of having their religion kidnapped by those purporting to speak for God and setting agendas of hatred, intolerance, and violence. To paraphrase an old quote, 'Religion is the greatest fomenter of hatred in the world.' Just as there rose an intolerance for war, the unending battle for religious dominance between Judaism, Christianity, Islam, Hinduism and others finally became too much.

"A man, Mohammad al Jar, came from the Mideast teaching that faith is a personal issue between you and your God. He showed the difference between faith and religion."

Katharine's face showed her lack of understanding.

"The organized religions fought the idea that individuals should consult God without clergy. Their survival was at stake, but al Jar succinctly said, 'Despite the appearance of goodness, the purpose of a religion is the furtherance of that religion and the support of the leaders. Faith is their tool to attain that.'

"Efforts by several groups were made to silence him, but by the time they organized, too many people began to reject the hatred and intolerance of their own religions," said Ron. "The major problem facing those trying to get rid of him was finding him. He would appear throughout an area, preaching tolerance and love, teaching people how to listen to God. Many times, he was killed, but he would resurrect and reappear within days. He created holograms to address people individually, and the broadcasts couldn't be jammed."

"This man just suddenly appeared?" asked Katharine.

"Almost simultaneously in different parts of the world. The movement separating faith from religion and religion from politics spread quickly. The rules of civilization, once the providence of religion and taught as 'God's laws' became the laws of the land. Faith was now separate. People were no longer controlled under the threat of eternal hell and damnation," Ron said.

Katharine was visibly surprised. This was a major change in the surface civilizations.

"What al Jar says is 'Focus only on <u>your</u> relationship with God, and do not concern yourself about your neighbors. They must find their own way. Treat others well, and God will tell you how to act. Your purpose in life is solely to learn to live as God wishes. When your belief in God is strong enough, that faith will guide your life. God will call you when you're ready.'"

"You seem to have a pretty good knowledge of this new faith," said Katharine.

"I was captured by it too. For decades, I watched the turmoil and hatred done in the name of God, and I knew this must change for mankind to mature. I welcomed the idea that only God could tell me what was right and what was wrong. I'm a convert," said Ron, without apology.

"Have you met al Jar?" she asked Ron.

"I had an audience with him which unnerved me at first. The power of peace took me away, and he opened my mind and created a defining moment in my life. He became a confidant at times.

"He overcame religious persecution by holding sessions with the religious leaders all over the world. They did not come out of the sessions the same. A few of them refused to meet with him and did not convert, but none denied his power of peace or the strength of his beliefs. His message of faith became known as Faithism."

"You feel strongly about this," said Katharine.

"Yes, his image seems to be everywhere, and his message isn't the same to everyone. Once he's shown you the way, he's in your head. It's been confirmed he holds simultaneous audience with many different peoples, and each address is individual. His message is always consistent: 'Believe in God, concern yourself only with your own relationship with God. Do no harm, do not judge.' He delivers it to each group in whatever manner is best."

"Has anybody traced the signals of the holos to their source?" asked Katharine.

"At first, everyone was trying to debunk al Jar, but as his message caught on, people didn't care where it came from. Several groups claimed to have traced the signals to a source coming from deep space. Al Jar dismissed these efforts as attempts to reintroduce meaningless minutia into faith. 'It's only about your faith and nothing else,' he said. 'Do not let yourself be misdirected from you and your God.' He would not let the trivial cause the dissension that had put the religions of the world at each other's throats. This was a pivotal moment in history."

"I hope to meet Mohammad al Jar someday," said Katharine.

"I'm sure you will," said Ron. He turned back to watch the sea pass by with the slow sweeping motion of the Traveler. His mind settled into the comfort zone of Faithism, and Katharine sensed it.

Chapter 12

As a part of the Traveler, Ron's energy drained as the huge creature's strokes slowed. Not only was he fatigued, but he was hungry. The layer of bubbles approached. Images formed in his mind, images from the residents of the city ahead. Communication by sensation became easier as he received messages made up of images, sounds, smells, tastes, and feelings. At first, receiving sensations had been overpowering and those sending messages put them into words for him. Over the days of the trip, he learned to absorb the ideas forming in his mind. Some ideas were foreign, obviously not his, but others he had to examine closely.

Soon, he learned it didn't matter because the experience and the thought were important, not the origin. When he relaxed, he expanded and became part of a huge body of thought, a giant intelligence that was the Collective. His individuality was another building block in the structure of this civilization, as important as every other. Never had he experienced a more intimate relationship.

Through the eyes of those awaiting the docking, he saw the Traveler's first touch on a bubble in the habitat, and it then slowly merged. He opened his eyes and stood from the soft couch as Katharine rose. They stepped into the room. The smooth walls had no adornment and glowed with a dim green light–the only light in the room. Two people walked forward and embraced Katharine exchanging hellos and turned to Ron.

Katharine said, "I'd like to reintroduce you to Dayton and Carol. They were with us on Kahchk Kihhim. You may remember them as our press department along with many other duties. The woman, a pretty, petite brunette, stepped forward. Shoulder length hair framed her pale unlined face and sensual wide full lips. Her eyes held his gaze as she extended her hand.

"It's nice to see you again, Mr. President," she said. "It's been a long time."

"You're as attractive as I remember, Carol." Ron said. He turned, "And I recall Dayton, too." The tall slender man stepped toward him, and they shook hands. Dayton had sandy blond hair and the good looks that had made him a TV news anchor many years ago before joining Kahchk Kihhim. "If I remember correctly, you were the reporter that started this by introducing Kihhim to the world." Both of them were pale from living their undersea life.

"Yes, sir. I was covering the death of an environmental activist near Kihhim and became enchanted with it. It's a pleasure to see you again, Mr. President."

"It's not Mr. President anymore. It took Katharine a few days to call me Ron. I hope you can as well."

"Welcome to Ajabada, Ron," Dayton said. "Let me introduce you to some of our other residents." He turned and walked toward a raised pool against one wall. As they approached, a creature rose to a stand. Ron instinctively jerked back. "It's okay, Ron. This is Cejani. She's an Altered."

The figure moved forward, holding out a webbed hand. He felt the power as her hand engulfed his. She towered over Ron, with dark shiny skin and a round head. He looked up into large black eyes. "A pleasure meeting you, Ron," her deep voice rasped from a wide mouth, revealing sharp triangular teeth.

"I'm pleased to meet you. I remember being introduced to another Altered many years ago at Kahchk Kihhim," said Ron.

"You must mean my father, Sean. He's living at Retseana. Perhaps you'll get the chance to meet him again." Releasing Ron's hand, she turned to the pool. A dolphin head rose from the water. "This is Norwen, my partner."

The dolphin spoke in a high squeaky voice. "I have never met a Surfacer before. It is my pleasure." He held out a flipper. Norwen noticed Ron looking at the hump on his back and the gill slits. "I'm a member of the Dahlfin species. We have been altered with larger brains and gills to increase my time underwater."

Another creature rose to the surface of the pool. Ron couldn't make out the shape, but he saw several arms or tentacles writhing and moving at the same time. Katharine came up behind him and placed a collar on his neck. "You'll need this to talk to Unweil. He has no vocal cords."

A voice filled Ron's head: [It's a pleasure to meet you, Ron. We have heard so much about you. I almost feel we have met before.] A tentacle raised out of the water toward Ron. On the end, a group of digits, like very thin fingers extended toward him.

Ron reached out, and the tentacles wrapped around his hand. In his mind was a sound, a giggle: [I do enjoy touching you humans. You are so warm. I'm a full Construct. My species was originally *genegineered* by Dr. Jamie Wong before we left Kahchk Kihhim.]

An image of a squid-like creature with tentacles of different lengths and types of ends formed in Ron's mind. Several had small tentacles at the end like fingers, others were wide and flat with suction cups, and others just tapered to a thin tip, a single long finger. Some of the tentacles contained eyes. The tentacles radiated from one end of a cylindrical body. The other end had a large fin. Wide swiveling eyes were all around the body and other sensors extended down the length. The voice again filled his mind. [If you would like, come on in.]

In his mind, an opening formed before him. It wasn't an image but a sensation. He moved forward and was absorbed, becoming the creature. His underwater vision was 360 degrees, disconcerting him—making him dizzy.

Katharine: [Relax. Just let it form, and your mind will adapt at its own pace.] He concentrated on thinking of nothing and became Unweil. Astonished, he was completely at home in the water, even more so than with the Traveler. He moved freely away from the habitat, his senses very acute. All the sea around Ajabada was visible but Ron sensed much more than he saw. Flabbergasted, he realized he was a true sea creature. He swam back to Ajabada and into the pool. Through Unweil's eyes saw himself standing with his eyes closed beside it.

Ron opened his eyes and looked around, blinking them into focus. Katharine watched him and smiled. "Unweil is quite a person isn't he?"

"It was like seeing for the first time. I... It's still too much to comprehend," he stammered. "My mind can't understand..."

"As with anything else, you'll get better with practice. Would you like to have dinner?" Katharine turned toward a table forming out of the floor. Carol and Dayton stood next to it, and when Katharine and Ron joined them, they sat, as chairs formed. The surface of the table seemed to be translucent liquid. Glasses and plates formed under the surface and then rose. Ron blinked, and before him was a glass of wine and a salad.

"I hope you like dinner. Carol set the menu. You're not allergic to seafood are you? It's really fresh here," Katharine said with a straight face. They laughed, including Ron.

"I bet," Ron said, enjoying the pun. The meal was delicious.

Dayton cleared his throat before stating, "Decades ago when we left, there was a serious erosion of rights taking place in America. I remember you were trying to heal the country and decentralize the government. What happened?"

"The threats to us have abated, so restrictions and government oversight are gradually being removed. The hardest thing to do is reduce the power of the federal government." The others at the table nodded.

"The United World Government has helped by creating worldwide peace. The biggest problem is still the inherent nationalism left over from the days of independent nations. The UWG only has jurisdiction in areas with international consequences though that can be stretched to include most of the worlds' inhabitants. It's similar to the situation early in formation of the United States when the state governments had most of the control, and the federal role was limited. Gradually the federal government expanded, and its role got larger, usurping the states' authority."

"I believe the Civil War was fought over that," said Dayton.

"There was a second Civil War, but it wasn't on the same scale and was finally settled in the Supreme Court. The cry of 'Homeland Security' still carries fear as the power given to it to protect us from terrorism was abused. Though we keep our guard up, we cannot do that at the expense of freedom. Through a series of Presidential decrees I began limiting the role of the federal government and shifted more power back to the states."

"I suppose basic human rights are preserved by the United World Government, just like the human rights protected by the US Constitution," said Katharine.

"There is a World Constitution outlining specifically what human rights are protected."

"Where would our Dahlfins, Cons, and Alts fall under the World Constitution?" asked Katharine. "What's the definition of Human?"

"Do nations have a choice about joining?" asked Carol. "Who decides what is perilous to human existence?"

"That sounds good," said Dayton, "but how does it work?"

Ron looked from one to another before answering. Those questions and others continued until Ron's weariness was obvious.

"Let's get you to bed," said Katharine. "You look beat."

Ron didn't remember much afterwards.

***

"Time to go, Ron," said Katharine in a throaty voice awakening him. Standing above him, she was lovely. "Get cleaned up. A meal is on the table beside the bed, and I'll be back within an hour. As soon as you're done, we leave for the next leg of our journey."

What a nice way to wake up, he thought. I wouldn't mind more of that. Less than an hour later, he stood alongside Carol and Dayton in the room with the pool. Through the transparent wall, he saw the dark sea. In the dim green light, he bid farewell to the residents, including Cejani, Norwen, and Unweil. They wished him well on his journey. As the wall dissolved, he and Katharine stepped into the room formed by the Traveler. The wall reformed as they sat, and the Traveler moved away.

When he put the collar on, the dark sea came alive. Seeing everything, but not with his eyes, he became the Traveler. The dizziness returned for a second with the sensory overload, but as he relaxed, they merged. He sensed Katharine's presence, and it stabilized him–reassured him.

"Second star to the right and on to Never Never land," she said.

He laughed at the thought of Peter Pan and the childish sense of adventure he now felt.

This time the pace was slower. Katharine explained: [The Traveler has far to go on this leg and needs to conserve energy.] Ron wasn't sure when he realized that he would fall irretrievably in love with Katharine if he didn't pull back. When they were linked, she let him see it was mutual, and she wasn't pulling back.

From the reclined chair, he saw that the cabin was darker than usual. The sea was black, and the green glow was softened. Turning to Katharine, she came close, easily moving into his arms. Neither moved, enjoying the closeness of their bodies pressing together. Katharine tilted her head back and found his lips waiting. Their kiss was more intimate than any Ron could ever imagine. Linked together as they kissed, their lips touched and their minds merged. Words were unnecessary. The passion that passed between them was as deep as the most fiery lovemaking ever, but much richer and more fulfilling. They broke the kiss.

"I don't know if I can follow that up," Ron said, gasping.

"Let's try," she said.

When Ron turned to look at the chairs, they had merged into a large bed. Katharine smiled at him. "We don't always need the collars to connect with the body-mind." She put her arms around him, pulled him close, and held him. "It's been a long time since I was with someone. I hope I can meet your expectations."

She must have plucked those thoughts out of his head. Those words calmed his worries, putting him at ease. He held her tightly, liking the touch and fit of her as he unwound. Her hands pulled his robe up and then her nails ran down his back. Goose bumps sprang up, and a shiver ran up his back. He felt a tingle in his loins and pulled her against him, touching her ear with his lips.

With a sigh, she tilted her head to one side, so he could kiss her neck, and his lips moved down. Her breasts pressed against his chest, and as his hands moved under her robe, her nipples were hard against him. He moved against them, and she moaned.

Her bare skin was hot in his hands, and she stepped back, pulling her robe off over her head. She was beautiful. Her breasts were firm and her waist narrow. As she turned toward the bed, he admired her hips and legs. She looked over her shoulder at him. It was the most alluring scene ever. "Perhaps you should take off your robe while you still can," she said.

Before it hit the floor, he'd moved to the bed. In the soft light, she looked up, licked her lips and moved her hands down the length of her body. His eyes followed the path they traced, and his excitement was a physical pain.

He laid down and kissed her while his hands paralleled the path hers made. As his hand moved across her bare midriff, her muscles tightened at the touch, and her legs moved. He kissed her breast, and she moaned. Her hand moved across the back of his head, pressing him tightly to her. Her legs wrapped around him and pulled him into her. Gasping, they lay still–enjoying the sensation–her surrounding him, he soaking within her. They moved, the electricity of intimate caresses going through them.

The rest of the trip was a blur of swimming and lovemaking as the Traveler undulated through the jade-colored sea. When he and Katharine put the collars on, it was if they were making love again. The intimacy that flowed between them was deeper than the surrounding sea. The end came too soon for both of them.

Chapter 13

With his enhanced senses through the collar, Ron watched as they approached the huge bubble city. He'd been in contact with Kit and had seen the Traveler nearing through Kit's eyes. Sadness touched him as the trip with Katharine drew to a close and the Traveler merged with the bubble. Reluctantly, he reached to remove the collar. The companionship while wearing it was not easily given up.

Katharine: [You can leave it on, if you wish.] He thought for a second before reaching up to remove it, preferring to greet Kit on his usual basis.

They stepped into the room where several figures waited. Kit stepped forward to hug him. God! The emotion of losing someone and getting them back was overpowering. Tears flowed from his eyes and onto Kit's shoulder. When they finally stepped back, he was speechless.

"Let me introduce you to the people who cared for me here," Kit said. Turning toward a tall, slender woman, with a mixed heritage cast to her, she stepped forward. The woman looked familiar. "This is Leticia Gardner. She has taken very good care of me since our wreck and Susan's death. It's been hard, but she's helped ease the way."

Offering her hand, Leticia said, "I don't know if you remember me."

"Of course I do," said Ron. "How could I forget the woman who held me and the most powerful nation on earth in her control? You're still beautiful and haven't changed at all." He took her hand.

"Thank you, Mr. President. It's good to see you looking so well. We've enjoyed having Kit as our guest."

"Guest?" said Ron.

"GreaPa, without their help, we all would have died. They saved my life," exclaimed Kit. "I've been treated very well. Leticia saw to my care." He looked at her and smiled. "The loss of Susan was a hard thing to handle, but I'm doing much better now." The look that passed between them wasn't lost on Ron or Katharine.

"Ron, perhaps you two would like to spend time together," said Katharine. "Kit can take you to your room. We'll get you in the morning or whenever you want us. If you need anything, just use this," she said handing him the collar.

Ron took the collar from her and looked into her eyes. Any mistrust fled under her steady gaze. "Thank you for my great-grandson, thank you all." He put his arm around Kit's shoulders. "Lead on," he said. They moved toward a wall and then through. The next room had Kit's things.

"This is my room…our room now unless you want one of your own."

"This will be fine for now. I'm hungry. We didn't eat for the last part of the trip. Have you had dinner?"

Kit donned a collar and a table and seats morphed from the floor. "What do you want to eat?"

Ron looked at him and said, "Seafood?" They both started to laugh. The warm pleasure of seeing him was so good. His heart had broken when he heard Kit was missing, and here they were—unbelievably together.

"Kit, I nearly died when I was told you were lost. Another loved one lost would have been too much for me to handle. This is nothing short of a miracle.”

“GreaPa, you do understand that we are prisoners here. Unless we can convince them we represent no threat, they cannot let us go.”

“I understand that more so than you. The fears I had about Kahchk Kihhim almost a century ago are back. I did not believe then that my species could accept a genetically engineered and superior species as equal partners. The prejudices within me against another native species on Earth having the same rights as humans rose. If I couldn’t accept them, what about the rest of the world?”

“Why didn’t you bomb them immediately?”

“They were very clever. They created a virus and loosed it in the world. It was a time-bomb that would insure the destruction of civilization if they weren’t around to release the antivirus. This ploy forced us to protect them. At first, they seemed to be just a group of scientists wanting to be left alone in their sea nation. Yet they were attacked on the day of their recognition by the United States. Our representative to the ceremony, Vice President Sanchez was among the causalities.”

“I remember reading that account in the history books,” said Kit.

"With the help of Kahchk Kihhim we caught those who initiated the attack. We knew who was behind it, but because of the politics and lack of evidence could not prosecute. The ensuing investigation revealed the true extent of Kahchk Kihhim's abilities. They had genetically engineered native species and humans.

"We kept that secret, but we had to form an alliance with the Chinese to protect Kahchk Kihhim while we raced to develop our own antivirus. Neither of us could let the other possess the technology of Kahchk Kihhim, and they had the ability to destroy us. We agreed to destroy them jointly once we had the antivirus."

"According to history, it was a rogue group of radicals who attacked the floating nation," said Kit. "And Kahchk Kihhim destroyed themselves."

Ron shook his head. "We had to fabricate that. It took me years to realize it was my fear and the reaction to 'kill the threat' that set the path. I didn't believe the human race would tolerate them, and war with them was inevitable. Forced into a corner, Kahchk Kihhim would do what any species would do to survive, and their biological weapons assured humans would be the losers. In all likelihood, there would be no winners."

Ron felt Kit's eyes on him as his shoulders slumped.

"Humans are my species, and like a father with an errant child, despite their shortcomings, I love them. Unfortunately, I've carried the guilt of destroying Kahchk Kihhim ever since, and it changed me. Throughout my terms as a leader, I taught tolerance in dealing with others. It earned me the label of soft, but my optimistic attitude toward people became contagious. The world is a better place today because I infected others with those beliefs."

"It is a better place, GreaPa, but enough better to accept Ocealla? Am I too optimistic?"

"If you or I don't know, we certainly can't convince Ocealla the world is safe for them. I do believe it, Kit. I've seen the changes. How do we convince them?"

"GreaPa, all we have to do is let them into our minds. They'll see what we see."

"Are we enough? History shows humanity will allow only one dominant species."

"History also shows humanity tolerated slavery, but they no longer do. Humanity changed."

"What about the other side of this? What about Homakuwa? They have the ability to change the world as they want, and in all this time they have remained hidden and haven't changed anything."

"GreaPa, I've seen into their souls, and they are not a threat."

"I've seen that too."

Both of them felt the weight of decisions to be made. After talking for hours, they fell into an exhausted sleep.

When Ron awoke, he lay quietly listening to the sounds around him: Kit's soft snoring, the sound of water, his own breathing. Quietly he reached over, put the collar on, and closed his eyes. As if he had stepped out of a building into a busy downtown street, he became aware of activity all around him. Voices materialized in his head, and many were not human. The sea pulsed with life, and the city throbbed with it. He thought of Katharine, and instantly she joined him.

Katharine: [We all believe this is the start of a new joint civilization on Earth. We're anxious to begin together.]

Chapter 14

Premier Hu sat behind his large desk as he scanned the latest coded message from their agent, Ahn. He glanced up at Robert Chaing, his western educated assistant and confidant. Robert Chaing looked the part of an Anglo-Asian. By Asian standards he was tall, his black hair was neatly trimmed, his western suit tailored. "Please summarize."

With a slight bow to the Premier, he began, "As you are aware, sir, the effect of the Prophet has been greatly reduced in China. Religion plays a much smaller part in our society. Religious groups representing a threat to our government are suppressed without mercy. Out of necessity, our actions remain covert as our country opens to the world, but those religious leaders trying to preach government policy from the pulpit are being retrained. In their place, we install leaders not averse to the government. Of course, life would be simpler without this opiate of religion, but it is better to control than try to suppress and create martyrs."

The Chairman nodded as Robert continued, "We restrict religions by reducing the stature and influence of those we do not control. This has reduced their numbers without driving them underground. Being subject to the United World Government has not changed life in China much. In many ways we remain a closed society with full central control. The UWG monitors see what we want them to see. We take much care with the publicity regarding human rights and the unrest over the economy so as to not attract attention."

"Yes, Robert, I understand we continue to extend our lead as the world's dominant economic power, but opening the country to the world has exposed China to the lifestyles of other countries. Now a desire has grown for more of the Western life."

"Yes, sir and as you are aware, wages and working conditions improved both at the demand of our workers and the UWG. We became less competitive by raising the costs of our exports. The people demand commodities which only a few decades ago were unheard of."

"Robert, our leap into the modern world requires we now address our environment and our people."

The Premier stood and walked around his desk. In comparison to Robert he was of average Chinese height, shorter than Robert, wearing glasses that emphasized his round face. A short haircut combined with a plump body completed the picture. He paced the perimeter of the spacious office, glancing at the paintings hung on the dark paneled wall. He paused in front of his favorite piece of art, a Ming vase.

Premier Hu understood the changes in his country and the world, but it was good to be refreshed. The pollution generated when they moved from an agrarian society to an industrial giant cost them. The lifespan in China dropped due in large part to environmental causes and a health care system aimed at younger and more productive citizens. However, that was not a bad thing. The cultural respect for elders was waning. The Great Revolution was founded on the basic concept that the few must sacrifice for the good of the many. People were used to benefit the society as a whole. The one child rule had been relaxed with the introduction of a lottery, where the winners were allowed another child. Alternatively, that chance could be sold. Though workers streamed into the cities for jobs, the skilled laborers were still in short supply.

He turned to face Robert. "Our acquisition of the Dow Engen-Michaels agricultural technology decades ago slowed the exodus from the countryside to the cities and in some areas reversed it. The food shortages, which created unrest before, are alleviated. Chinese biologists continue the Genetic Engineering programs to maximize areal production though there were some problems when people developed allergies to some of the foods. Chinese produced GE food is still prohibited in areas of Europe because of this, but the demand for inexpensive food is changing the market. Europe is gradually becoming available again."

He continued. "Our infrastructure is unrivaled anywhere in the world—both in scope and technology. Our political experiment of a strong central government directing a national economy has proven much more successful than the regulated capitalistic system of the West. We are able to respond to changing conditions directly, rather than wait for market forces to come into play. We move rapidly on decisions without waiting for legal challenges to take place, and our economy is so large as to absorb problems without a ripple."

"Yes, Premier. You are correct. Chinese technology has accelerated to the point we are unrivaled in the electronics industry, supplying most of the computer and communication equipment to the rest of the world. Now we import engineers into our industry. Your plan for this has given us the opportunity to build into the chips whatever we want."

"I am quite satisfied to allow the UWG to run things while we are able to monitor everything that goes on. What did concern me was the lack of domestic resources and raw materials. We have moved to address that."

"Premier, your plan to acquire the foreign companies we import resources from gives us control in a worldwide arena. As you foresaw, we have used the capitalistic system to take over without firing a shot. The long-term goal of a world dominated by China is taking place through economics."

"Robert, the one area where we must gain control is energy. We already supply virtually all the photovoltaic panels in the world. Our subsidized industry has driven the competition out, and we have secured the raw materials necessary for manufacture worldwide. No competition exists. But now the United States has gone into the energy business, and our position is threatened."

Robert understood that Premier Hu was engineering a takeover of the Orbital Energy System. Since private industry now controlled the system, China continued to quietly buy up controlling interests in those companies through shell companies. The purchases recently reached a point where further acquisitions would start to attract attention, so they needed a diversion.

The corruption of the Justice system of the UWG would do nicely. Thus, Hu found himself in bed with the other dissidents. China was willing to support the Foundation from behind the scenes and let them take the fall. No doubt existed in his mind their effort would be a failure. They fought for all the wrong reasons, and the world would not go backwards, digressing into a tribal state. China would not allow that.

"Robert, a single world government is the proper philosophy to follow, but it has to be directed. Amid the chaos of this upcoming war, the systems we have hidden within the technology will give China the position of director. They so eagerly purchased our technology at cut-rate prices, and now we have fingers throughout the world. This has been a long-term project, but we Chinese are used to thinking in generational terms. We remain unseen. Our involvement in this war must never be revealed."

"Yes sir, all our contacts with the Foundation pass through an agent, Kwang, with no direct connection to us. He is only known as 'The Asian.' His country of record is Korea. We allowed his family to immigrate covertly."

***

Leticia and Kit had become an item as much as possible at Ocealla. Kit looked over at her as she slept beside him. Through the collars, they knew each other more intimately than a couple married for forty years, and they were comfortable with each other. Their bond was strong. Kit already considered Ocealla his home. When he tried to imagine living back in Idaho, the picture blurred. The desire to be at Ocealla was too strong.

Leticia wanted to integrate him into Homakuwa society, and Kit embraced it. With his skills at diplomacy and knowledge of world politics, he would be invaluable as the nation began to join the world community. Content, Kit leaned over to kiss Leticia. Her eyes fluttered open. Smiling, she kissed him back, her arms pulling him atop her.

"Shouldn't we join the Collective soon? I need to learn more of this wonderful organism Ocealla if I'm going to live here permanently," said Kit.

"We have a little time, and I thought we'd join from here. I promise not to be a distraction." She kissed him hard and felt his passion rise along with hers. They became one without the collar.

***

Afterward, they held hands and lay side-by-side. "Are you ready?" asked Leticia.

They donned the collars, and the bed enveloped them and began to move their bodies through an intricate exercise routine. Their minds entered the Collective as they took over the operation of Ocealla from those exiting the Collective.

Ron was also in the Collective and watched them, remembering love at that age. Though he could only see what another person wanted to reveal, Kit's feelings about the loss of Susan had been genuine. The pain and guilt remained, but they didn't overpower his reason. This must be the magic of Homakuwa. Kit isolated those feelings and brought them out when he was alone and able to deal with them. Ron had been fond of Susan, but he had seen she was not the political animal needed to be the wife of a successful politician.

Katharine's presence broke into his thoughts: [Are you disturbed about the death of Susan?]

Ron: [I had to go through the deaths of all of my friends and relatives, and that built callouses allowing me to deal with the idea of my own death. My acceptance of Faithism alleviated a lot of the pain.

[During my long lifespan, everyone I knew left me behind as they journeyed into the next life. The loneliness was painful, as if I had been abandoned. For a time, I did not allow myself to get close to others, my family being the sole exception. I now accept this physical life as one classroom in the school of our existence. Death is merely the graduation to the next class.]

Katharine requested: [Show me some of this Faithism.]

Ron opened the pathway and Katharine joined him. He led her to a point where she looked out and sensed his strong belief in God and the certainty of a passage from this life. She felt the well-being within him from the belief that through this transition resided those he had loved and known. They belonged to an ocean of knowledge and love. The comfort from this would have helped her deal with the loss of her husband Robert decades before.

Ron: [This belief always existed within me as with many people. What the Prophet did was open the gateway. Once I was able to see it, I became a Faithist.]

Katharine: [There is no doubt I must meet the Prophet,] she said as she withdrew until they again entered the Collective.

***

Ron mused over private thoughts. He and Katharine had formed a deep bond because they knew each other completely. When you are able to behold another person's soul, you truly know who they are. The Collective also allowed him to peer within himself. After his extended life, he thought he knew himself well, but now he had a depth of understanding previously unknown. Again, Ron wondered if the Collective was influencing him or revealing parts he had not been able to understand before–like the Prophet. He and Katharine would be together for a long long time. He hoped Kit would choose the same with Leticia.

***

Kit and Leticia lay asleep in each others arms. After their session in the Collective, they exhausted themselves in unbelievable sex. Even without the collars, their minds meshed, and they shared sensations. A new dimension was added to their lovemaking because each could sense what the other wanted and needed.

Leticia awoke first, listening to Kit's soft snoring and enjoying the warmth of him beside her. Never before in Leticia's life had she had such a complete relationship with another person. While a Surfacer, she had always placed career and work goals ahead of everything. When Ocealla had been created, managing and protecting it had taken all of her time. Now she had someone she wanted to share it with.

Soon Homakuwa would begin the discussions with Kit and Ron about revealing Homakuwa to the surface world. Leticia knew this would eventually have to happen, but they risked so much. Their existence depended on the good will of mankind, and she had found humanity's good will in short supply.

Over the decades, since they built Ocealla, she had enlisted Jamie Wong's help in a covert plan to prepare for re-entry into the community of Earth. From Kahchk Kihhim years before, they had launched a virus which changed the nature of a few men in order to avert a war. The tactic had proven a temporary solution. From Ocealla they had embarked on a more ambitious plan in preparation for this day, one that could never be revealed to the Surfacers. It would be viewed as the ultimate betrayal of mankind. She kept that secret well buried because not even all of Homakuwa would approve.

When Kit stirred beside her, she quickly tucked the whole topic into a deep recess.

***

Kit and Ron participated in several discussions with all the city/states making up the nation of Homakuwa. The discussions went much faster than Ron was used to for this level of decision-making. Through the Collective, Ron familiarized them with the surface world and made his points for Homakuwa to reveal itself and join. Leticia remained the strongest opponent, but with Kit's arguments, she finally appeared to be persuaded.

***

Kit looked at Dave and Jackie. Ocealla had kept them unconscious in the med cells since the wreck. As the fluid drained, they coughed, their eyes fluttering open. At first, they were unfocused–rolling about–but gradually they stilled, settling on Kit.

"Dave, Jackie, it's me, Kit, Try to relax. Recovery from the med cells takes a while." Dave gave an inarticulate gurgle. "Don't try to talk. Just settle back. It'll all come back in a little while." Hearing their friend's words, their heartbeats calmed.

"You're in a medical facility. These people rescued us and brought us here. When you're better, I'll show you around. It's a pretty amazing place."

"We'll be going home in a week. Go back to sleep, and I'll come back soon." Their eyes closed, and he turned to leave. As he passed through the wall, Leticia joined him.

"Kit, they'll be fine. By tomorrow, we'll have them moving around without any problems. We should be able to leave in a few days. You'll get to go home."

"Leticia, as much as I've missed the surface world, I've started thinking of this as my home. You've made it so for me. I don't want to live away from you."

A grin on her face, Leticia said, "I feel the same, Kit. After all these years, I've finally found someone I want to be with." They stared at each other, awed by the magnitude of their mutual revelation. Their deep embrace left them both wondering where this path would lead, knowing that together they could face whatever would come.

PART 3

RETURN AND DISCLOSURE

Chapter 15

Jack Laurer answered Ron's call. "You've got a pair of balls calling me! I got fired over your disappearance. Should have retired years ago. I only kept working for you. Though I didn't do anything wrong, when you disappeared, somebody had to pay."

Without allowing Ron to interrupt, his rage continued. "The main criticism was in letting you go to Mexico without an escort. And the government of Mexico was really pissed that you entered without the normal dignitary fanfare, and then you disappeared from their shore. I didn't dare reveal you were spirited away in a submarine in their waters without their knowledge even though that was the only explanation I could think of.

"As far as they are concerned, you and that woman drowned, your bodies never recovered. You created quite an international incident. Our president had to apologize, and you know how much he likes to do that." He started run down, his ire vented.

"Jack, I am sorry. I didn't know we were going to leave, but I probably wouldn't have told you anyway. You would have tried to stop me."

"Goddamn right I would!"

"Are we going to talk or yell at each other?"

"I'm sorry, Mr. President."

"Ron, remember?"

"Okay, Ron, It's really good to hear from you. Where are you?"

"Actually we're on our way back to the US. Kit and his friends are with me. I also have a world shocker with me. Want another job?"

"With you, sir, anytime. What do you need?"

"I need you to rent a van and meet us at the Blue Moon Beach House on Camano Island, Washington, in three days. It's sixty miles north of Seattle. From Interstate 5, you'll exit onto route 532 west and…"

"I can find it, sir."

"We should arrive about five a.m. Hopefully, not a lot of people will be around to notice us coming out of the water. We are a party of six plus you for the drive to Idaho."

"Wouldn't a plane be faster?"

"To get the plane to Idaho requires a flight plan, and we don't want anyone to know of our return until we are ready to make an announcement. Is the plane back at the ranch?"

"Yes sir. We brought it back after we abandoned the search."

"We have our reasons for opting to drive. I'll explain when we see you. Please keep this completely confidential. Tell no one."

***

Seeing Katharine with Ron did not surprise Jack, but he was stunned to see Kit and his friends in good shape. "Susan didn't make it," Kit explained. "She was killed when the boat broke up."

"I'm sorry to hear that," responded Jack.

"Jack, this is Leticia Gardner. She's the leader of Ocealla."

"What's Ocealla?" asked Jack.

"Have we got a story for you!" said Kit.

On the drive back to the ranch, Ron and Kit filled Jack in on what had happened. When the discussion turned to Ocealla, Jackie and Dave couldn't stop talking. They literally gushed about the city, the citizens, and the trip back in the

Travelers. Jack tried to absorb everything, but the revelation of a new civilization undersea was hard to believe.

Ron said, "Now you understand why we need secrecy. We're going to introduce the Homakuwa civilization to the world at a full UWG meeting. We can't have leaks and speculation before that release."

"You mean we can't go home?" wailed Jackie.

"Not right away. We need time to prepare for the presentation of Homakuwa. Dave, do you believe Jackie can keep this a secret until then?"

Dave laughed loudly. Jackie elbowed him in the ribs. "Jackie, do you think Dave can keep this secret until we release the news?"

Jackie roared. "All right, we see your point. But we do get the book rights, okay? Dave, we could start writing while we're at Ron's!" They all laughed. Even Jack smiled.

***

From the ranch, Ron called the president of the United World Government. "Mr. President, this is Ron Carson speaking."

"I thought you drowned in Mexico."

"No, I'm alive and well. I'm sorry for the commotion my disappearance caused. Heinz, I need to brief you about a matter of world security. It's critical we keep this mater completely confidential. I have someone to introduce you to, someone quite remarkable. I can fly to DC tomorrow. Could you schedule us in?"

"I will cancel meetings if it's that important."

"It is, and I think you'll agree after we've met. I plan to make a news announcement later, so we'd appreciate your keeping this under wraps for a few days."

"I understand."

***

The private fanfare and jubilation of the Carson family celebration over Kit's return lasted several days. Dave and Jackie's families were there to share, but the ranch was closed to outsiders. Ron wanted to give themselves some peace before their return broke, so nothing was said, but it had to come out. Wanting to give the local press a scoop, Ron notified them of an announcement to be made. They were astounded that he was alive. Mostly, they kept the news a secret–mostly.

Ron stood on a pickup truck bed at his gate and addressed the press. "Ladies and gentlemen, today is a happy day for the Carson family. We're celebrating the return of my great-grandson Kit and his friends from a disastrous shipwreck. Unfortunately, Kit's wife, Susan, perished when their boat, caught in a storm in the South Pacific, sank."

Ron watched the crowd react with smiles. Hands frantically waved. He ignored them.

"As fortune would have it, they were rescued by a group from a place called Ocealla and nursed back to health. Our celebration today will be private and closed, but I will take a few questions." Ron pointed at a frantically waving hand.

"Wes Jackson of the Boise Tribune. Sir, you disappeared from Mexico a while back, and now you've returned with your great-grandson Kit. Would you please elaborate on that story."

"First, I want to apologize for my hasty and covert departure and the consternation it caused. I didn't plan it that way, but I didn't have any choice. We'll be issuing a full account at a later time. I was picked up in Mexico and transported to Ocealla to meet up with Kit and his friends. We were then brought back after they had recuperated. We're extremely grateful to Ocealla for their assistance and aid. That's all I'm going to say on this topic at this time. Next question." Another hand went up.

"Janet Blake of the Pocatello Times. Sir, will Kit be representing us again? The governor has appointed his replacement until an election can be held."

"This episode, the death of his wife and the near death of him and his friends has changed Kit, and he is reassessing his future. Next question."

Having given the local press first questions, Ron pointed at another reporter–one he didn't know.

"Gloria Sanchez, AP. Sir, I've been trying to find out anything I can about Ocealla. It not up in any of our data bases. What and where is Ocealla?"

"Gloria, we'll be making a full disclosure about Ocealla next week. Your questions and many more will be answered at that time. Thank you ladies and gentlemen. Now I'm going to celebrate Kit's return." He stepped down, got into the cab of the pickup and drove back to the house, shouted questions receding behind him.

***

"Whew!" Ron said as he entered the house. "I'm glad that's over. I need a whiskey." The group laughed. He walked over to Katharine and Leticia. "I suppose you watched the coverage?" They nodded. "Ocealla is going to cause quite a stir next week. How are you both doing?"

Even though the gathered group was small by Idaho standards, after decades of living in the closed-in society of Ocealla, Leticia and Katharine were still overwhelmed. "Your guests are most gracious and have not crowded us too much, but we both had to take breaks in our room to escape the continuous press of people."

"They're just grateful you were able to save Kit, David and Jackie. I also asked them to give you some consideration." He chuckled.

Since their arrival, Katharine had met with many people. Leticia had stayed back to acclimate at a slower pace. Getting used to the surface world was arduous. The brightness, direct sunlight, and colors leapt at them. The temperature changes and the numbers of people made her feel exposed and vulnerable causing her to miss the close press of the sea.

Chapter 16

Katharine looked from the dais at the huge hall before her. Delegates from the nations of the world filled the seats. Not all of them were physically present, but their holograms attended. At this distance, she was not able to distinguish image from real. Katharine knew those visible in the hall were only representatives; the world watched through the holo transmissions. The crowd quieted.

"It is with tremendous gratitude that I come before you today. I want to thank you for making the time for me to address you. As you know from the docket, my name is Katharine Levey, and I bring you greetings from my city of Ocealla and my nation of Homakuwa. As their representative, I am here seeking to join the community of man on Earth.

"Perhaps a short story of how we came about is in order. Decades ago a group of people living in the desert of Arizona formed an isolated community we called Kihhim. That is the Tohono O'odham word for village. Our group wished to form our own country, and since all of the land in the world belongs to someone, we decided to build a nation at sea, Kahchk Kihhim, Tohono O'odham for sea village. We did this and started to adapt ourselves into citizens of an ocean nation. We became a new species, one with the ability to evolve ourselves through genetic engineering, areas forbidden by international treaty. The penalties for these transgressions were severe, and we had crossed over that line. Fearing for our existence, we disappeared." Katharine watched the audience. Some were rapt, their full attention on her. Others studied their tablets, seeking more information.

"We grew in the succeeding decades, expanding and becoming a civilization, a nation in every respect. We now feel the time has come to unite all the peoples of the Earth. We are a new civilization of different people, very different. Some of your present scientific definitions of species will have to change. But we are like you in many ways. We hope that our diversities will combine with yours to make a truly unified and strong world for the future. Let me take you on a tour."

Katharine pressed a button, and a large bubble appeared above her. "This is how we started." The bubble started multiplying; forming a layer of bubbles floating in the air, and the hologram of Ocealla grew above her and the representatives. An undertone of murmurs arose, as the delegates looked at the glowing green layer of bubbles, not understanding. The layer grew, rapidly filling the hall. The cloud of bubbles started to descend toward the upturned faces. Momentarily, some of the delegates showed a panicked look, but this was just a holo. A titter of excitement grew as the transparent walls revealed waving figures inside, and the true scale of the vision became apparent. The city began to rotate, other shapes peered out at the crowd in the hall, obviously not humanoid. Like the satellites surrounding the Earth, figures swarmed around the bubble city.

"I would like to introduce you to some of our citizens. Their appearance will be strange."

The holo moved toward the layer, one bubble growing until it hung above those in the hall like giant moon. A large soft gray squid-like creature swam into view. "Some of our citizens are very different from you because we live in a different world. We are much more varied, with many altered shapes. Some are homo-sapiens such as I am. This," she gestured to the squid-like creature now dominating the view, "is Unweil, one of our oldest citizens. He is a Construct–Con for short. Homakuwa created him."

As the image focused, more than ten arms of different shapes and different sizes became apparent. "As you can see, the tapered body at the center has eyes and bumps giving it spherical perception. This Con has the ability to see 360 X 360 degrees. The arms seemed to wave to each delegate, and the many eyes sought them out. The delegates' mouths gaped in total silence.

"Unweil doesn't speak as we would understand, but we have translators." A dolphin swam into view beside the Construct. At first glance, it was a dolphin, but on its back was a growth. Gills were visible. "This is another of our citizens, Blue Streak. He is an Altered–Alts for short, and he has been part of our civilization almost from the beginning. He is a modified dolphin."

The hall was stunned into silence. A high pitched but clearly understandable voice spoke. "We are sooo honored to meet and speak to you at last and look forward to establishing the best of relations."

Suddenly the air filled with deafening voices as all the delegates tried to speak at the same time.

Nothing could be heard. Her question board was a solid mass of lights. She stood watching the frantic activity, listening to the shouting, waiting for things to calm enough, so she could speak. When that didn't happen Ron walked to the microphone. "SILENCE!" he roared. The sound echoed within the chamber. Slowly it grew quiet. "Ms. Levey and the others cannot speak or respond to questions until order is restored. When she is finished with her address, all questions will be answered." Smiling, he gestured for her to return to the dais.

"Unweil and Blue Streak are only a couple of examples of our people. We have others who are anxious to join with you. I can take a few questions, but if you submit them electronically, all will be answered." Almost immediately delegates began speaking into their communicators. Those with implants stood quite still, eyes closed, lips moving. She looked at the message board and spoke the name of the first delegate from the South American bloc. He appeared before her in the air.

"Where exactly is this nation located?"

Katharine repeated the question then answered. "We have habitats throughout the oceans in every part of the world."

She chose another name, this one from Asia. "How long ago did this civilization, Homakuwa, start?"

"It's been more than two of your generations since we left the surface of Earth."

In the background, she could feel the millions of inquiries going to Homakuwa. Activity in all of Homakuwa had been focused on this event–this moment–when their history would change. The Collective mind absorbed the flood and sent back answers. The questioners talked to someone who answered them one-on-one. Beside her Ron shook his head. None of them had realized how immense this was. The crowd was fully enraptured in the questions, the answers, and the answerers. When they finally realized the extent of logistics exhibited, jaws would fall. She and Ron watched the bedlam. "At least it's organized," he said, his eyes on her. They both laughed.

"The aliens have landed, and they are us," Katharine said. Again, they held their sides with laughter, but they both understood this was serious history. Hours later, Ron guided the exhausted Katharine toward the door. The applause from the standing delegates that followed them out of the hall was deafening. Stepping out into a quiet hallway, they hurried to a secure exit used to leave without making a statement. That would come later.

Ron held her arm as they stepped onto the moving walkway. Suddenly, they moved under a clear roof and looked up at the darkening sky overhead. The surface of the moving walkway disconcerted her at first. As they sidestepped toward the center, their speed picked up until the buildings outside flashed by. "The walkway is a liquid with low shear along the direction of flow, but very strong vertically," Ron explained, gesturing down at the transport surface.

Katharine peered at what appeared to be syrup, but felt like a plush carpet. Katharine looked around. Those people in front and behind her were moving with her while they passed those on either side. Some of their eyes flashed recognition from the press coverage of the UWG meeting, but no one moved toward them. One man in front glanced over his shoulder, nodded, then turned back.

"Privacy has become a benchmark for us because it is so fragile–so easy to violate. We guard privacy with fervor," said Ron. They edged to the left and were swept along a branch moving away from the main flow. Suddenly Katharine's stomach lurched as they dropped into a tunnel, a huge spiral carrying them below the earth's surface.

The ceiling was well lit, and the walls smooth–plastic or metal or a combination. Katharine couldn't tell at this speed. Toward the center of the spiral was a huge column of storefronts with people moving in and out. Several layers later, Ron moved her toward the column, and they slowed until they stepped onto solid ground. As they walked along the sidewalk and under the transport spiral, people on the far side whizzed around them. In front of them was a door. Ron spoke quietly, and on silent hinges, it opened for them.

The far wall looked out over the Potomac. The setting sun glinted off the water, and birds–ducks she thought–flew down to settle onto the surface. A few boats with their running lights on glided past toward docks down the river. She walked across the room and put her hand on the glass. "We can put any view on you want," Ron said.

"This one's fine, magnificent in fact," Katharine said. She turned to look around for the first time. The room was spacious. A marble floor had alternating black and white tiles. The walls were a soft creamy white, and in front of her hung the Mona Lisa. She walked over to it, and its spell took her attention. Gently she moved her hand forward to touch the frame, but her fingers touched only smooth wall.

"Redecoration's a snap," said Ron. "If you want, we can tour any gallery in the world. Even private collections, or we can make up our own collection." With a mischievous grin on his face, he asked, "Would you like to sit? I can get us something to drink."

"Please," said Katharine, as she dropped into a soft white chair, reminding her of a tall beanbag. Ron went to a panel in the wall. He spoke and returned in a few minutes with two glasses of deeply amber liquid.

"Scotch," he said, handing one to her. As he sat beside her, he held out his glass. "To a united world." She nodded as they touched glasses. Only recently re-introduced to scotch, the liquid was like a fire going down her throat. "This is a moment in history," said Ron.

"Whatever the outcome, you're right," said Katharine. "Now begins the work of trying to assimilate."

Chapter 17

Rhualla Hussein sat quietly with Ayatollah Aiassi Komini and Abayat Hussein. Rhualla had left his position as security agent in Washington with the United World Government, but he actively followed world events, logging on several times a day. Returning to the Mideast, he now was the assistant to the Ayatollah and followed events throughout the world to report. He offered an assessment of the potential influences and problems.

He showed them the video of the Homakuwa woman's presentation to the UWG assembly, and they were numbed into silence. "At first, I was fascinated, but a troubling knot began to grow as I grasped the enormity of the threat represented by this civilization. Humanity could be swept away by this species, just as Islam and the other major religions of the world are being decimated by the Prophet. I believe a crisis of epic proportions is growing. Yet the world does not understand what is at stake. Homakuwa presented a benign image, but they hold the potential for total domination of the human race."

Ayatollah Aiassi Komini and Abayat Hussein had absorbed his report in silence, waiting to ask questions until he finished. "Since this revelation," asked the Ayatollah, "what has this Homakuwa done?"

"Ocealla City has offered a few tours to government officials from various countries. They established an embassy in Washington D.C. The woman who gave the presentation is the ambassador to the UWG. Homakuwa developed a website with virtual tours available to anyone who wants to take them. They are trying to integrate into our civilization though they are closed as a society."

The Ayatollah raised his hand to his chin, obviously thinking. "If we had a closed society, as they do, we would be forced to open up." "Do they have the education control and monitors as we do? Do they have the justice control that we are required? Do they have the Prophet corrupting their religion? Do they even have a religion or are they Godless?"

"We know very little about them because they are so closed," said Rhualla. "The vote for membership is scheduled next year following one week of open discussion. No country seeking membership has ever been denied, but this is intriguing. Surely, many points will be brought up both for and against their membership because they are so different from us."

"What could be the outcome if membership is rejected?" asked Abayat Hussein.

"If our previous rulers had not signed up, we would not be subject to these outrageous conditions. Can we secede?" asked the Ayatollah.

Rhualla shrugged. "No country has ever asked to leave the UWG. That would probably require a popular vote. We would need to convert a lot of people to our Islam. The election would be overseen by the UWG, making it difficult to control the tally."

The Ayatollah understood the scope of the problem and the need for new thinking. In the past, he would have been able to motivate the faithful and mount a movement, but their numbers were too few. Even if all the religions of the world combined, who would lead, who would follow? He lamented to himself, the organization no longer exists to fight this. He understood the Foundation needed to meet face-to-face to discuss this and what to do, despite the danger. In its own way, this was more monstrous than the Prophet. He hastily scribbled out a message and handed it to Rhualla.

"Copy this and distribute it to all members of the Foundation. This is critical." Rhualla rushed out. "If Homakuwa is accepted into membership, we may be able to mount a campaign to control our own government and then find a way to secede. If they are not accepted, we can yet use that to unite and form a government and then secede from the UWG. Either way, we must gain control. Presently only a few delegates stand in our way. I propose we suggest they support us."

"And if they choose not to?" asked Abayat Hussein.

"We will suggest in such a way they must, or they will be replaced."

"Will they step down?"

The Ayatollah merely stared at him.

Chapter 18

Once again, Katharine looked out from the dais at the assembled delegates of the United World Government. "Ladies and gentlemen, as you know, a vote is pending for the acceptance of Homakuwa into the United World Government. I am here to personally answer questions in your consideration of membership. Homakuwa has been receiving a continuous stream of inquiries, which we tried to answer. Many took advantage of our virtual tours, and we tried to accommodate visits. Unfortunately, due to our limited staff and resources, those have been few. "I previously described our civilization. What more can I answer?"

Her board lit up, and she took a question from the representative from Iran. "All members of the UWG are monitored to assure basic human rights policies are followed in each country. How would we be able to do that with Homakuwa?"

"As you know, the electronic monitoring system used on the surface does not function underwater. We agree to allow representatives of the UWG in each of the cities of Homakuwa to assure that species rights are met. This will be the same for the education system and the environmental compliance."

Another light. "All the nations on the Earth contribute to the UWG so there are funds for it to function, yet Homakuwa does not have an economic system for funds to be paid. How would you handle that?"

"We are working on things to sell or trade with the surface world to allow us the wherewithal to pay dues as needed."

The Chinese delegate rose. "I looked into the history of Kahchk Kihhim and Homakuwa, such as I could. I find some things troubling. We have laws regarding human genetics and manipulation. You violated those laws as Kahchk Kihhim and continue to violate them as Homakuwa. Those laws are in place to protect the human species and the world environment. You also pursued nuclear development and destroyed Kahchk Kihhim. Whether this was in the development of a bomb or not, is not clear. Again, this is a violation of the basic tenets of the UWG. What assurances do we have that you will follow the laws and rules now when you blatantly failed to do so in the past?" He dragged the last word out for several syllables.

A confused stir arose within the hall with angry undertones. This was the crux of the discussion, and the agreement to accept Homakuwa into the UWG. Katharine could not reveal that the United States and China had jointly tried to destroy Kahchk Kihhim. Without proof it would ring false, nor would it solve the problem before her. She needed to face this issue and respond. "Homakuwa has no interest in nuclear power. We have no program to develop or even study it." She took a breath, letting it out slowly.

"With regard to the human genetic laws, they are loosely followed by you now. Under your definition of species, we are made up of many different ones, but we consider all of Homakuwa as one species. Our genetics is a technology basic to our ability to adapt to our environment. We will not share it outside of Homakuwa. Our species does not represent a threat to humans. We live in entirely different worlds with no desire to compete."

The delegate spoke again. "So we are to accept your word that your created species and your technology will never threaten humanity? Your past record speaks otherwise. China, for one cannot support your admission without strict oversight."

Katharine's ire rose. About to lash out, she felt Ron's steadying hand on her shoulder. The questions continued, but none were on the same level. By the end of the session, Katharine was exhausted.

***

Taking the tall scotch Ron handed her, Katharine exclaimed, "Boy, do I need this!"

Ron nodded. "The grilling by the Chinese delegate was pretty rough. It was not a move to deny you membership, but one to increase the oversight of Homakuwa. In the end, you must be approved for membership."

Leticia spoke up. "And if we aren't approved. What does that mean? Would the UWG attack us? Without assurances of protection, would we be subject to attacks by individual countries? We cannot be at odds with the surface world, Ron. We will do whatever is necessary to survive, and that will bring out the nightmare action that the surface world fears. What I'm saying is we can be provoked into actions we abhor in order to survive. I'm sure your species will do the same."

"It's not productive to focus on the worst case until we know more," said Ron. "That will sap our energy and sour our attitude. Let's see what they propose. I suspect those countries voting to reject the membership application seek other agendas. The critical issue here is the oversight. Much of the technology they try to apply will not work. Certainly, the electronic technology will be of limited value. What's left is representatives on site, and they know nothing about the Collective which you must keep hidden. Do not resist oversight. Make the statement you will accept any level. Your actions will allay their fears."

Her brow creased, Leticia said, "They truly don't understand how different we are. Once we gained the ability to adapt ourselves to whatever environment we chose to live in and control our longevity, we ceased to compete for resources. Humanity has not risen above the genetically driven need to compete, even when resources are not the issue. They may not be capable of doing so. I'm sure the monitors will come to realize we are not a threat. This alliance between the surface world and Homakuwa will be interesting."

Leticia continued, "Knowledge of our capabilities to control longevity and the Collective will create a demand to share–something we won't do." We'll make sure of that she thought.

Kit said, "In one respect, it's too bad the Collective can't be shared, because it would be the one way to assure Homakuwa is not a threat. The openness and true understanding would ease the process. But then, I'm not sure humans would open up either."

Chapter 19

The crisp fall air greeted Leticia and Kit when they left their hotel. Summer had given way to fall, and the leaves on the trees in Washington D.C. were changing. The colors were beautiful, almost an assault on Leticia's eyes. The world of Ocealla, two hundred feet below the sea surface, was dim with colors muted in shades of green. They had learned to use color as part of their enhanced senses, but the colors remained pastels in comparison to the surface world.

Stepping onto the transport strip, they moved toward the fast part. Slower passengers and the few above-ground buildings passed by, and then the strip dipped underground, and the smooth walls rushed past. Glowing signs sped by overhead, showing branching tunnels and destinations. Leticia wasn't used to the speed in this surface world where everything happened so fast. Kit pulled on her arm, and they stepped to one side where they were swept down another tunnel. Lights flashed by, and they moved to the slow part. As they neared the side, they slowed almost to a stop.

In front of them a sign glowed, Anika's Atrium Restaurant. They walked through an arched hallway to approach the small counter. Katharine and Ron stepped into view. "Have you been waiting long?" asked Leticia.

"We just got here minutes ago," said Katharine, turning to tell the monitor their party had arrived. Wooden doors opened, and a spot of light moved across the floor showing them the way to their table. Sunbeams struck them as they entered the room. Leticia saw a glass dome and the sky above. Plants hung everywhere—some of them several stories high. This reminded her of the atrium at Kihhim. The floor had tables with rooms and private alcoves built into the walls. Booths were located vertically up the sides, and as they watched, one of the booths descended slowly. As it settled, the spot of light indicated it was to be theirs.

They moved into the circular booth, which closed around them. To their delight, the table surface lit up with a question. *Freshen up first?* When Katharine and Leticia stood, the booth opened again. Lights in the floor led them to one side. Ron and Kit watched them go. "You and

Leticia have grown quite fond of each other, haven't you." said Ron.

"As have you and Katharine," responded Kit, smiling. "Leticia's not like anyone else I've ever met. She's kind and knowledgeable yet there's steel inside her. She's funny, but is wise in so many ways. When I asked her how old she was she said 'Much older than you, kiddo' but wouldn't say more."

"We knew each other when I was President of the United States," said Ron. "And that was a long time ago. She, Katharine, and the others at Homakuwa are the reason I'm still here today."

Kit's mouth hung open. "But they seem so young, certainly not over forty."

"We're a long, long way from forty," said Ron. "When I knew them they gave me some gifts setting the direction of my presidency, and I used them to change our world for the better. They also gave me the gift of extended life, though at times I felt it was a curse. The blessing of longevity was exciting at first. But as everyone I knew and loved left this Earth, the loneliness drove me to despair.

"I threw myself into establishing the stability of the World Government, but the world had moved past me decades ago. When you disappeared, I waited for my time to die, and then Katharine showed up. She saved my life and has now given me Homakuwa and the integration of a new species as my cause."

"If they did so much for you why did you try to destroy them?" asked Kit.

"I was afraid for the survival of my species, and I reacted the way humans have reacted since they stood up on two legs. I thought their destruction would ensure the survival of homo-sapiens as the dominant species on Earth. What a relief it has been to find out my attempt to annihilate them ensured their survival. The load of guilt haunted me for decades, and now it has been lifted." As the women returned, Ron stood to welcome them. When they were reseated the booth sides encircled them again before rising to a position overlooking the atrium floor. The table top displayed the menu. Sounding serious, Ron said, "The seafood is probably not up to your standards," which made them laugh. Within minutes of pressing their order, an opening appeared in the wall, and their drinks moved onto the table. "This is pretty impressive," said Leticia.

"Some of the older restaurants still use human staff for a special ambience, but many of the upscale ones use this method," Kit said. They sat quietly, observing the huge atrium containing people above and below. A tone sounded, the wall opened again, and their meals moved out onto the table. The food steaming on the plates smelled delicious. The taste proved as good as the aroma had promised.

As they finished, Kit ordered coffee, the rest had tea. Kit addressed his great-grandfather. "Leticia's resisting the I.D. chips for their newborns. I don't understand why. We all have them."

Before answering, a knowing look passed between Ron and the women. "You need to understand the generation we came from. No chips existed then, and Americans were suspicious of government. It was a feeling left over from the actual founding of the United States when the Constitution specifically prevented the power of a strong central government from becoming onerous."

The hatred of government intrusion still resided within Leticia. When she had refused to set aside her oath of justice, she'd been forced out of the FBI. As a result, she joined Kihhim, her hatred growing from the forced exodus when Kahchk fled the persecution of the surface world. Her loyalty to

Homakuwa was absolute, and her refusal to start the chip program was the result of distrust of government.

Controlling her anger, Leticia calmly responded, "Kit, we won't retrofit the adults, and the chips won't work underwater. The birthrate in Ocealla, in fact in all Homakuwa is very low due to our long lives and our need to live within our environment." Population control and longevity were areas that humankind lacked the maturity to handle.

Ron took over the conversation. "Before the formation of the United States, governments regarded the citizens as subjects to be ruled. Predictions that a democracy, a representative government, couldn't last almost proved true when the social programs became so burdensome they robbed the people of incentive. The controls put in place to limit government eroded over the decades as people demanded more from their government and less from themselves. To deal with this, I had to severely cut the role of the federal government. By Executive Degree, I moved much of the power back to the states and reduced federal social programs. Only after that did I believe it was safe to embark on a program where citizens would voluntarily have chips installed. I had to assure the citizens that any oversight was severely restricted, and all programs subject to public scrutiny. The press was critical in being the watchdog that abuse didn't occur."

"From what I read," said Kit, "critical is too kind. It was hell."

"Until those restrictions were in place, it would have been all too easy to slide into a totalitarian system and a repeat of the historic cycle of oppression and rebellion—war and death. Once I felt assured the chips could not be used as a spy device, I had a chip installed to demonstrate to the country my faith in World Government." He pointed to a spot behind his right ear.

"Computers gather and collate tremendous amounts of data, with the ability to actually monitor individuals among millions of citizens. The watchdog and the rules to prevent abuse were fluid and altered with the changing needs. Freedom from government surveillance was traded for security during the world war against terrorism—the war against the civilization we had built."

"That was part of what drove us out," said Leticia.

"As the watchdog heralding abuse, the press is also subject to influence and bias. The competition between news agencies to capture the public attention led them to magnify minutia–influence public opinion rather than present facts, at times manufacturing news. This fact was not lost on politicians, and an evil symbiosis resulted in public suspicion of both those who ran government and those who reported the news. It was all subject to the frailties and inconsistencies of the people, and that pushed us toward computer monitoring of government. Now it is virtually impossible for government officials to abuse their positions or grab power. More than two hundred years ago George Orwell wrote a book called _1984_, in which government regulated every aspect of human life. Individuality was viciously suppressed as was love." Ron smiled at Katharine and took her hand.

"Where Orwell set the citizens against each other to monitor behavior, the computer age gave government the ability to realize that kind of control. But those very computers also offer the ability to impartially ensure that basic rights and freedoms are fairly applied. By absolute control, they cannot be suborned, and their watchfulness is not subject to influence or changes in government officials, or lifestyles.

"Consistency is the bedrock of our way of life. The fact that an impartial judge monitors us is more reassuring than having people snoop into our lives. Access to data is granted only when a justified specific request is submitted to the computer. And those requesting without proper need are themselves suspects. We don't trust each other but we do trust our machines. Machines are without ambition, or the drive for power, or animosity, and they are un-biased."

"Who monitors the machines?" asked Leticia, suspicious.

"That is the key." said Ron. "The machines report the decisions to a committee for assessment, but any change in the decision recommended by the committee is reviewed by the machine. A final decision must be agreed to by both the committee and the computer. The oversight computer is in reality an artificial intelligence."

"Okay," said Leticia, "but who programs that intelligence?"

"Initially it was programmed by the UWG Justice Department, but now it programs itself."

"There were a lot of science fiction stories written about machines taking over the world and warring with humans for supremacy," said Katharine.

"There was also a whole series of stories where the computers had immutable rules called Prime Directives they operated under. These could not be violated without destroying the machine. All artificial intelligences have these built into them. Any attempt to subvert those rules sets off alarms."

There was a silence as they mulled over this information.

"If you read the World Constitution closely and check the laws, the installation of chips is still voluntary," Ron continued. "De facto, everybody has them installed, because the suspicion of government has ceased, and people believe government exists for them. The surface world will need to demonstrate to Homakuwa our confidence is justified. Their view of history certainly doesn't accomplish that."

Kit's face showed his surprise at the revelation. "We'll need to close the voluntary chip loophole."

"Only by keeping the chip installation voluntary can you maintain the confidence that it's beneficial. If you force it, chip use will be seen as a loss of freedom to choose, which it would be. The image of government as the protector of freedom must never be threatened."

"Actually," said Katharine, "we also have a system of monitoring our citizens. Members of our habitats are all a part of our organism, Homakuwa. Just as you are aware of a problem with a part of your body, we all are aware of each other. People can still keep things private, but the signs of a problem manifest themselves in detectable ways. In our case, we use a biologic system, which in its own way could be considered even more invasive than yours."

"Yes, but your system is not accessible by the World Government," objected Kit.

"So local autonomy isn't a reality?" asked Katharine, with a wry smile. Ron looked at Kit, raising his eyebrows. Kit sighed. They were right.

Chapter 20

By the time winter hit Washington, Leticia and Katharine needed a break from the surface world including an escape from the cold. Ron remained to aid in other issues. Back in Ocealla, Leticia sat with Katharine and several other citizens. They wore collars and were operating Ocealla on their shift.

Katharine: [Leticia, I'm so glad to be back. The surface world is a continuous grind. It never stops.]

Leticia projected: [There's no place like home. I really missed the familiarity of Ocealla. Homakuwa may not be in competition for resources with humanity, but the surface worlders will try to use us in their competition for domination. Only the United World Government will restrict those efforts.]

Unweil opened up: [Perhaps Homakuwa needs to lead humanity away from the plunder of resources. We see serious problems with the fish populations near Retseana. The surface creatures are depleting the schools to the point they will not recover for seasons. You have voiced concerns.

Perhaps we could make some sort of deal with them.]

Katharine had heard of this from surface oceanographic scientists. [I believe we should approach them with the idea of Homakuwa managing the industry. Who better than us?]

Blue spoke up: [If we designed and operated a farming system, we would save the species, and the farm would be more productive. It would protect our interests and integrate us better into the surface world.]

In agreement, Katharine contacted Ron to explain the situation and proposal to him.

Katharine: [Initially we'd meet with resistance from the fishing industry being regulated by a non-human species. Kahchk Kihhim worked with a number of fishermen who were more successful with our help. We should use that,] Katharine projected. [Let's start with the Oceanographic community. I believe we can get them on board. I'll arrange a delegation visit to Ocealla including some of the international corporate industry leaders.]

Ron: [In order to save the food species from the ravages of overfishing, the Canadian and US regulators restricted the industry. Over the last two decades much of it has been devastated.

Generations of fishing tradition and demand expanded the industry to the point it was overgrown. Without restriction, it would have totally collapsed with the loss of food fish for decades. The violators from the other countries pay no heed. The UWG now directs the oversight, and it is much stricter, but there are still violators. Thanks, this is a very good suggestion.]

Katharine: [We'll make arrangements as soon as we can establish the visit schedule. How are other things going?]

Ron: [We're having problems with the maintenance of the Orbital Power System. The last contract bids came in and the cost of keeping a maintenance team in orbit has become exorbitant. That's taking up a lot of my time right now. The union wants extended hazardous pay with one month on and two months off. It's not unreasonable when one considers the damage a month in space can do to the human body. The price of power is going to go up. It's the major export from America now, so we must keep it cost-effective.]

Katharine: [I'm sorry you're facing this. Two months apart is diverting my mind from Ocealla, and I really wish you were here.]

Ron: [I wish I were there with you. Are you enjoying your time at Ocealla?]

Katharine: [Perhaps you can come with the oceanic visitors?]

Ron: [We'll see how this goes.] He left.

Unweil: [The control of the sea farming would be to our advantage in relations with the surface.]

Leticia added, [It would be of great benefit. Under our direction, it will be more productive. Unweil and Blue, you work with the herders and put together a presentation with show and tell.]

Katharine mused: [What can we get in return? Their currency is worthless to us except to pay our UWG dues. We need to figure something to buy.]

Unweil spoke again: [Perhaps it's time we considered expansion for Homakuwa. I don't mean on Earth either. Humans are made only for life on Earth–not space; it's expensive to send and keep them there. Perhaps we should embark on a new design program for ourselves with that in mind. A design similar to me would be a great improvement for space life over surface worlders, and some modification of my design wouldn't need to be extensive to be a vast improvement.]

There was total silence as the multiple minds turned the thought over. Jamie Wong offered: [The limitations of humans dooms the species. With their physical form, they cannot exist unsupported, in mass, anywhere other than Earth, even with great technology advances. They have dreams of space colonies and colonies on other planets, but the reality is their bodies cannot survive in any environment other than Earth or Earth similar for extended periods.]

Leticia: [Maintaining Earth-like environments is expensive.]

Jamie Wong: [Eventually, there will be a cataclysmic event, which will change their environment on Earth faster than they can adapt, and thus destroy their civilization. They are headed for extinction, and time is the only variable. For survival, a new species capable of adapting to any environment is critical. We are that species.]

Leticia: [Jamie, work with Unweil and see what you can come up with. If you think it's possible to meet the schedule, we could bid the next contract and exchange transport and habitat construction for maintenance and operating labor. Expansion into high orbit would give us unlimited opportunities.]

Katharine thought to herself, 'Leave humanity behind to their fate? Are we like that? Aren't we better?'

A wave of excitement not felt for decades rippled through the group. All of Homakuwa was thinking about it, but no one was more excited than Jamie Wong. Homakuwa had become a static society, and this offered a chance to become dynamic again. There was unanimous agreement to keep this confidential within Homakuwa until they were ready to submit the bid.

***

Robert bowed low to Chairman Hu. "I have good news to report on our bid to take over the maintenance and operation contract for the Orbital Power System. The American unions are demanding substantial raises and shorter work periods, and it will be quite easy for us to underbid them. We will start training crews immediately, so we are ready to take over the system when the existing contract is up in six months. With the contract award, even though we don't own the system, we will control it which will represent a major gain for us."

The Chairman smiled. With the management of the Orbital Power System, China would control most of the world's supply of power. They already controlled much of the world's food supply, and through their wholly owned subsidiaries, the world's resources. Regardless of the position of the United World Government, China would hold the world by the vitals. Not a shot had been fired. The uprising of the Foundation against the UWG would be a great diversion from the true takeover.

Chapter 21

The contingent of oceanographic and fishing industry specialists arrived on US Naval aircraft carrier USS George H. W. Bush. They and USS George Bush's Captain, Fredrick McCain, boarded several Travelers and were conveyed to Ocealla. This fifteen-person group was the largest single group ever to visit at one time. As they entered the bubble room created for the discussions, there was only one closed mouth, which belonged to Ron. Katharine, Leticia, Blue Streak and Unweil were in attendance, and introductions were made.

"Gentlemen and Ladies, I welcome you to Ocealla." Seats formed out of the floor. "Please be seated. I hope the trip was comfortable. The Travelers you rode here in are constructs we use to move air breathers such me around. We have many things to show you. First I'd like to explain a little about Ocealla and take you on a tour."

"We are presently located two hundred feet below the surface. As you saw coming in, at this depth the sea is quite dark." She gestured toward the bubble wall. "I'm going to enhance the view for you." The bubble wall lightened, and the sea became transparent, teeming with life, enabling them to see for almost a mile.

"What you see is a projection of the outside made up of light, heat, sonar, and input from the many citizens, all integrated into a visual display. For us the sea is a busy and living organism in which we participate."

The eyes of the audience were riveted on the bubble wall.

"This habitat," she gestured at the bubble around them, "was genetically engineered and grown, controlled by our continuous input. We consider ourselves a single life form of many parts. Above us at the surface, we farm algae and plankton, which supplies us with the oxygen you are breathing plus food for us and the fish we raise. The light is supplied by phosphorescent algae. We've modified it to produce more light than is naturally produced. Normally we keep the habitat darker, but the surface world is brighter, so this is for your convenience."

Faces full of wonder gazed around the room.

"As you know, we offered a proposal to take over the Directorship of the International Fishing

Oversight and Control. We live in the sea, and thus have a unique perspective on how to manage the resource represented by the oceans. I know those of you from the fishing industry are concerned about us regulating your industry, so let me put this on a dollars and cents basis for you.

"We propose setting up large farming areas at sea where you presently fish, maintaining the entire food chain from feed to fry to fish. With this system we can triple the areal production of fish, reduce the time and distance to beds and ensure catches. On our side, we would maintain the viability of our oceans by overseeing and enforcing the regulations to ensure everyone is meeting those requirements. In exchange for this, we would charge a modest fee per ton harvested, resulting in lower cost to you and ensured catches."

There were looks of doubt in the audience.

"On the scientific side, we have been actively maintaining successful farming operations for decades. The species we grow are now more numerous in our growth areas than the worldwide populations. These species are not modified but natural. We are able to achieve high areal productions because we control the base of the food chain and the predators. By maximizing the algae and plankton growth and minimizing the predator losses, we can grow to higher densities. After our tour, we'll have lunch–all of it our catches. Are there any questions at this time?"

Apparently, the group had not recovered from the ride and the view. One lone hand went up. "Yes?"

"I'm Yaki Inoushi, Representative from Japan. As you know we have been much maligned over our fishing practices, but fishing is the life of Japan. How are you going to assure we will be able to get the various species we need?"

"All of you will supply us with a list of the species you need to harvest. In addition, we need the annual tonnages you expect. I'm not saying we will meet all tonnage requests at first, but we have a better chance of meeting those needs than anyone in the world. Any other questions?"

No other hands went up. "If you will proceed again into the Travelers, we'll take a tour of our own farms." Hesitantly they approached the wall, watching it dissolve to expose a number of Traveler chambers. The USS Bush's captain held back. "This is astounding. I'd like to talk to you a lot more about your technology, especially the viewing technology."

"I'm sure you would. Proprietary at this time though." The captain entered, and the bubble reformed. Katharine turned to Ron. Once the Travelers moved away from Ocealla, the chamber bubbles became transparent with a small area showing the interior of each Traveler to Katharine in a heads-up display.

"What do you think?"

"Great, and great to see you again." Their hug pushed the world away, leaving just the two of them. When Ron's lips met hers, she felt the hunger rise within them. At last Katharine broke away.

"Of course you'll stay for a few days after the delegation leaves." It was not a question as they knew the answer. "Time for me to play tour guide. Want to join me?"

Ron nodded, and they both sat and put collars on. Katharine was part of the Travelers. Each one contained a speaker to carry her words.

"You'll notice the sea life is dense around the habitat. Much of it is our constructs going about various tasks. First we'll head toward the surface so you can get an idea of the scope of our algae and plankton fields. The total area is about one hundred square miles in many modules." As they neared the surface, the water got much brighter. There was a colored thickness to the surface not seen from below. Mid-sized sharks were below the surface.

"We patrol this to keep the munchers out. On the perimeter are other patrols to keep out the larger munchers, including whales. We feed some, but they consume way too much, and we get no return. We fertilize the upper surface with both nutrients and the carbon dioxide from our habitat to increase the plant growth." As they moved further out, another bed of algae and plankton appeared. Long tentacles of huge jellyfish surrounded it. Inside was a swarm of small fish. At times, they were so dense it was impossible to see more than a few yards. When they cleared, another curtain of tentacles was visible hanging down, but not as dense. Inside were schools of larger fish.

"We farm concentrically, where the outer ring consists of the fry. They are protected by the stinging tentacles. Inside that ring is the next sized fish, the fingerlings. They can't penetrate the curtain to get to the fry, but the fry pass through to become feed for the fingerlings. This continues toward the center, which is full of our harvest.

"Below are membrane shelves where we collect the fish waste to use as fertilizer and grow the bottom feeders and scavengers, such as crab and lobster. The whole structure is loosely held together by circumferential strands. It can move and deform as the sea pushes it around, but we rarely have a break."

With the explanation, new looks of wonder appeared on the visitors' faces as they gazed out.

"We would propose to open corridors to the interior sections of the farms for your fishing. You would pick the section you wanted to fish to determine the type and size you want. The boats would be weighed going in and returning.

"By building a series of these, we should be able to meet your needs in supplying fish. We know the size of the farm best suited for control, and we understand how to do this. The farms would be managed and maintained by us, as we are much more adapted to that type of work. Importantly, this would not impact the natural environment.

"Those wishing to continue the traditional fishing could do so within the regulations. But they will find they are not competitive with the farming system."

A hand went up. "Joe Canteau, rep for British Columbia Fisherman's Union. What's to stop independents from just barging in and taking fish, you know, like poaching?"

"Thanks for the question, Joe. I'll let Captain McCain answer."

"Joe, there's a bed of plant growth surrounding this area so thick it will foul any propeller. I'm embarrassed to say we found out the hard way when we tried to steam in. We had to get help from Ocealla to break free."

Another hand went up. "Dr. James Duncan, Pacific Oceanographic Studies. What about bottom species like clams and other mollusks and bivalves?"

"We'll create that habitat. It's a critical part of the ecosystem because it is where waste gets processed."

Another hand. "Dr. Alfredo Sanchez, United World Government Director of Ocean Preservation. A couple of questions, at least for now. How do you propose to integrate with the departments we have now, and how long will it take you to bring these farms up to production?"

"We're willing to consider any type of organizational structure, but we do feel we're in a stronger position of authority over how to set up and operate these farms than anyone else. We feel we can both learn a lot from each other in this endeavor." In an aside to Ron she added, 'Like the politics.' "Let's head back for lunch and address more questions there." She directed the Travelers back and removed her collar.

"Well, how do you think the meeting is going?" Katharine asked Ron.

"You explained the program well. The problems will be political, especially how the various agencies will keep their authority, funding, and people. They will guard their turf aggressively."

"Ron, we're also looking at something which may help you with the Orbital Power System. Please keep this strictly confidential for now. We plan to offer a bid for the operation and maintenance contract. Just as we built Constructs for life within the sea, we would do the same for the OPS. For the next contract term, we would use the Constructs with only slight modifications, but we would embark on a program to develop a design specifically for life in space."

Ron appeared stunned by the idea.

"We would partner with companies to provide the transport as we haven't that ability. Our problem will be the political structure for this. Think it over and let's talk."

Ron opened his mouth to speak, but the concept was still rolling around in his head. He closed his mouth. He snapped his fingers. I almost forgot. The Prophet would like to meet with you on your next visit to Washington."

Katharine thought this over. Although she was anxious to meet the person who had made such a difference with the world, after experiencing Ron's visit, she was nervous.

Chapter 22

Katharine returned to Washington in early spring. Soon after her arrival, the message reached her with a date for the visit with the Prophet. On the day of the meeting, she looked around the apartment she and Ron shared. The décor was much the same, with the holograms of the Mona Lisa and the view of Baboquivari Peak from Kihhim lighting the walls. She loved that desert view and the towering granite peak, filling her with a sense of history and renewal.

A flutter of trepidation tickled her stomach when she heard a knock on the door. She had waited a long time to meet Mohammad al Jar. Perhaps the single most influential person of the 21st century waited at the door. Katharine took a deep breath before opening it.

At first, Katharine's eyes had trouble focusing on the figure standing before her. A glow seemed to emanate from the brilliant white robe obscuring her view of the downturned face beneath the cowl. Was he a hologram? He looked up and held her eyes with a strong gaze. Depths of knowledge were within those lapis lazuli eyes, and she started to fall into them. Her instinct pulled back in fear of the plunge, but she sensed no challenge, no pressure, only peace.

Neither spoke, and inside her mind the others of Homakuwa saw and felt what she did. Her eyes focused on his face, and a smile touched his lips, breaking the spell. That smile said he was aware of more than just Katharine standing before him. He closed his eyes before dipping his head in a slight bow.

Katharine stepped back without saying a word, and he seemed to float by like an aroma wafting on a breeze. Before she could identify the scent, it faded. The white walls of the room camouflaged him, leaving only his hands and face, and those eyes visible. The shadow on the floor betrayed his position at the chair she was going to offer him. "Green tea?" she asked, pointing–already knowing he would accept. He nodded, but as she approached the table, he reached out and poured from the delicate ceramic pot into the bone china cups. This wasn't a holo. Katharine sat opposite him, as if in a dream, not quite in touch with the reality around her. The combined mind of Homakuwa snapped into focus within her, crystal-clear and secure.

The comfort of their presence filled her, but there was more–someone outside her family. She seemed to know him, and he knew them. Her senses returned to the room, and she looked at his face again, trying to assess her feelings. She picked up her cup and sipped the barely cooled tea. "Tell me about yourself," she said.

"What you really want to know is where I come from, though some of you already know," he said. "But I won't start with that. Where I'm from isn't as important as who I am. Very early in my life I experienced a connection with God that changed me and has directed my life ever since.

"You see, I nearly drowned while swimming. Actually, I did die that day. At that time, I experienced what was to be my life's work. What I realized is the way you are taught math is not so you can add and subtract, but to teach logical thinking. Math is just the tool used to learn that lesson. The same goes for history. Certainly, we need to understand what happened in the past, but it is also about teaching yourself to memorize things– learning a system that works for you. It's about understanding people of the past and how they are different from us and yet the same as we are.

"English is about learning how to communicate, which is much more than just the words. So much is transferred by tones and usage. What I learned that day was my purpose in life. Since then I've learned how to open other people's minds, so they too can find their purpose in life. Let me show you."

Soundlessly, he placed his cup in the saucer, before looking straight into her eyes. His charisma overpowered her. This stranger was so familiar, she thought. She put her cup down and reached out to touch his waiting hand. She had to know more.

At the contact, a current flowed like electricity, but it was more. Just as with the collar, she and he joined, and his mind lay before her, open and inviting her to explore. Katharine did, moving with him back through his life, like a movie of sensation on fast forward. As a boy, she experienced al Jar growing spiritually, saw his focus sharpen as he came to know his God. He grew older, and his faith became as natural as breathing. She felt his fear as he met his Imam, then confidence surged through him as he became the questioner.

For the first time, he became aware he sensed another's mind. The thoughts had always been within him, but now he understood those thoughts weren't his. Soon, he met others, Emirs and Imams of the Middle East, Lamas and masters of Asia, priests and Popes of the west. Some feared him as his reputation became known, but he calmed their anxiety when they met. Others refused to meet. Some tried to kill him.

Many of the attempts were successful, and she experienced the unbelievable pressure and pain of his body being blown apart in a bomb attack, the fiery pain as a bullet penetrated his heart, but worst of all was the burn of hatred from those who feared him. His outpouring of love toward them cooled the heat of hatred like the ocean on lava.

Katharine formed a question in her mind: [You're not the first or the only, are you?]

The Prophet: [There are many of me, as many as it takes. We are much closer than you and I are now for we are one. As you understand, it's the only way I could survive to do the work God laid out for me.]

Katharine: [I can only see back to you as a boy. Who are your parents? Where did you come from?]

The Prophet: [Look inside yourself, and you will see.] A scene from her past formed in her mind, a dream within a dream. She and Leticia were sitting together on the deck of Kahchk Kihhim, the huge catamaran, looking out over the blue sparkling Pacific Ocean at a brilliant orange sunset. The smell of the sea assailed her, and the serenity of home settled over her like a cape. Recognizing the memory of what had been a defining moment in their history she was comfortable.

Kahchk Kihhim had sent out one of their own with a designed virus–a disease–to be used as a weapon to kill an individual enemy set to destroy them. The mission had been successful. They had built a biological guided weapon, performing a surgical strike. As she and Leticia sat, the understanding of that power formed, and the moral dilemma facing them followedt. She and Leticia mulled over what to do next.

"We could create a virus that would alter the nature of humankind so they are less aggressive. They might find us more acceptable and distrust us less. Without fear of us, we might be able to live together. Though changing the basic nature of humans will require undoing millions of years of evolution," said Leticia.

They both understood that basic nature is what makes humans what they are. In the end, they decided to flee the surface world in order to survive and leave man to his own fate.

As she watched, a scene of Leticia and Jamie Wong sitting in Jamie's laboratory formed. He was the geneticist who began the whole program of genetically engineering; first their food and later themselves by creating the biological computer that could form the strands of DNA into viable creatures.

Jamie and Leticia were discussing whether one altered man could make a difference in the surface world. Maybe that one man wasn't just one lone man, and certainly not just a man–maybe not a man at all. And maybe, given enough time, the changes in humans would be enough that the species making up Kahchk Kihhim would be accepted.

Upon opening her eyes, she saw al Jar smiling at her, his eyes sparkling with laughter. His thoughts filled her mind: [I am your son, put upon the Earth to save humankind and pave the way for your return.] The enormity of those thoughts crashed in on her like the tsunami from a magnitude 9.0 earthquake.

Leticia had not gone back on her word, but Katharine felt betrayed that she had not been a part of the decision. Yet, she knew she would have opposed it because if anyone of the surface world found out, the hatred and fear would arise again tenfold. Humans would feel deceived and manipulated, but most of all inferior. This time they would not be able to escape and hide. The danger of this path would have stopped her, but Leticia made bold decisions, and always for Homakuwa. She understood that humans had to change to accept them, and this could well be the only way for that to happen.

With the aid of hindsight, Katharine resolved that Leticia had been right. Ron would know something the next time they shared the collar. He would sense she had something she didn't want to share. Eventually she would have to reveal this secret of the Prophet to him, and she cringed.

The Prophet: [Do not despair.] The words formed inside her mind. [He will look into your soul and all of Homakuwa and know that your manipulation was to save humankind, and he can't fault the success. Have you so little faith in him? I have looked into his mind and seen that his wisdom will overcome the momentary petty fear. Believe in him and in yourself. He will understand that regardless of how I came to be, my presence here has made the difference. Who is to say what is the hand of God?]

Peace settled over her. Worry wouldn't change anything, and she did believe in him, for she'd also seen into his soul.

"Now let me show you something wonderful. This is the reason I am here," he spoke aloud. He again took her hand in his. "Close your eyes." She complied.

Again, his mind opened, exposing another scene. This time she gazed over an endless wheat field, the golden stalks stretching before her to the sky. Behind her, as if rising in the dawn, low on the horizon, sat the sun. Pinpricks of light sparkled in the black sky ahead, and the low angle of the sun lit the golden tufts. The stalks moved in undulating waves as if pushed by a breeze.

She drifted forward, brushing the tips. As they contacted her, thoughts filtered in–thoughts from other people! Each touch brought her into contact with someone else, and they filled her being. The sensation was similar to becoming acquainted. Her pace through the field increased as she flew away from the sun.

Miraculously, she surged forward, and her mind expanded to absorb all the contacts into her consciousness. When she moved into the blackened sky, the tips of the stalks became lights. She soared upward into space, moving through the galaxy toward the blindingly bright center. The stalks had become stars, thick around her, touching her.

Her mind expanded again, and as she moved into the intense light of the center, knowledge and love opened. What she experienced was infinite knowledge and infinite love of which she became a part. Leaving behind her physical being, her senses no longer were comprised of sight, sound, touch, taste, and hearing, but only of her mind. Instead of seeing the brightness, she felt it with her mind.

As the awareness of self slipped away, her very essence emerged like a butterfly from a cocoon. She was now a part of the light, and it was a part of her. All memory of her life and being was gone. Total peace and awareness engulfed her as she floated on an eternity. Never had she known a feeling like this.

A force like gravity started pulling her back. She didn't want to leave this place of peace, but couldn't stop the spiral. A thought filled her. "It's not your time. You have much to do." With this she ceased efforts and was whisked away. When she opened her eyes, she had returned to the white room sitting before al Jar.

Disoriented, she stared into his eyes. "Now you understand what I am trying to bring to humankind. This is my purpose in this life. I am here for them, but you also have tasks to do. Homakuwa is the future of humankind, but not as they are now. We will only save them, but you will go forward." With a whisper of soft cloth, he rose as he glided to the door.

In a daze, she walked behind him and reached for the door. This time, when he took her hand, no shock passed, but a wave of confidence surged through her, and a familiarity remained. "I will be with you always. You have only to quest with your mind if you need me."

"Thank you," she said, letting his hand slip from hers, as he turned and drifted down the hall. She closed the door and stumbled back to the chair and her tea, which had stayed hot! She felt Homakuwa as they struggled to understand what had happened. There was fear and pride at what had been revealed.

Leticia: [I couldn't tell you. At last it's out, and a great burden has been lifted from me. Whether it was right or wrong doesn't enter into the picture because it was the only way for us and humanity to survive.]

Katharine: [Did you infect him with a virus, a disease to change men so he could overcome their opposition?]

Leticia: [No. You remember we decided not to change man. Instead, we created al Jar from parts of us. He is our child, but so much more. Parts of his mind we enhanced, but after his drowning episode, they expanded on their own. You sensed that power when you first saw him. He has the ability to open people's minds to a much larger purpose. Their individual religions don't matter any longer for they are able to understand that all religions are humanizations of true understanding. He opens up a pathway in their minds so they can see that understanding. He is an Envoy from God.]

Katharine: [I should be upset with you, but I'm not. What you and Jamie did created an opportunity for us that couldn't exist otherwise, building an opportunity for humankind. Eventually the origin of al Jar will come out, but perhaps not for a great while. Hopefully by then, mankind will look upon this as the gift it truly is.] A sense of warmth, love, and trust enveloped her as their presence diminished into the background. My God! It suddenly hit her. They had created a man who could control others with his mind. She'd felt his power. She'd also known his goodness, but would that be enough? Needing to think, she leaned back in the chair but her thoughts were interrupted.

Leticia: [Katharine, al Jar said something just before he left, and it has had a great impact on me and Jamie Wong. Something we've often thought about. Always remember 'Who is to say what is the hand of God?']

The tone of the phone jarred Katharine back to the reality of the room. "Identify," she said, and the phone answered: "Ron Carson"

"Open."

"Ron, how are you?" Her mind wasn't fully back yet.

"Are you okay? How'd the meeting go with al Jar?"

"I'm fine, thank you. It was very revealing. He's quite remarkable."

"That's what I thought too when I met him. Are you free for dinner?"

She hesitated. Was she ready for him? "I'm pretty tired, but I wouldn't mind a quick bite."

"I'll be home to get you in about an hour. Is that enough time?"

"Sure. See you then. Bye."

"End," she said, collecting her thoughts. She would have to plan the revelation with Ron carefully. Though assured of his final reaction, his initial response might not be accepting. Carefully, she tucked the nature of the Prophet al Jar into a corner of her mind, and closed it off.

Chapter 23

The three month test period during the summer when the UWG placed monitors in Ocealla went as expected. As predicted, the trials of the surface system ID chips failed because the signals could not be received through water. The majority opinion of the Homakuwa nation was to opt out. The citizens would not accept the chips. They reached a compromise whereby the central system accessed by all citizens tied into a monitor. Leticia disagreed to even this, but it could be dealt with. Linking an organic system to an electronic system provided unbreakable firewalls. Only filtered information went out. She made sure of this, also considering the link to Homakuwa a pathway into the surface system. All in all, it wasn't a bad tradeoff.

Leticia had been busy over the last month, and they had access throughout much of the surface world system. Unwilling to allow monitoring she didn't understand, she began to trace the lines of control to see where they led. Beginning with the archives, she compared the system in time intervals and noted what changes had been made.

Kit had moved to Ocealla to work with Leticia in their private bubble. Through the collar, she and Kit were able to access the mechanical monitor.

Kit: [Leticia, this distrust of government is a thing of the past. The safeties in the UWG program assure its integrity. You're wasting time and effort testing the system.]

Leticia: [Maybe, but it's my time. Let me show you what I'm doing. Some of the things I've found are interesting.] Leticia created a graphic display of the submissions and approvals for changes. She pointed the trend out to him. [The system is self-correcting and self-analyzing. In the beginning, proposed changes were submitted to a committee headed by the President of the United World Government for review. With the older records, a panel oversaw these reviews and rendered judgment. Most were accepted. As time went on, fewer and fewer changes were reviewed until the approval became automatic with little review. None have been submitted in ten years. The system now changes itself.]

Kit: [It is an Artificial Intelligence. I self corrects.]

[Yes, I understand. Now look at this. Last year, changes were made to the education system. No review took place, and each is listed as a local change in the Iranian education system. These changes are tweaks to the history being taught, specifically with regard to the Islamic control of the government and the change to the UWG education installation. Other changes involve the Prophet. These are small wording changes, really minor.]

Kit exclaimed: [What is troubling is that the changes have been made at all! Where did they originate?]

Leticia: [The computer initiating the changes was in Washington DC. Why would someone in Washington change things in Iran?]

Kit asked: [What other changes have occurred?]

She started a program to search for more changes and inconsistencies in the UWG system, linking in to the Homakuwa Collective so they could see what she had.

Chapter 24

Gazing at the fall sunset across the Idaho plain, Ron and Katharine acknowledged they needed a break from Washington. "Getting a new nation membership in the United World Government has proven more stressful than I would have believed," Katharine said. "Politics is something I dislike and don't do well. I don't understand how you were able to do it for so long."

"Political life is definitely something one has to grow into," Ron laughed. "I've always liked the negotiation, the give and take for a better good. This situation is particularly difficult because factors never considered before are involved."

Ron continued, "The oversight normally applied to other nations won't work in the city/states of Homakuwa. Satellites can't see them, and radio waves can't penetrate. The link between central control of Homakuwa and a monitor for the UWG was helpful. I appreciate your intervention with Leticia on that. Having Kit as the Ambassador helps too."

A thought came to Katharine. "We need to link in to Homakuwa," she said, as she went to get the collars.

What was this about, thought Ron. She handed him his collar. They settled into the chairs and donned them.

Leticia's thoughts formed: [Katharine, Ron, you need to see this.] She led them through her explorations of the surface computer system.

Ron's surprise was clear as he grasped the extent of what she'd found: [I was looking into this before Kit disappeared. I thought it was minor, but it is much more, and I don't understand how this could have happened. Obviously, we've become lax in our oversight. Luckily, it's a small thing we can correct. I'll contact the president.]

Leticia: [If this were limited to minor changes in the local education programs, it wouldn't be so bad, but there's more. The changes initiated from Washington D.C., so I created a sniffer program to compare programs. A year ago, the number of differences greatly increased.

[Differences in the judicial system appeared. Small decisions have been tweaked. Some changes are minor, like a reduction in sentence, but others are a change in the wording of the law resulting in different decisions.]

How could the system be corrupted? Ron was stunned: [When the public learns of this it will be a calamity! The one thing that could destroy the World Government is loss of confidence that it is fair and incorruptible.]

[Equally important, Ron, is who is doing this? I'm running a trace back through to seek the origins. Somehow, I don't think one individual or even one organization did this. In addition, I'm running probability programs to learn what the results of these changes have been.]

Ron: [Let me know what you find out. We're going to have to present this evidence to the World Court.]

Leticia: [Unless some of them are involved.] That statement shook Ron. Removing their collars, they broke the connection. She noticed how totally depressed Ron was that his dream had been corrupted.

"Let's wait until we learn what Leticia finds out before we take this anywhere. In the meantime, you need to make a list of those who are absolutely above reproach, those you trust implicitly. Let's do everything we can before returning." Anxious that he not dwell on this disturbing news but concentrate on how to fix the problem, she left.

***

Even though Ron and Katharine had withdrawn, Kit felt his great-grandfather's pain. Leticia watched the emotions flow across his face reflecting his concern. "Look, we'll find out who's behind this, and we'll get it straightened out," she said.

"I know," said Kit. "It's just the feeling of betrayal."

"Let's trace the changes. As the names come up, you let me know if any are names you recognize. Possibly this came from an outside source."

"Inside or out, we consider the whole world inside now. We still have to deal with human nature, and that includes greed and the need to prove status and power over others. We haven't been able to move away from those basic drives. Even if we had a world where everybody had enough to live well, some would still want more and would scheme to take it. Won't we ever learn?" Wearily he reached for the collar to help Leticia.

Their minds joined and flowed as a stream through a duct of information until they stopped before a wall.

Leticia: [This is the first level of firewall. Just to be careful, we'll disguise ourselves so any alarm points elsewhere.] She pulled in data to form a cloak around them. [Now we're an investigative branch doing a security survey.] Carefully Leticia touched the wall. They both felt a tingle. [Okay, we have to find a chink.] They moved along the wall peering closely. Kit didn't understand what he was looking for until they came to what appeared to be a pipeline.

[This is a major in/out data port. Let's find out what kind of info's going in and try to blend.] They watched the stream in an effort to recognize a change. [Student reports. Perfect.] Leticia did something to cause their cloak to change color so their appearance was the same as the stream going in. Once inside the wall, they moved with the flow toward an evaluating program. Before getting to it, they detoured around the program to enter from the back looking at the comparison data. They followed the stream back toward the source.

[This is where the changes will show up. If we follow this, we'll know when it was changed. I did the comparison with the archives, so I know what I'm looking for specifically.] Like the pages of two books, the current files and the backup files flipped in front of them until she stopped. [Here's the change.] In front of them were two pages with some of the wording highlighted. [See, this is different from this.] She pointed. [Now we know when. Let's find out how. We'll follow the source back.]

They tried to trace a path leading from the document, but it branched several times.

Leticia: [Clever. See, he's trying to cover his tracks.] Leticia sent programs out. They looked like dogs sniffing a trail, racing ahead along the branches. One trail started flashing. [This is the one. Let's go.] They flew down the trail which ended at another wall.

Leticia looked carefully: [This appears to be an official site for education. Either this guy works for the education bureau or this is false.] She probed lightly. No reaction. [It's false. No firewall. Let's go.] She pushed, and the wall in front of them dissolved. Behind was a block with a number. [This is the computer that entered the change.] Leticia touched the block, and after a second a name and address appeared on the side. Placing an electronic insect within the block, she moved, and it disappeared. Another wave of her hand [I'm making this visit appear to be a routine check with no interest. Okay, we're done here. We need to go back.] As they moved down the path, it disappeared behind them. [Covering our tracks.]

Kit opened his eyes. They were back in Ocealla. He removed the collar. Leticia was still in the couch wearing her collar. He watched her face as it contorted. She was doing something.

Leticia opened her eyes and looked at him. "Sorry, I had to do a few more things before I left. Now the question is what to do with this information. I'm going to set up a whole series of sniffer programs to track down the sources of other changes. We should soon have a complete list, but we need to talk with Ron and Katharine."

At the same time, they put the collars back on so their minds could join and seek Katharine.

Kit: [Are you and Ron able to join us?]

Katharine entered their minds: [Ron will be here in a moment. I gather you've had success.] Ron entered. He and Kit did the mental equivalent of a hug.

Leticia: [We've traced the first anomaly back to the source. The computer is registered to the

Security Department located in Washington D.C. I've placed a bug within it, and we'll be able to monitor it completely. A virtual clone of the computer now exists. So now what do you want to do?]

Katharine: [Let's follow this guy–where he goes and where he's been. He's our path into whatever organization he's with.]

Leticia: [I can set up programs, so we'll have more information than he thinks he had. Within a few days, we should know a lot more. The biggest problem is sifting through the data. I'll install filters as soon as we get keys to work on. Ron, what are you going to do?]

Ron: [For now I'm going to look closely at those who need to deal with this and start to evaluate. I've been listing those I trust. At the right time, I'll go to them with what we have. For now I'm in assessment mode.

[Katharine will help. She's shown remarkable talent in reading people. First, we have to compile questions to get us a response. We can do this while we're making the Washington circuit introducing the Homakuwa ambassador. To clarify the answer to your question, we're going to be eyes and ears.]

Kit: [Leticia and I will start the sniffer and filter programs to get a handle on this.]

Kit opened his eyes again to Ocealla. The enhanced view of the sea was full of life. Joyfully, he expanded his vision to include those working around Ocealla. Watching and being a part of it was the most peaceful sensation Kit had ever experienced. He was a part of a whole, yet remained an individual.

Chapter 25

Ayatollah Aiassi Komini listened to the report from Rhualla. In addition to the education realignment program against the UWG, they were now modifying the surveillance programs. Within the Foundation, important information was relayed face-to- face, minimizing the chance of eavesdropping. The levels of computer and internet security were raised to a higher degree. Monitoring programs of the UWG security detected no activity to signal knowledge of the Foundation.

"We have embedded operatives," said Rhualla, "within the UWG system to give us information and act at the proper time. We are formulating virus software to be inserted at the time of our attack and, Allah willing, we will destroy the Satan UWG. Our viruses will destroy the computer system with a series of changing attacks that continuously morph. The Sword of God will render their technological weapons worthless, and making it impossible for them to defend against us. Their weapons and communication systems will be useless. They will be forced to fight hand to hand, and that is how we will beat them. As soon as our allies see our success, they will flock to us."

This was going well, thought Aiassi, but he had several major concerns. Their attack must be coordinated with the others of the Foundation so a multi-pronged attack took place across the world. But foremost in his mind was what to do after the successes. Without a plan they would soon fall into chaos, plunging back to interfaith skirmishes which would give rise to the UWG again. With a coordinated attack, the Prophet would be found and finally destroyed. When he was dead the mystic hold over his followers would vanish.

"Set up a meeting with the others of the Foundation. We must meet to coordinate our strategy," said Aiassi. "Minimize communication," he added, knowing Rhualla understood the danger and pitfalls better than anyone. He had worked for the Security Department of the UWG and built much of their security system.

Officially, Rhualla was dead. At birth the spy chip was inserted–the same for almost every child. While working at UWG he was monitored as were all security employees. During intense sunspot activity after he left the US, he removed his chip and inserted it in a cadaver. To the UWG he was dead.

Ayatollah Aiassi Komini stared at Rhualla. "We must learn from the hard lessons from the past wars. Yes, we learned how to stay covert under the very noses of opposing forces. We understood the necessity of using the civilian population as unwilling soldiers. When their faith in their government to protect them was destroyed, that government was ready to be deposed."

Rhualla nodded, listening carefully.

"The outcome has been far from satisfactory. In Afghanistan, the Taliban negotiated from a position of equality rather than weakness by achieving sovereignty over sections of the country and earning a place on the ballots. By changing the result of the elections, they moved into power. But the UWG laws on human rights prevented them from following the Kuran, and the education system has corrupted the youth."

"Yes, Ayatollah, and we have made changes in the education system to correct that."

"It's a good start, Rhualla. My grandfather lived through the uprising when Egypt achieved a form of democracy. Many other Arab countries changed governments at the same time. The western world forced democracy upon them. The Islamist parties were much more organized and won the elections easily. Within each party though, the fundamentalists warred with the progressives, and the extremists began an internal rebellion. My grandfather supported the winner of the Egyptian election and helped to consolidate power. Through a series of decrees the elected leader moved to create a position of absolute ruler and a return to the dictatorial states of the past. Grandfather knew that was the wrong way to advance an Islamic state."

"The Western governments would not allow that," said Rhualla.

"Even though it was the elections that paved the way, as a young boy, I watched the populace again rebel, and in the end, the military took power. They staged a series of bogus elections to legitimize their rule, but the UWG would not allow a fundamentalist Islamic state if it violated western human rights."

Rhualla glanced at his tablet. "All is set. A meeting will take place in two weeks in Dakar, one of the least watched regions. Best if we fly into other cities and arrive by boat, rail, or road. Much safer. This will be the only face-to-face meeting. Other discussions must take place over hard-line communications or hand carried notes. There will be no attention drawn. Not only can we not be hacked into, we will continuously sweep for bugs."

"Very good. Compile a list of assets, commit it to memory and then destroy the list. We must not have any record. You will be my record of all that transpires. See that this is followed by the others."

"Yes, Ayatollah."

"Rhualla, the appearance of the Prophet has changed everything. The people were hungry for a moderate religious leader and the Prophet offers a form of Islam where the people don't have to listen to the Imams. This loss of control has devastated our religious hierarchy, practically destroying traditional Islam.

"Islam is not alone in this struggle. For survival, we must form alliances with the infidels. The peril has been the same with the other major religions, and the Catholic Church is the hardest hit. For them it is worse than the schism created by Martin Luther. The exposure to the Prophet is toxic, but they didn't realize this until after the Pope met with him. The Pope was corrupted. Under the edicts of the Pope, most of their priests became

Faithists. Those bishops able to go into hiding have become a part of the Foundation. Our strength now exists in Southeast Asia and parts of Europe, where Islam grew strong. Catholicism has always been strong in places like Latin America. Much because of the isolation offered there."

"You are correct, Ayatollah. I have seen the Protestants in America, and it would seem that they would fare better because of their diversity and non-centralized organization. Yet their members are the easiest converted.

"Hinduism has been completely taken over. The masses were eager to follow a new spokesman for God. Rhualla, we must build alliances temporarily with the remnants of the world's organized religions. Though these religions still exist within the Faithists, none of us has the autonomy we once had when separate. These Faithists now fully accept the others, and it is impossible to raise the fervor that leaders have used in the past.

"The people will return to the old religions and the leaders only if they are driven back into their arms by the fall of the Prophet and the UWG. Once again it will be possible to control men by holding their souls for ransom. When we've re-established ourselves, Islam will again fight to become the one true faith. This is a war for our existence, and we do what we must to survive."

Chapter 26

Robert Chaing knocked politely on the Chairman's door. "Enter" called a voice.

The large paneled office was empty except for the man behind the desk. Showing respect, Chaing bowed. "Sir, we have received a communication from the Foundation, and a meeting will take place in Dakar next week. The agenda will be the uprising against the United World Government."

"Very good, Chaing. Make your arrangements; limit all communications. Do not reply to them. Ask Mr. Xian to come in."

Chen Xian entered and bowed.

"Xian, go through your Dragon program to assure we will be able to activate it at the proper moment. We will need to restore the order of the computer system after the attack by the Foundation's series of viruses. At that time, we will bring them under our direction, but without outside knowledge. That is all."

Xian paused before bowing again. "You have a question?"

"Sir, do we know anything about the viruses to be used in this attack?"

"Chaing will give you the links to get them." Xian bowed, spun and retreated to the back of the room.

Hu was more than a little excited. Here was the chance to defeat the Western World laid at his doorstep. China would play the game, and a small portion of their troops, disguised as rebels, would join the Foundation forces and attack the UWG as soon as their computer systems failed. Allowing the battles to rage on, China would step in to restore the UWG computer systems, and let the UWG destroy the Foundation forces with their technology. China would enact their systems after the war while the UWG thought they again had control. They will be allowed to think that, but the control will rest with China. No reason to go to war when you control the enemy forces. The thought swirled within his head, and it was delicious.

The only mote in the Chairman's eye was this new civilization, Homakuwa which was unknown. He had directed Xian to perform a major research effort into finding out more about them. No doubt they could be dealt with. History said so.

Xian started his report. "Chairman Wu's memoirs told of a nation called Kahchk Kihhim. Decades ago China entered into an agreement with the United States to protect this new nation while a method was found to control it. Kahchk Kihhim had the knowledge and technology to manipulate life on the genetic level. This was a world-changing technology, and if China could have gained control, we would rule absolutely.

"Kahchk Kihhim extorted this protection, holding human life on Earth hostage by releasing a virus capable of fully destroying humanity, promising that the antivirus would be released in the future. If they were destroyed, there would be no antivirus. The first nation to find a cure would be able to take control of the world. We were so close that we had already designated who would get the antivirus and thus be the survivors and the rulers. In the end, the United States and China both arrived at the solution simultaneously. Kahchk Kihhim was destroyed to prevent their genetic technology from falling into other hands. Now, it appears they are back and working with the UWG."

Hu wrestled with ideas of how to gain control of Homakuwa and their technology from the UWG.

Chapter 27

Stupefied, Leticia and Kit watched the list of thousands of anomalies scroll before them. Leticia explained: [I've set up an extended filter to back-source each one, eliminating legislated changes after checking the specifics of the legislation. At the same time, the remainder is ranked. Those directed by officials have the lowest importance, and those with less clear origin have the highest. A separate program takes the low-ranking changes and checks the background of the change originator. As this would take more time, it runs independently, eliminating those fully checked out. Those changes initiating from a common source are also flagged.]

Kit nodded though not fully understanding.

Leticia: [Once ranked, the predicted effect of each change will be projected and prioritized again. The computing power required is huge, and I've called in all the power from the Homakuwa nation.]

Kit asked: [How long before we can see results?] In response Leticia indicated a new list forming.

Leticia: [The education changes are eliminated from this first list because they are long-term effects. What you see are the modifications resulting in personnel changes. I've sorted them by the job description. The top of the list is security related. The group in military–sorted by job and rank–follows. These groups potentially have the greatest immediate effect if they have been corrupted.]

Following this, she ranked funding sources for elections and the lawmakers elected. Decisions and votes on bills were ranked, with those of flagged lawmakers a priority. The investigation would continue with other categories.

***

HOMAKUWA ACCEPTED INTO THE UNITED WORLD GOVERNMENT

The members of the United World Government vote to accept the marine nation of Homakuwa. In an almost unanimous vote, membership was approved with the requirements that Homakuwa allow monitors in their city/states to assure that human rights are maintained. Since the personal ID chips worn by most citizens of the world do not function underwater, a transmitter system will allow additional monitoring. Trade groups are already applying for travel visas to visit to establish trade and tourist operations with the newest member.

*Washington Post
Staff reporter.*

Unlike Ocealla, Washington D.C. had four seasons. The United States Representative to the United World Government had agreed to host a Christmas ball presenting the Homakuwa Representative. The vote for acceptance into the UWG was anticlimactic. Homakuwa was approved easily. The ball was formal. Ron struggled with his tie until Katharine helped. Now arm in arm with her in an elegant off the shoulder white gown, they entered the ballroom. "I still don't understand how you got that gown so quickly," Ron said.

"It's the same dress I wore to the UWG address–just modified a little."

"More than a little! You took a nice summery dress suit and turned it into a designer formal gown. The colors change like an old CD disc in the sun, and the way it moves with you is stunning. The eye of every man here is on you. And where did you get your necklace? Are those pearls?"

"It's our collar modified into strands with simulated pearls that glow and change color."

"So you're in contact with Homakuwa?"

"We want to read the guests as we greet them. We couldn't think of a better way to contact so many so quickly. It's a working party."

Ron quietly muttered "They all are really. You make me look dowdy."

She laughed at the term. "You're never dowdy, but thanks."

As the diplomats and wives filed by, they stood in the greeting line. Katharine's first statement was "Homakuwa is pleased to be accepted by the Earth's surface world community." She and the Homakuwa mind would then watch the eyes and body language carefully as she shook hands. The Collective mind also allowed her to recall names and backgrounds instantly. Her second statement was, "We are happy to see the world together under the United World Government. I don't believe there's been this level of peace before." Lastly she would say, "The level of technology seems to have greatly improved living conditions for the whole world."

Katharine didn't keep track of the reactions. Homakuwa would track and compare those reactions to the lists Leticia and Kit were compiling. She concentrated on being the gracious Ambassador from Homakuwa. For the most part, they were greeted warmly. One notable exception was the Ambassador for China.

"So very pleased to meet you." said Ambassador Chaing as Katharine offered her hand. "We are anxious to know more about Homakuwa. Our search of records offers very little of your history. At one time, we had relations with Kahchk Kihhim, but with their destruction, we lost track. Perhaps we can again become allies."

Katharine bowed graciously. "Perhaps we can. China has become a major influence in the world."

"We always have long-term plans for the benefit of mankind."

Katharine nodded as he continued to hold her hand until finally letting go to move on. She turned to the next delegate.

At long last the evening ended.

"Whew, I'm glad that's over," said Ron. "No matter how many times I did that in the past, it was always exhausting."

"Even without Homakuwa input, I found the Chinese Ambassador's comments disturbing," said Katharine. "China will prove to be troublesome."

Ron nodded assent. "I always found them so." They trudged back to their room to enjoy the rest of the night together.

Chapter 28

The next morning, Leticia and Kit connected with Ron and Katharine as they finished the room service breakfast. Leticia related the search and filtering criteria, displaying the list they had compiled. She began with the first name on the list.

Leticia: [Several anomalies were initiated by the same computer. That computer was assigned to Dr. Robert Adams in the Computer Security Division. These changes were installed on weekends and holidays when he was absent, but Rhualla Hussein was present. Rhualla established a history of working when the office was deserted. He was in the computer security section but resigned and was then reported dead by his chip. In our search we found activity on the system from a computer with an IP address listed for Rhualla. Looking at the style of the activity, I think it is Rhualla. Without the chip, we can't directly trace him to a specific location, but we have been able to backtrack. I was able to enter his computer and create a clone.

[We see messages too innocuous to be real and believe they are coded. We're working to break that code. The results of the tracing reveal several of the IP addresses are registered to people with strong religious ties. Those ties span the globe with a spectrum of traditional religion from Jewish to Hindu. We may be seeing an alliance of traditional religions attempting to subvert the human rights regulations and revert back to religion controlled states.]

Ron asked: [But how are they going to bring this about? The UWG military can crush any uprising.]

Kit added: [We've been asking ourselves the same question.]

Leticia: [We've started looking into what could level the playing field so there could be any chance of success. That's where the search became interesting. We've found references to "The Sword of Allah" neutralizing the UWG forces. This could be a new weapon, but we haven't been able to confirm that.]

Katharine: [What about a virus?]

Leticia: [We're combing through the system now, but it's slow since we're not supposed to be there–plus we need to be careful not to set off alarms and trap ourselves. I don't think the UWG would look favorably on the newest member snooping.]

Kit jumped in: [We've started looking at the military chain of command, especially the field commanders. A few made rank rather quickly. In looking at the recommendation for promotion, a line leads to a few individuals we're investigating closely.]

Ron showed them his list: [These are the people I'm confident of. I believe they are above reproach. We have to bring some of the UWG in on this.]

Katharine: [If you're comfortable, go ahead. Let's get opinions besides our own to see if we're chasing ghosts. I'll go with you if you wish.]

Leticia: [In the meantime, we'll continue to refine our lists. It'd be nice to know what the "Sword of Allah" is and why their faith in it is so strong.]

Leticia and Kit removed their collars. "We must find Rhualla," said Leticia. "We can trace back to his computer, but that won't pinpoint him. Any ideas?"

"Perhaps we can make him call us. What if we initiate a fake diagnostic program on his computer which finds a problem component. To access or recover his hard drive information he has to order a special part."

Leticia smiled at him. "That's not bad. Remember, he's already an expert, so he's probably capable of repairing his computer, but the component needed would have to come from the factory."

"What if we put up a diagnostic alerting him to problems, and then we crashed his hard drive. In the diagnostic we give him a recovery service. He can either send in the hard drive, or we can send a technician."

"Good," said Leticia. "We'll make the problem a virus. The diagnostic will read 'Virus detected. Your computer will attempt to shut down to protect your data. Do not attempt to remove your hard drive as it will destroy your data. Please contact ____ for assistance.' Then we'll freeze his screen and lock him up. He'll have to call us. We need to get him to physically contact our hardware."

"Why?"

Leticia stood. "Let me show you something we've been working on." She led him through several chambers to a small one he hadn't seen before.

In the center was a raised table holding a clear bubble with a glass plate inside. "What do you see?" asked Leticia.

Kit peered in and saw nothing. He moved around trying a different angle, but nothing was there. "There's nothing but that plate," he said.

Leticia placed her hands on the bubble, forefinger tips and thumbs touching. She spread them apart, and a lens formed, magnifying the image of the plate. At one side, numbers scrolled until she stopped at four hundred. A part of the bubble showed microbes madly swimming about.

"Now what do you see?"

Bacteria swarmed, moving, multiplying, and forming a mat. "What is it?"

"That's the new model collar. By just putting a dab on your skin, the bacteria will multiply and form a two cell thick membrane and become a part of your skin. It's invisible and self-replicating. We can design it for a specific lifetime or permanent. We can limit the replication, so only the initial person has it, or we can increase it, so anyone coming in contact with him will carry it. We can also limit the power. The form I want to give to

Rhualla will give us access to his ears and eyes and a little of his thoughts, but not give him any access or awareness of us. He will become a walking bug."

Stunned, Kit's mouth hung open as the concept burst in his mind. He became more disturbed by the second. Being able to hear what people hear, see what they see, and read people's minds. This is monstrous! "How will you control this? Who uses it, and who is it used on? What if you made a small error and everybody became infected?"

"Those are not new questions to us. As of now, the design is very specific to a person's DNA and will only survive on that person. We have his DNA from his time in Washington. We do not intend to change that. We will offer this to all citizens of Homakuwa as an alternative to the collar. It will be their choice. They can continue to use the collars, or do away with them and be connected at all times. Kit, we're not monsters. You've seen into our souls."

"I'm not worried about you. This is a world changer should it get out."

Eyebrows raised, Leticia said, "This concern from someone who wants to monitor everyone with chips? I'm sure many people think the same about your chips. I know I do. If this becomes known, we would be destroyed. Others would either want to possess it or eradicate it."

Leticia continued, "We do have self-restraint. Let me tell you a story–one your great-grandfather already knows. We told him about the longevity, but he also asked us to modify the behavior of some world leaders to prevent a war. We did what he asked. The war took place later anyway, but after enough of a delay that the American elections were over. He was elected to a second term. And look what he did during that term."

"One thing he only suspects is we killed a man, a very evil man, by tailoring a virus to attack only him. This man threatened our total existence, and if we were to survive he had to go. You are the only person to learn of this ability outside of us. The situation before us now is much the same. The survival of the UWG could well depend on this cabal being thwarted in their efforts to bring us down. I do mean us, all of us. Certainly millions of lives could hang in the balance. Do we do proceed or not?"

She was right, of course, but that didn't make it any easier to swallow. "Okay, as much as I don't like this, we must."

Chapter 29

Ron and Katharine were escorted into the office of President of the United States. Ron stepped forward offering his hand as the man behind the desk stood. "John, good to see you again. Thanks for arranging the wonderful party at Christmas. I'm sure you had some influence in that." They shook hands, and Katharine stepped forward.

"It was a great opportunity for me to see and be seen, and I'm sorry we haven't had a chance to meet less formally. Thank you again."

The President clasped her hand in both of his. "I enjoyed your address to the UWG Assembly, and it's a pleasure to meet you. Did you really know Ron on Kahchk Kihhim? You look entirely too young."

"Thank you, Sir. I have a good doctor, eat healthy, and have good genes."

"You must send me a copy of that diet, but enough chitchat. What could be so secret we required this emergency meeting?"

Ron chuckled. "John, you always did get to the heart of the matter quickly. Before I went to Ocealla to get Kit, I was looking at some anomalies in the central computer system. In the excitement since then, it was forgotten. During the integration of Homakuwa into the UWG system, we found additional anomalies in the computer system. Some of them are troubling, especially a systematic change made in a number of programs. At first I found it in the educational content of local programs, but the changes expanded into the judicial system."

The president's eyebrows rose.

"As a result, favorable decisions held toward a specific group of individuals within the old organized religions and the power they exerted over their populace. Additionally, we've found corruption in the education curriculum skewing history. We became complacent in our oversight. Our investigation is now focused on the security systems. With these changes in place, it is certain there are viruses which will open us up to much more damage."

"You're saying our computer system may be compromised!" exclaimed the president.

"Because of differences between past programs held in the archives and those operating today, we are able to detect these changes. They were made without authorization or review and in many sections of the UWG. We suspect a potential uprising of a fundamentalist religious sect, perhaps Islam, but it may include others on a world-wide scale."

The President's face registered shock. Ron laid out a list of the anomalies arranged by date.

"The oldest ones were two years ago. They seemed innocuous at first: a background check specification reworded, a judgment voided, a word in a law changed from 'should to shall.' The changes were minor, but opened the door to significant alterations: the hiring of a technician who would have been rejected, a convicted felon released under parole, a security check okayed when it should have been flagged, a security guard placed in a sensitive operation. These are individually small things, but as a whole, they corrupted the system."

Katharine spoke, "The changes in history soft-pedal the fundamentalists' terrorist activities and elevate them to heroic deeds, and the UWG is always cast in a harsh light. These are small wording changes, but in lesson after lesson, they become instilled in the minds of the children.

"Wording changes in the laws, though minor, result in judgment changes where sentences are reduced and prisoners who remain a danger to society and the UWG are freed. This is a systematic and insidious attack on the foundations of the UWG and made possible by the trust in a supposedly incorruptible system."

"How could these changes have been made?" asked the President.

"We are looking into that now, trying to trace the source machines," said Katharine. "The traces led to the Security Department, so we started to review background checks and work history of that department. One technician has become a suspect."

"This technician grew up in a fundamentalist Christian family," explained Ron. "As a boy, he showed great promise in computer technology, and his family encouraged a career in computers. He left them for a special school. When the family met the Prophet in a large stadium, they converted to Faithism. Unfortunately, the boy was absent that day. Upon his return he was crushed to find the loss of their religion. His rage with his family resulted in violence against them, and he ended up in prison where he continued his education with computer science. Rhualla became very adept.

"A felon's work program allowed him a job upon release, and after illustrating his talents, he was moved into a work program for the UWG. Somehow, his history was changed, allowing him to transfer into areas of sensitive operations. We suspect he altered his history files. The archives of the penal system had not been affected, and we found his name there as a parolee."

"Although his chip lists him as dead, we're not sure that is correct. We're looking for him now," said Katharine.

Chapter 30

Through the Collective, Leticia spoke to the minds from all the city/states of Homakuwa who chose to attend.

Leticia: [In the two years since we assumed the Directorship of the International Fishing Industry, our contact between Homakuwa and the surface world has grown. We established ourselves as a part of the Earth community, and our assets in the surface banks continue to grow. Even though we invest much of it back into the various nations, we need to come up with a plan to utilize it–one that benefits Homakuwa.

[Thus far, these investments strengthened our ties, but we have not become dependent on the surface world. I think we need to maintain our ability to survive apart from them. Our Directorship has benefitted the international fishing industry, in fact saved it. Who better than us to manage the resources of the sea?

[We increased the total tonnage of fish taken by a factor of five, while growing the workforce of the fishing industry worldwide. More importantly, the populations of food fish are sustainable, and we protected our own environment. In a world where food is always a concern, this comes as welcome relief and enhances the image of the UWG. The Directorship and the fish farming operation result in a huge trade surplus, as Homakuwa rarely imports anything from the surface. Despite the disparity between the civilizations, we live in harmony.

[Visits to Homakuwa are rare, not because of lack of interest, but because we haven't the staff or facilities to accommodate surface worlders. We also lack the desire to open up fully.]

Kit and Ron were part of these discussions, and they had not faced a situation such as this before joining Homakuwa. The surface world was interrelated with little isolation of one region from another. They depended on trade.

Leticia continued: [Homakuwa needs to grow, but we cannot put more pressure on the seas, nor do we want to appear to the surface world as supplanting them as the majority. I believe it is time to revisit Unweil's suggestion of expanding into space. We should consider establishing space colonies orbiting Earth. Just as we moved into a habitat unpopulated by humankind when we left the Earth's surface, space is uninhabited.]

Rich Lewis spoke up: [The largest obstacle is the lift platforms to get us and the materials for habitat construction launched into orbit. The trade surpluses could be used to build orbiting platforms where colonies would be housed. But the surpluses are not nearly enough to fund this venture.]

Katharine: [We will need other economic projects to fund such a development.]

Jamie Wong: [We will need to start a new biological modification program to create citizens more adapted to very low air pressure and weightless environs. I have been working on this ever since the original suggestion from Unweil.] An image formed within the meeting. [The basic adaptation looks like a species of jellyfish. The arms are shielded such that they can operate in a vacuum while the braincase and vital organs are housed in a protected cavity. The shielding gives protection from the vacuum and moderate radiation exposure. They are able to survive in very low air pressures.]

He continued: [This is the basic space life-form. We will modify from here. Others will be grown as support life for the habitats. In an ecosystem, they could survive for long periods in the vacuum of space, perhaps permanently. With these adaptations and proper habitat design, the habitats would be much easier to build and maintain than those humans require.]

Rich spoke again: [Initially, we will be able to design species that will take raw materials and grow habitats as we did when we grew Ocealla. Unfortunately, those are not robust enough to withstand long-term. They would be susceptible to radiation damage and impacts that would penetrate the shell. We need hard shells, and we need to design the life forms to exist within. We are considering some design options for long-term habitats.]

The excitement of seeing plans and ideas to move ahead caught everybody's attention. The hurdle was still the initial launch and materials for habitats, and the money required.

PART 4
War and Expansion

Chapter 31

The first notice of problems came as a call to UWG headquarters. It was routed to the headquarters of the United World Government Middle East Operations and General Bradley Alexander. "Who's this?"

"Sir, this is Colonel Rodriquez UWG Commander, Baghdad. We have a situation developing here you need to be aware of. Our routine monitor of the Baghdad computer traffic here alarmed at 06:45 when the education computer system dropped offline. We tried to reestablish communication but that has not happened. We followed that up with calls to the central facility here in Baghdad with cellular and landline. All queries have been met with silence. Attempts to contact the UWG site personnel have been unsuccessful."

"Have you found out anything?" asked the general.

"Sir, we had a surveillance drone in the area and diverted it for a flyover. At 08:23, we lost all communication with it. The drone had programming to return to base automatically if communications were lost, but it has not returned. Our radar had it on screen. One moment the ping showed the location, the next it was gone. Radar had the blip for a while, but it spiraled down and was lost at 09:22."

"Ground forces?" asked the general.

"General, before I send in a ground unit, I want you to be informed of the situation. As you are aware, we have had some reports of antigovernment unrest, though no real activity has taken place."

"Colonel Rodriquez, we have a satellite tasked for that area. I'll get it repositioned and see if anything shows up. I'll be back to you."

The general called and had the satellite positioned for surveillance. The first real-time view showed nothing out of the ordinary until the roof of the computer center opened. A bright light flashed and the satellite went dark. Now things were getting serious.

While attention focused on Baghdad, a report came in that the computers in Lima, Peru had blinked out. Subsequent attempts to contact and reestablish control failed. Things at headquarters were starting to get exciting. The General called Colonel Rodriquez.

"Colonel, our satellite went dark right after the roof of the computer center opened up. Lima, Peru also reported the loss of communication with their computer center. I want you to dispatch a platoon to the central computer facility for a recon. Have your troops take precautions. This could be the beginning of something. Get back to me as soon as you have anything." He wouldn't pass this on until he knew it was a problem.

***

"General Alexander, this is Colonel Rodriguez."

"What's the sitrep?"

"Sir, at 13:30 we dispatched Air Cav to fly over the central computer building. They were about a kilometer from the building when they went completely silent and disappeared from the radar. All attempts to contact them failed. Their GPS markers went blank, pingers went silent. They were just gone. Smoke was visible in the city, and we believe they crashed or were shot down, so we sent

1st Platoon with armored support to find them. They approached the first crash site when we lost communication with them. The weapons carrier pinger went blank too. There's been some small arms fire reported, even a Ma deuce, but no cannon fire. Sir, we're still trying to contact anyone from 1st Platoon but have been unsuccessful.

"Their last report put them about a klick from the crash site, which put them about two klicks from the communications center. They hadn't reported any activity–nothing–then they dropped off the Earth. Honestly, sir, I'm not sure where to go now. We're considering sending out all of A company with a full package–armor, Air Cav, and support from the warthogs."

"Colonel, just so you know, we sent in an armed Predator, and it's gone. We've also lost the satellite. We're trying to re-task another for that area, but it'll take a couple of hours. In the meantime, we're sending another Predator to orbit at extreme range. I want you to send a patrol to the one and a half kilometer border and start looking at everything. Have them try to creep further in, and at the first sign of trouble pull back. When we have intel in place, we'll take 'em with A company."

"Just give us the word, sir."

General Alexander leaned back and looked around the conference table at his staff. "What the fuck is going on? I want answers and not tomorrow. I want ideas, wild ass guesses, anything. Get whoever you think can give us info to work from. Dismissed!"

***

Sniper team Alpha, the best in the Middle East Sector, had set up an observation post atop a five-story building. They had a clear view all the way to the block-sized computer center building. Lt. Bob Harris accompanied Sgt. Harry Begay and Lance Corporal Joseph Whiteshoe to supply recon information to headquarters while team Alpha prepared to support a probing squad from 2nd platoon. This squad would advance to the computer center. The remainder of 2nd platoon had set up a post on the ground floor below to secure the op above and await orders to move into the computer center.

"Colonel Rodriquez, this is Lt. Harris. We're maintaining radio contact both with the team below and our probing squad." Through his scope, Harris watched his squad, eight hundred meters out, await orders. This was a standard Advance Under Fire

Tactic. "Advance and cover." Begay spoke, "Nothing showing anywhere between you and the computer center."

"That's the eerie part," said Sgt. Jacobs, "The streets are empty. Nobody's moving, so something's going on. No sign of 1st Platoon either." Suddenly, the squad grabbed for cover. The ground shook, and one second later the sound of an explosion rocked the air around 2nd Platoon.

"Sgt. Jacobs, what happened down there?" asked Lt Harris. His question met with silence. He repeated, the calmness in his voice becoming ragged. With his eye to the scope, he repeated the query, "Anyone from 1st squad, respond." Nothing.

In the quad below, Lt. Harris watched men with scarves and rifles spring from cover and engaged his troops. They fought back, but their firing was ragged–misaimed. Begay began firing. The shock of the Barrett 50 firing pounded the air around them, and enemy began to disappear in a red cloud. The fifty caliber bullet from the big sniper rifle utterly destroyed whoever was hit. The enemy troops took cover, but they still inched forward until they were among 1st squad. Begay ceased firing lest he hit his own men. Within minutes it was over. His soldiers were escorted or dragged away, even the bodies.

Lt. Harris talked constantly to headquarters describing the event until nobody could be seen below. They packed their gear and left. The sniper fire had marked the position of their op, and the enemy troops certainly already dispatched toward them. Time to go.

***

Lt. Harris and Colonel Rodriquez conferenced via satellite to General Alexander back in Washington about the situation. "Yes sir, General," relayed Lt. Harris. "There was an explosion, but no smoke or sign of the blast, only the shock and noise. The men hit the deck for cover and all communication ceased. Then the enemy emerged from cover and surrounded the squad. The men started firing, but their hit ratio seemed awful. Within seconds the enemy was upon them. All became casualties, either killed, wounded or captured."

"You didn't see where the explosion happened?"

"No, Sir. We saw no of sign of it. Just felt and heard it."

"Could you see where the shock wave came from?" asked a female voice.

"No, Ma'am. We just felt the ground jolt."

"Thank you, Lt. Harris."

"Colonel, I want you to send out another team and set up an observation post. Put in a sniper team close enough to protect them but far enough back to stay out of the dead zone. We'll relay the Predator recon to you as we can. Unfortunately, if the Predator gets within three miles, we'll lose it. Keep me informed of any changes. Colonel Rodriquez, stay on the line."

The General then turned and faced the woman at his side. "Well, Dr. Jolet. Any ideas on what happened."

Dr. Marion Jolet, a physicist from MIT was consulting on a contract. The small woman combed the bangs of her short blond hair from her eyes with her fingers. "If I had to guess, and that's what you're paying me to do, I'd say we have an electromagnetic pulse knocking out their electronics. That's an EMP, and it can fry solid state electronics. In addition to the communications equipment, I assume the targeting sights on the men's weapons are electronic?"

"Yes. They are all equipped with the standard holographic sights. They should have been able to fire them," said the General.

"Yes sir, but without the sights, they'd be trying to point and shoot. With the shock of the explosion and the confusion of communication loss, I'm not surprised the ambush overwhelmed them so quickly," said Colonel Rodriquez.

"Dr. Jolet, how does one generate an EMP?" asked the General.

"A large explosion will create one. A nuclear explosion can knock out electronics for a hundred miles. This one was not nuclear, but what is interesting is it affected your troops only. Another effect, if it's strong enough, is it will momentarily disorient human brains. That and the loss of your Predator aircraft makes me think they may have found a way to generate a focused EMP.

"This is something we've been working on for several years, but we haven't been greatly successful. The equipment is extremely bulky and not fit for tactical application at all. We haven't been able to successfully focus one. If they can, then they are ahead of us."

"If they have an EMP weapon, what can we do?"

"The only way for electronics to survive is a well-grounded Faraday Cage."

What's a Faraday cage?"

"It's a mesh of conducting material which redistributes the charge. The cage can be made of copper screen for instance. If it's connected to the ground, it's much more effective. That's not too helpful for the Predators, but we'll be able to dissipate the pulse around the body. The body must be isolated from all of the components. "

"Looks like we have some work to do. What's the range of this EMP?" asked the General.

"I have no way of knowing, but if it knocked out a satellite in orbit, it can reach out hundreds of miles. We can develop and deploy shielding in a few months, but what we really should be worrying about is the things we can't shield, like those satellites.

"However they are able to focus that beam, they are also able to aim it, so it must be mobile. That's a formidable weapon, not because of its power, but because it will negate our technological superiority. They have hit us directly in our Achilles heel. All of our wondrous toys get us nothing."

"My God!" exclaimed the General. "We'll be fighting hand-to-hand. Without the kill ratio that technology bought us, we're back to a war of numbers, and we can't win. What about the Baghdad computer center?

"Colonel Rodriquez, Are you there?"

"Yes sir."

"Here's the situation as we see it. They appear to be using an EMP weapon. Without going into the specifics, this weapon disables all of our electronics. We have to capture that weapon. Strip anything electronic off your troops and send a force strong enough to capture the computer center. Remove all communication gear, electronic sights, computers, everything. Replace the holo sights with iron. You'll be in close quarters contact. And we need enough men to take over the place. Questions?"

"Understood. We're on it sir. I'll call you when we're set up."

Marion Jolet spoke up. "In the meantime, Colonel, get as much metal mesh, that includes screens, aluminum or whatever metal mesh you can find and tack it up completely covering the communications room, and then ground it. Put a disconnect on the dish antenna so there is no physical link to the outside. Got it?"

"Ugh, I think so."

"Put as many of your laptops inside as possible, too," continued Jolet. Cover your mainframe with screen and use emergency power only to operate. Try to shield everything you can."

"Roger." The Colonel was not nearly as sure about what was going on as he sounded. What was he sending his men into?

"Out," said the General. He turned toward her. "Will it work?"

"For a stopgap, that's the best we can do. The results will tell us a lot about their capability. Sir, if they can focus the EMP tightly enough to hit a satellite in space and take it out, a focused beam may still overload and penetrate the shield."

"We're going to have to come up with something. On a one-to-one basis we'll get our ass kicked. Gird your loins and grab your coat. We have to brief the White House." The General signaled his aide to have his car ready, as they passed through the conference room door.

***

The first success happened when all of the high-tech equipment was left behind. Colonel

Rodriquez watched in person. A piloted recon plane, an old Super Cub, without electronics flew over the communications center. While circling, the pilot watched the rooftop open and a tube track him. There was a flash, but nothing else happened. He felt a momentary dizziness, but it passed. His camera snapped away even as the small arms fire erupted.

As UWG forces assaulted the communications center, the casualties mounted, but the force of numbers carried the day. When they entered the communications compound, a tremendous explosion shook the ground, followed by the collapse of the central section of the building. There were no prisoners taken alive. It was a success, but also a failure, as the only thing learned was that fighting must be on a face-to-face basis. Only the wreckage of the technology was found. When the Colonel tried to send his report, the communications were down. The weapon must have knocked out the communications satellite before they blew it. He found an old landline telephone, and was able to call. After numerous routings and switching around, he was connected to the operations center and made his report to General Alexander verbally.

Chapter 32

Chairman Hu sat with his head down listening to the report from Chen Xiao. Things were spinning out of control. The Foundation, more successful than he had thought possible, now actually was threatening the UWG. In a master stroke, their "Sword of Allah" weapon had struck the UWG with unbelievable success. They had taken the military satellites out, which had blinded them from orbit. It cut their communications, which grounded all of the remotely piloted aircraft, blinding them from the ground and isolating all of the units from central command.

Xiao continued. "The attack is two-pronged and brilliant. First the EMP device knocked out the electronics, and when the UWG made efforts to reestablish them, they inserted viruses rendering them inoperable. It has crippled the ability of the UWG military and that of the United States. The problem is that it has also knocked out our monitoring capability. China is now unable to either monitor or control the systems we inserted into the world's computers."

Chairman Hu closed his eyes. By default they were actual allies with the UWG and would have to fight with them. This electronic war was not completely new, but it certainly favored the less technological forces. Letting the Foundation wage the war as proxies had backfired. They had been too successful, or Hu had overestimated the UWG.

"There are further problems," said Xiao. "We received a communication from the UWG to isolate all systems. Within two days, our mobile systems, the internet, cell phones, GPS, television all stopped. We were not able to break all connections and isolate before troubles began. Our financial systems are frozen–some compromised before the backups were protected."

The depth of the troubles began to dawn on Chairman Hu. The reality of how dependent the world was on technology began to explode in unimaginable proportions. It was a crash of serious gravity. All of the plans for economic control put in place so carefully over the decades were for naught. The world was back to pencils and paper and adding machines. It was like returning to the pre-Sputnik era. Now China would have to help the

UWG and quickly, to defeat the Foundation and put the world back in order. This was a setback.

"Get me UWG President Schmidt."

"Sir, communications are out. We're trying to reestablish the overseas cable system now."

Chairman Hu shook his head.

***

From his command center, Abayat Hussein watched the film of the whole scene again. Inevitably, the UWG forces would discover how weak they were. The viruses unleashed into the civilian systems became the most devastating of the attacks. The electronic terrorism collapsed the systems, leaving people alone and in the dark. With the viruses spread, he escalated the EMP attacks to include all satellites and communications systems. The Sword of Allah had done its work and opened the pathway for the destruction of the Western System.

"Rhualla, start the calls to the faithful. We must take to the streets and recruit followers now. Get the people to the mosques. Get a list of the operable Sword of Allah weapons left, order them to silence and hide them. They performed better than we had hoped. The world is in disarray."

In its way, this bested the 9/11 attack of 2001, as it hobbled their enemy and limited their ability to attack. The public raised a huge cry of dismay requiring much attention and isolating them. The people were alone, deaf, mute and powerless. The power and utility systems dependent on computers and satellites had shut down. The world ground to a halt.

"Send out messengers to the Christians, the Jews and the others to tell them the time has come to go forth. A flood of recruiters around the world will overpower the ability of the UWG to contain us. They no longer possess operating computers to watch us. The mosques, temples and churches will again become the center of communication."

Chapter 33

Katharine and Ron sat together in their Washington DC hotel with collars connecting them with all of Homakuwa. Ron: [It's chaos here. From what we gather, the war being waged by the Foundation has hit at the very core of modern civilization. With the loss of communications, the UWG can only meet in session face-to-face, and air transportation is seriously compromised without GPS creating great delays in travel. This is the ultimate terrorist attack and has struck at the basic belief of the people in the government. Unless organization can be reestablished the UWG is in danger of collapse.]

Cejani: [I would propose we try to place Homakuwa citizens with as many of the leaders as possible. We do not communicate electronically, and thus we are not compromised.]

Leticia: [To do that would reveal the capabilities of our communication system. It is something we haven't let out yet.]

Katharine: [If you've been following the events, you know the integrity of the UWG is at risk. Without government, who do we deal with? The attitudes might return to the days of Kihhim. The Foundation is a coalition of fundamentalist religions, and their re-emergence would spell our doom. If we don't fight them alongside the UWG, we are all in big trouble.]

Leticia: [Let's send representatives to the governments around the world to act as communications terminals. But we must never allow outsiders to use the system.]

They all agreed.

Chapter 34

With the communication systems down, several weeks has passed without any idea of the status of the United World Government and the nation members. By using the Homakuwa translators placed with as many of the world leaders as possible, the UWG again convened using the Collective for communication. Things had calmed. The actual fighting between the Foundation and UWG did not last long. The size of the Foundation forces, though quite small, created havoc out of all proportion to their size.

As the EMP sites were found by the UWG forces, their locations were swarmed and destroyed. The leadership was pursued, isolated and captured. The process of rebuilding began. At the top of the priority list was the electronic systems.

***

Katharine and Ron conferred with UWG President Heinz Schmidt, United States President

John Sorenson, Canadian Prime Minister Joliet de Gaul, and Mexican President Julio Perez. Representatives of the EU, Venezuela, North Africa, China, Australia, and Japan communicated via Homakuwa representatives.

Heinz Schmidt summed up. "We are getting our computer systems back on line here on Earth. It is time-consuming, but the power grids are coming back, though we are having to use power generated on Earth. That limits what we can do, because we depended on the Orbiting Power System for much of the world's power.

"We are recovering much of the transportation systems and gradually moving back to automated systems from the manual programs. The banking systems were backed up, so we didn't lose most of the data, and we're restoring those, too. Our major problem is reestablishing the large system of satellites. Presently the communications satellites have first priority, with the GPS system on a par. Next is the power satellite system followed by the visual data satellites. I want to thank all of the governments and corporations making the launch facilities available and the manufacturing sector for the crash program to build new systems. As has become painfully apparent, we cannot repair the satellites already in orbit as quickly as we could manufacture and launch. This program will take years, maybe decades."

Katharine translated the assent from those members not present. She then translated for Unweil of Ocealla. "As I understand it, the greatest shortcoming is the lack of trained personnel remaining in orbit for perhaps a year or longer to make necessary repairs. The International Space Station Complex is still functional, though sections will need work, especially all of the electronics. Is this correct?"

John Sorenson confirmed, "Our manned space program had been mostly supplanted by robotics as the support systems needed for humans were cost prohibitive. Needless to say, the robotic systems have been destroyed in the attacks. Much of the ISS Complex originally set up for humans has been mothballed."

Katharine for Unweil: "You have hit upon the crux of the matter. Homakuwa has residents and life forms much more suited than humans to life in space. If the nations of the world would supply the lift platforms and repair materials needed, I would propose that Homakuwa embark on a joint program to rebuild the satellite system. What would take decades could be reduced to a few years."

The world leaders sat in stunned silence as they tried to assimilate this. Finally President Schmidt spoke. "Have you discussed this with Homakuwa, and are you in accord?"

"We have," Katharine said. "Our Constructs can be modified for work in space while we develop a species adapted for life in space. We are working on those designs now. The great advantage is these species will be more mobile, exist without ill effects from zero gravity and live at greatly reduced air pressure."

"The point is we can have a team in orbit as soon as a lift vehicle can get us to the ISS Complex. We would depend on you here on Earth for support, such as equipment replacement supplies and staples for existence. Initially we would team up with human astronauts to get the living quarters in shape to support the repair team. We would like to form this team immediately to begin the planning."

The room erupted with everybody talking at once. Katharine was overwhelmed with the translations coming in. She looked at Ron, equally deluged.

***

TRAINING BEGINS FOR HOMAKUWA REPAIR CREWS

Training sessions have started for Homakuwa repair crews for the satellite systems. The first satellites slated for repair are the communications satellites, and the GPS satellites. Homakuwa personnel are much more suited for extended stays in space, and thus offer compressed repair schedules for the damage sustained during the attacks by the Foundation.

Homakuwa has also embarked on a species design program for personnel adapted specifically for long-term life in space. These species could live in space permanently, maintaining the satellite system continuously. Negotiations have begun with the International Space Workers Union to represent the Homakuwa workers.

Associated Press

The world went into overdrive. Committees were formed to address the integration of

Homakuwa life forms into the various sectors for the repair of the multiple satellite systems around the Earth. Homakuwa grew space suits for their crews of Cons. The Homakuwa workers were forced to join the union.

Russian and ESA Lift Vehicle Construction Program Accelerates

In response to the transport needs to lift materials into orbit, Russian and European Space Authority programs have accelerated. Additional spaceports in India and the United States will be opened up to accommodate the increase of launches. Replacement satellite construction at the various American facilities have moved into 24/7 schedules. Chinese computer systems are being supplied to meet the needs for rebuilding the satellite systems.

Aerospace News

The surface world understood that the Homakuwa collars enabled a communication system outside of the electronic age. The Collective remained hidden.

Chapter 35

Leticia watched the instrument panels with the technicians glued to them. This launch by the Russians/European Space Agency was the result of hurried and intense negotiations with the UWG and those nations having a space program. Once the UWG saw how helpful Homakuwa was, they agreed to include a Construct in the first crew.

This was the first of many missions to start repairing the satellite system, reestablishing communications, the Global Positioning Satellites, and the Orbiting Power System. Launches would soon be taking place at the NASA Kennedy Space Center in Florida, Vandenberg in California, the Russian Space Center and the Chinese Space Center. Those launches would happen after the International Space System was operational and could accommodate the additional personnel. There had been no talk of the military satellites, but several nations watched the progress with interest.

Homakuwa had talked about Constructs for space habitation, and Chetnaz was only one of several who had been modified for that purpose. Many more were designed and being grown. Leticia smiled to herself. This opportunity to utilize the surface nations to establish a series of space colonies greatly benefitted Homakuwa. Once the habitats became established, Homakuwa would expand and take over the maintenance of the various satellites systems orbiting Earth. It would put Homakuwa in a position of control and ensure their security. No nation would allow their power system, their communications, or their navigational systems to go down.

This symbiosis between the surface world and Homakuwa would truly strengthen. They already were integral in the fishing industry, insuring the long-term survival of the seas. Now they would be in space assuring communication systems and the continued supply of power to a world needing ever more.

Initially there had been substantial resistance from the companies owning those satellites, but when Homakuwa bid the repair, maintenance, and operation contracts at less than half of the present costs, even China had seen the dollar signs grow and inked the contracts. The Chinese could never resist a great deal.

***

Chetnaz floated in her water-filled tank, blissfully unaware of the crushing force exerted by the acceleration of the Russian booster rocket hurling the European Space Authority shuttle toward the International Space Station complex. On one side sat Clay Pickering of the United States space program. On the other sat Felicia Van der Meir of the ESA. She was Belgian. Both of them wore G-suits. Through their faceplates Chetnaz saw their faces sagging under the g-force.

This was the first shuttle in the satellite reestablishment program. It had been fast-tracked and was to prepare for the start of the operations. Only six months had elapsed since the end of Foundation War, as it had been dubbed in the press. The three astronauts had been training hard for the last four months as technicians capable of upgrading and repairing the equipment on the space station. The shuttle cargo was test equipment and replacement equipment to bring the ISS back to fully operational status. Felicia and Clay planned to remain on the station for a four month tour. As a

Construct from Ocealla, Chetnaz would be able to stay much longer.

She had originally been a Construct grown for undersea life. In appearance she looked like a large elongated jellyfish with thick tentacle-like arms. The tips of her arms differed. Some had fingers, others had claws, while others could deform into different shapes. She had eyes in several places around her bulbous body and on some of her arms. She had been similar to a cephalopod designed for life around Ocealla, but she had been modified for existence in zero gravity and at low atmospheric pressure.

Chetnaz could use any of her arms to pull herself around or inflate and expel gas as a jet and shoot about. Without bones, she would not experience the loss of bone mass her companions would. She breathed either through gills, as she was doing now in the tank, or with the lung tissue coating her interior. She existed quite easily at atmospheric pressures of 0.1 atmospheres, even less for short periods. She was designed to live in an orbiting habitat and become the ISS's first permanent resident.

She felt a jolt as the first stage of the booster dropped off, and then she felt the thrust of the second stage as it fired to push them into orbit and match the speed of the ISS. Docking would happen in one day. She relaxed and opened the channel with Ocealla.

As a new Construct, she didn't need the collar, because the function was built into her. Many of the original residents of Kahchk Kihhim and Ocealla still used the collar. Those created recently had it integral. Homakuwa had the ability to add it to the others, but they still somehow needed the periods of isolation of the older generation. Not her. She was fully integrated into the Collective mind of the Homakuwa.

Chetnaz was in Ocealla, Retseana, Ajabada, and the other parts of Homakuwa, and they were with her. She pictured the Collective mind as a water bubble floating in zero gravity. The cohesiveness of the parts held it together as a whole, but it could be broken into units as small as the individual molecules. Yet, it would pull back together into a single unit. Like a water molecule in that bubble, she was an individual, but she was also part of a much larger whole.

The lessons she learned were also learned by the Collective, so retention was no problem. Her experiences would be felt by all. Homakuwa prepared to grow and expand. A voice brought her back to the shuttle.

"Chetnaz, what's the orbital status readout?" Leticia used the vocal channel for the sake of the Surfacers.

"I'll key them in for you," said Chetnaz. She looked at her indicators. "I hope they're the same as yours." Her fingers danced over the keypad linking the speed, altitude, distance to the ISS. "I'm going to give you the shuttle readouts too for comparison." Again her many fingers danced across the keypads mounted inside her tank entering atmospheric pressure, oxygen content, temperature, fuel inside, fuel reserve, any anomalies on the shuttle exterior and a myriad of other operational data. This necessary check assured the electronics were functioning properly. If the shuttle were hit with an EMP, it would be disastrous.

She already knew all of the readings agreed because she was connected to Leticia Gardner in the launch headquarters. Homakuwa chose not to reveal the full extent of their Collective mind to the surface people. It might be an unnecessary precaution, but did no harm. Somehow, being too different from the surface world seemed dangerous.

Chapter 36

The reestablishment of the ISS took a month. As soon as it was habitable, a string of ships were launched for six months with mixed crews of humans and Cons and loaded with repair parts. Their primary task was the repairing of the satellite systems around the Earth. Initially under the direction of human supervisors, it quickly became apparent that the humans were more of a detriment than a help. Repairs expected to take years happened in months. The UWG began to return to the pre-Foundation attack normalcy, with one important exception.

The space civilization of Tashogith Kihhim (the Sun Village in Tohono O'odham) was born. Chetnaz remained on site as the commander of the Homakuwa expansion.

Chetnaz: [Leticia, we've finished refurbishing the GPS and the weather satellites, and we're ahead of schedule on the Orbital Power System. In addition to the inactive and abandoned satellites orbiting Earth, our lunar mining operation has brought us more material to begin constructing additional habitats.

[As we construct them, we'll need the raw materials such as water, carbon, and oxygen and the many other materials to make them self-sustaining and support life. We're beginning construction of our first tow-ships now. We've detected a comet that will come close enough for us to harvest materials when we complete the fleet of space tugs.]

[Leticia, this is Rich Lewis. We've been working on the tow-ship design and will make them small, but with a huge mirror and sail system. Rather than use standard rockets to power them, we'll use a concentrating mirror to focus sunlight through a laser and then a reaction mass to create a jet. The first ones will be crude, but they'll work well enough to tow ice back.

[This ice and comet material along with what we're mining from the moon will get our habitats going, so we can produce food and oxygen. Our intent is to have at least two self-sustaining habitats within the next two years. The Cons we've developed for space have freed us from the restrictions of the human body.]

Leticia smiled to herself. In a bid to take over the operation and maintenance of the Orbiting Power System, they had no equal. The bid for the contract was no contest. With their new Cons, they didn't require nearly the Earth support. Soon they would require none. This was the beginning of a new series of city/states and the expansion of Homakuwa.

Jamie Wong: [Leticia, you know we've had problems with the radiation damage caused to our Cons. The damage is much less than humans would sustain, but remains a concern as we are required to increase our rejuvenation program for them. The teams we will send to mine the asteroid belt and the comets won't have us available to help them, so I've asked Rich to look into ways to build in enough shielding to protect them. We are trying to design species more resistant to radiation but with only moderate success.]

***

Chetnaz' report to Homakuwa on the status of their efforts in space after the first year was remarkable: [We sent a tow team into the asteroid belt to bring back several sizeable asteroids. We plan to use them to construct the habitats when

Rich comes up with the design. They should be back in eighteen months.

[Once completed, these structures will be ready for the final additions and bio-systems to become homes for the new civilization of Tashogith Kihhim. With shielding and protection offered by the massive rocks, we can continuously regenerate those Cons damaged by the intense radiation in space. The genetically engineered bio system will thrive, and we are on our way to being creatures of space–a space civilization.]

Leticia: [This will be a huge boon for Homakuwa, and it is also the death knell for the exploration of space by man. Anything needed from space, including knowledge, can be purchased from Homakuwa at a fraction of the cost to send man or even robots aloft.

[Homakuwa now controls life in the seas on Earth and soon space above. We are expanding, with colonies on the moon mining water. Our asteroid mining system will expand our growth into the Solar system.] Through Chetnaz' eyes, they saw Mars and its moons for habitation. [Upon arrival, we will again build Cons, but compatible with life on Mars. This will be Homakuwa's next step.]

Chapter 37

Ayatollah Aiassi Komini, Abayat Hussein, and Rhualla Hussein sat together in a small hut near the Pakistan border. The Foundation uprising had been put down but not completely stopped by the UWG. While the UWG was still in disarray, they increased their fundamentalist following, but the numbers were not as great as hoped. It was the same for the other religions involved in the Foundation.

The UWG forces now actively hunted many of the Foundation leadership. The good news was they were having to do so on foot though the technical systems were coming back online. Generations of the true believers had successfully eluded pursuers in this part of the world, even when they used their high tech. They would be safe for a long time.

Ayatollah Aiassi Komini spoke. "Rhualla, the Sword of Allah has proved a huge success. With their technology inoperable, the UWG forces had to face us directly, not kill us from halfway around the world. We had foreseen that they would find a way to negate that but not before we leveled the field of conflict. How many remain, and where are they?"

Rhualla glanced at a sheet of paper. "There are six left. They remained unused and hidden and are thus unknown. We can bring them out when we need them. The most valuable ones are in China, the United States and Germany. These give us coverage that, with the blessing of Allah, will deliver another strike when the time is right."

Abayat Hussein smiled. "Rhualla, your computer viruses were successful beyond our dreams. We have set back the computer control and monitoring by decades. Did you think we would do so well?"

"The Sword of Allah blinded the satellites. Somehow the virus mutated to become even more powerful than we designed. It moved past firewalls and piggybacked onto the satellite control directives to infect those systems. As the controllers tried to repair the damage done by the EMP, they infected them. We did not plan this. Our attack was aimed at the education and justice system computers. Allah gave us this blessing."

Abayat Hussein spoke. "What about this spawn of the devil society Homakuwa? They are surely an abomination against Allah and all of humanity. How do we destroy them? They are as great a threat as The Prophet. Where the Prophet steals our souls, they threaten to destroy mankind. They have teamed with UWG to restore the satellites using creatures they have created while playing God. We must declare a Jihad against them and stop them at all cost."

"It is one thing to declare a Jihad, but a way of carrying it out must exist. How do we attack a civilization that lives under the sea," said the Ayatollah.

"We can attack their representatives wherever they are. We can maximize the deaths of all those who are near them and turn them into pariahs driving admirers away," said Abayat Hussein.

"A representative is in Guiana supporting the European Space Authority launch. The security is not tight. We could strike there first," supplied Rhualla.

"Once we strike, security will become so tight as to make further action very difficult. This strike must be defining, for a long time will pass before the opportunity arises for another," said Abayat.

The Ayatollah spoke. "Perhaps we need more than one strike at the same time before the opportunities for others disappears. We must take advantage of the times, and our resources are limited. Perhaps now would be the time to bring in our other allies. The Christians could form another strike to coincide with ours. Perhaps the Hindus and even China as well. We all agree that this nation of Homakuwa comes from the devil himself. Let us formulate a plan and send messengers. This will take careful planning."

***

Chairman Hu glanced at the many silk paintings on the paneled walls of his office. He listened to the report by Robert Chaing. It was not good news. Hu was in danger of losing his seat as Chairman. The negotiations with Homakuwa had cost China absolute control of the Orbiting Power System. Refusing to accept the maintenance and operation bid put forth by them would have raised questions and exposed the control China had over the industry. His political opponents nipped at his heels over this loss. He only half listened.

Robert continued. "We have received a query from the Foundation regarding a possible attack on

Homakuwa." Chairman Hu sat up. "The Foundation is planning a series of attacks on the representatives of Homakuwa in an attempt to create fear toward them. They want us to participate by supplying them with materials and even suggested that we initiate an attack as well."

Chairman Hu mused. If fear is associated with them, certainly their aura of power would suffer. Perhaps an opportunity had arisen to gain back some control. There was little downside as long as China had deniability. At the very least, if the plan was weak or faulty, China could step in and save the representatives. "Send a representative to meet with them. Find out more."

Robert Chaing bowed as he backed out the door.

Chapter 38

Katharine rose to the quiet knock. She opened the door to see the Prophet standing before her. Mutely she beckoned him in. He glided to a chair and sat. She joined him in an adjacent chair. His eyes focused on her.

"Distressing news has come to my attention by way of a recent convert. The Foundation is still active and is planning a coordinated series of attacks against Homakuwa personnel. These bomb attacks will cause as much collateral damage as possible, creating fear of association in anybody dealing with you."

Katharine was shocked. Attacks against Homakuwa representatives!

"The fundamentalists put you in the same category as me, an enemy of their God. I'm not sure this is an honor." He smiled. At once

Katharine wanted to laugh at his small joke and shrink at the idea of being a target.

"Just a minute. I'd like to include others from Homakuwa in this," Katharine said. Donning the collar, she brought Homakuwa into her mind. Homakuwa quickly understood the revelation. Her mind tingled as the Prophet's mind touched theirs. She was surprised he was able to do this. [Don't be alarmed. If you want me to leave, I will do so.] No one objected.

Leticia posed, [The question is what to do with this information. How can attacks be turned to our advantage? There are several choices. We can step up the security to thwart the attacks. The outcome of this would be to maintain the status quo.]

The Prophet: {This would weaken the Foundation slightly but leave them viable.]

Leticia: [We might allow the attacks to take place but without success against our people. The collateral damage would then be used to ostracize the Foundation.]

Katharine wasn't the only one shocked with the idea of using the loss of innocent lives that would result as a tool. This proposal to use people's deaths even if for some higher purpose seemed wrong.

Leticia: [If we allow the attacks to take place, we then use that to battle the Foundation in an aggressive manner. We would suffer the loss of some of our representatives, but their minds are within the Collective, and they would not be truly lost. With more information of when, how, and who, we may find more options. If our people are injured but not killed, we can recover them in med cells provided we are able to get them to the tanks before they die.]

The Prophet chimed in. [Another possibility exists. Perhaps if we have some control of the incident to minimize the collateral damage, and if I were present, we would resurrect them and claim I did it. Your abilities would remain secret, and my stature would gain while theirs would wane. It would actually become a negative for them.]

Ron sensed Katharine's revulsion, but added, [Such an action would make them seem impotent against the Prophet, something already apparently true. How would you resurrect those killed in the attack?]

Leticia explained, [We have clone bodies of several of us. It's a program we began decades ago. The clones are empty shells and inert in stasis, awaiting the introduction of mind and memories.]

Katharine: [Leticia, when did this take place?] She was shocked about this new revelation—wondering what else she didn't know.

Leticia: [We decided as we were growing Ocealla we might face this need. When we considered rejoining the surface world, and those of us living on the surface would become vulnerable, it became more important. The clones have been grown so they are approximately the same age as we appear now. We must limit those involved in the attack to the bodies we cloned.]

Ron: [How would you introduce the minds and memories?]

Leticia: [We would use the Collective to create a duplicate mind and implant it using the collars. We would create the duplicate without actually opening the mind completely. The private parts would be maintained as a file.]

Katharine: [Have you done this before?] She sensed Leticia struggling to answer.

The Prophet: [It has been done many times before.]

Katharine felt Ron recoil from the implication. She'd need to open up to him, and that may not be pleasant. He still maintained loyalties to the surface world. [Later,] she flashed at him. His mind clamped down on his questions. Compartmentalizing was a talent learned from decades of politics.

Leticia: [Will you be able to find out more about this plot?]

The Prophet: [I will. As I learn more, I'll be back with you.]

Leticia: [I think the last option holds out the best for us, but dying in this way is going to hurt. A lot]

The meeting broke up.

***

Katharine and Ron looked at each other. The house they had rented in Washington, now the Homakuwa embassy, was quiet around them. "Tell me about the clones," said Ron.

"You know as much as I," said Katharine. "Leticia has fierce loyalty, and she does things in the best interest of Homakuwa, even if she believes I would object. There exists a tie between the Prophet and Homakuwa. This connection is something I was unaware of until I met with the Prophet."

Ron sat silently.

"When we fled the surface world," Katharine continued, "we knew we could not come back until mankind could accept us. To create this tolerance, Jamie Wong and Leticia created a man with special powers, the Prophet. His sole purpose is to minimize the hatred generated by the various religions in the name of God and create a more tolerant world. He has done so and continues to. I was unaware of this until I met him."

"So you didn't leave the surface world alone." Ron's voice was harsh.

She sensed his ire rise at the thought of betrayal. Katharine felt the need to defend Homakuwa. "We planted a seed. Was it wrong? Did we help or hurt humanity?"

"In one respect, I feel manipulated. I believed the Prophet to be a messenger from God, and now I find out he was created by Homakuwa. Certainly the rest of the world will feel their faith in God has been manipulated if this ever comes out. It could easily unite the world's religions and lead to open warfare against Homakuwa."

"I understand feelings of betrayal. It's what I felt when I found out. But when I examined Leticia's actions, she was right. Ron, you know we will not allow ourselves to be destroyed. A war would put the human race back thousands of years, perhaps into a society of warring tribes. We cannot argue that the world is better because of the Prophet, Do you disagree?"

"Of course not," snapped Ron, "but I cannot rid myself of this sense of treachery."

"This from a man who tried to destroy us!" Katharine regretted those words as they left her lips.

Ron reacted as if struck. "I think we both need to take a time out. Any revelation about this will never come from me." He spun and left the room. Katharine stared at the closed door. Her heart was like lead in her chest.

***

Ron's mind whirled. He could be trusted to hold this secret, but his trust in Homakuwa as a benevolent partner had been shaken. It wasn't fair to take it out on Katharine, because she didn't know, but she was a part of Homakuwa. Just as he maintained loyalty toward his species, they did the same. That did not mean they were in conflict. Still, the sense of betrayal stung and also made him wonder what else lay unseen. Homakuwa certainly had the power to destroy humanity, yet they had striven to live in harmony. At least it appeared so. But now it seemed to be on their terms, and that was where the distrust lay.

In all of his time in the Collective mind he had never sensed animosity toward humanity, and he didn't believe any existed. Yet their goal was not clear. The recent contracts putting them in charge of the Orbiting Power System would give them unrivaled opportunity to take over the world though he didn't sense that was their aim. Their actions were to improve life for humanity, live in harmony, and keep a proper balance with the Earth. In his heart he believed this was their objective.

But to what ends would they go to achieve accord and recognition of their species? The picture formed in his mind of a loving parent trying to guide a wayward child into growing up. Despite the sting of the characterization of mankind as rebellious children, perhaps this vision was a more accurate image than he wanted to see. Perhaps humanity needed a parent. History seemed to say so.

Chapter 39

**Rebuilding the Earth
Satellite System Ahead of
Schedule!**

With launches taking place throughout the world, Homakuwa crews are repairing the satellite systems around the Earth at a pace unforeseen with human astronauts. In the year since the start of the repair program, the Global Positioning System is fully operational, and the numerous communication satellites will be operating at pre-Foundation attack levels within months. Work has begun on the Orbiting Power System. With a central base out of the Jet Propulsion Laboratory in California, liaisons all over the world are coordinating with the launching of materials to replace the damaged parts on the various satellites.

Crews made up mostly of Homakuwa Constructs are replacing and repairing the components to get the systems back up and operating. The Constructs are showing their value by being able to remain in space longer with lesser needs than their human counterparts. What was predicted to be a ten-year program to get the satellite system back is well ahead of schedule.

Pasadena Sentinel

Leticia: [Chetnaz, you are amazing. You've remained on the ISS while several teams of human companions have come and departed for Earth. Your abilities have shortened the estimated time to get the station operational by more than three months, and the new crews will be all Constructs. You've demonstrated your abilities to work outside with only a minimum of protective gear and oxygen supply for short periods. Your need for only a low-pressure atmosphere extends your working time greatly.]

Chetnaz: [Thank you. Jamie Wong deserves much of the credit for his design of me. The larger problem now is getting the life support materials transported to the ISS and the replacement parts for the damaged satellites.]

Katharine and Leticia were at the Jet Propulsion Laboratory putting in their term as ground support for the growing number of Constructs. They were enjoying each other's company, having not been together for an extended period in a long time.

Leticia related the status report directly from Chetnaz to the human satellite repair staff on Earth and to governments around the world via direct link.

"The Constructs along with Rich Lewis developed several highly mobile craft we call 'Sleds.'" Leticia pointed to the hologram. "We use these to move crews and materials to the various satellites for repair." A holographic display formed showing the ISS and the small craft floating nearby. The view zoomed in on the sled. "These small craft carry the basic life support systems needed for the Constructs, replacement fuel and replacement parts for the damaged satellites."

The hologram changed to show a satellite with the sled approaching. Leticia continued. "The technique we developed for the repairs is to envelop the satellite in a bubble of low atmospheric pressure, which allows our crews to make the repairs." A transparent bubble grew around the satellite in the display. Constructs appeared inside and swarmed around the satellite.

"Stray and wayward parts are contained within the bubble and collected after the repair. This will all be done in the satellite's existing orbit. Once completed, the bubble will be collapsed, and the satellite released. Control will then be turned over to the owner." Leticia watched the smiling faces nod.

"Materials like fuel, water, and food are being lifted in a continuous stream of automated rockets from launch pads throughout the world. Without the extensive need for life support systems, we've been able cut the costs per pound tremendously."

Leticia clicked a button and the view changed. "We are presently working on a system to minimize the fuel requirement for the sleds." The hologram again showed the ISS. "A laser power system is under development. Sunlight is collected and focused into a chamber creating a laser." A large mirror similar to those on the OPS formed. "This laser will then focus on the sled."

The hologram now showed a sled with the laser focused on it. "The light will push the sled to the desired location. When we need greater thrust, the laser will be focused by the sled on a thrust chamber." A mirror formed around the sled and directed the laser into a ceramic chamber. "Reaction fuel is fed into this chamber where it is vaporized and forms a jet, driving the sled. The mirrors allow us to direct the beam regardless of the sled orientation." Seen in the hologram, the sled jetted up to a satellite, and then the mirror changed orientation and focused to slow and stop the sled.

"All the material recovered from the satellites and stray orbiting material is recycled. Recovery and scavenging are now our basic way of life. Circuit board testing equipment is now on the ISS, so those boards unharmed in the attack can be used again without having to lift replacements from Earth. At a cost of $500 per pound to lift equipment to orbit, everything saved is a bonus."

The scientists around her at the JPL nodded.

"A solar forge has been constructed to melt metals, so they can be reformed into useful parts. The rocket booster bodies are used to expand the

ISS and construction is underway on additional habitats. The technology for us to permanently exist in space has started to develop rapidly."

To those watching the report, the changes seemed wondrous. Only later was the idea of a non-human species having control of the space around Earth troubling. Especially worrisome was the powerful lasers orbiting overhead.

Chapter 40

"CAR BOMB ATTACK ON US SOIL KILLS THE PROPHET AND HOMAKUWA REPRESENTATIVES!"

"Katharine Levey and Leticia Gardner, representatives of the new nation of Homakuwa were killed in a car bomb explosion as they were exiting the Jet Propulsion Laboratory in Pasadena, California. The Prophet was also a causality. The three had met late in the day to discuss Homakuwa's travels into space. Because of the late hour, the parking lot was almost deserted and there were no other causalities. The Foundation has claimed responsibility for the bombing, the first on US soil in several years. The investigation is being conducted in a joint effort by the FBI and the Bureau of Alcohol Tobacco, Firearms, and Explosives."

"PROPHET RESURRECTS HOMAKUWA REPRESENTATIVES KILLED IN ATTACK!"

"Homakuwa representatives, Katharine Levey and Leticia Gardner, murdered in a car bomb attack have been resurrected by the Prophet. Resurrections of the Prophet have occurred many times before, but this is the first time others have been brought back to life. The Prophet states, "This was possible because he was with the representatives at the time of the attack and otherwise cannot be done." The representatives have resumed their duties for the nation of Homakuwa.

The explanation for the resurrection has not prevented thousands of people from assailing the Prophet seeking resurrection of their loved ones.

Pasadena Sentinel

Ayatollah Aiassi Komini and Abayat Hussein listened to Rhualla Hussein's latest report. "The assassination was successful. Katharine Levey and Leticia Gardner were blown up along with the Prophet using a bomb placed under their car.

Unfortunately, little collateral damage occurred. They left the center late, and their car was isolated. We at once claimed responsibility. The statement read, 'God had struck down the false Prophet and struck a blow against the blasphemous nation of Homakuwa.'"

"The condemnation from all nations of the United World Government is loud and long. Vows to arrest and punish those responsible were swift in coming. The hunt is on, and we must be cautious," said the Ayatollah.

He continued, "Our friends in China and North Korea gave sanctuary to all of our forces able to cross their borders. We still possess the Sword of Allah in several countries, and though the Global Positioning Systems are operating, communications yet require more work. But repairs are proceeding more quickly than we had anticipated, and Homakuwa is proving very useful in aiding the United World Government. Their prowess in space cannot be matched by humans."

"You are correct, sir," said Rhualla. "Our strike against their representatives has slowed their efforts only minimally. The reappearance of the Homakuwa representatives and the Prophet makes us seem impotent. The strike has not resulted in the flood of converts as we hoped,"

"Instruct all of our forces to go deeply underground," said the Ayatollah. "I foresee another opportunity coming, but not soon. We must maintain our strength for that time. Pass this message on to our allies. We must withdraw, or we will perish. Change is coming. I can feel it, and Allah will provide."

PART 5
Civilization Falls and Rises

Chapter 41

Sylvix: [Leticia, a large meteoroid has entered our Solar system and crossed the orbit of Pluto. The projected path does not intersect the orbit of the Earth, but the object will pass close to Saturn. Saturn's gravity may cause it to break up in a similar event to the Hale-Bopp strikes on Jupiter. We will watch and analyze as we can.]

Sylvix was a new type of Construct. Though a bio-system, she could integrate with some of the mechanical components of a spaceship directly. Her bio component was still independent of the spaceship, but she was much more than a pilot.

[Thanks,] returned Leticia. She was in her latest rotation period. Their resurrection was easier than she had thought, with the memory imprints having only a very short lapse. That lapse included being blown up and the pain, thank goodness. The reappearance of Katharine and Leticia had indeed caused the image of the Prophet to strengthen. Followers seeking resurrection for their loved ones besieged him.

Patiently, the Prophet explained the resurrection was only possible because of the close proximity he had with them at their death. Still requests poured in for his help. Now people flocked to him as a way to escape death.

By association, Homakuwa was also the target of requests for miracle medical procedures and resurrection from death. They declined all discussions on the topics. This increased the awe of their civilization, but it did not endear them.

After the revelation of Homakuwa's involvement with the Prophet, Ron had spent more time in Washington, but his understanding of Katharine pushed the doubt and feeling of treachery out of his mind, and he longed to be with her. Ron returned to Ocealla and moved in with Katharine, making only short sojourns to the surface world.

Leticia walked over and spoke to JPL Director, Dr. Martha McGuire. "Are you tracking the incoming object now crossing the orbit of Pluto?"

"We just found it. We're trying to assemble a path projection now. It will cross Saturn's orbit in about four months. By then we'll know a lot more.

Thanks for mentioning it," said Martha. "Sylvix just sent us the images, so we'll assign someone to keep track as part of our Near Earth Object program.

"I wanted to mention we continue to be astounded by the capabilities of the Constructs in maintaining the space near Earth. You're building your third habitat now, aren't you?"

"We're trying to," Leticia said, "but the shortage of materials has slowed our program. The Earth launch facilities still have control over us, so we've tried to minimize the needs for support. Our asteroid mining program is successful, but to tow the asteroids into Earth orbit takes a long time. We're considering a program to increase the Lunar mining operation, and I'm sure we'll raise some hackles. We understand there's a move before the UWG to limit usage of the moon. Even though Earth's surface people no longer have the capability of putting people on the moon, they still consider it theirs."

Martha was sympathetic toward the growth hopes of Homakuwa and disagreed with the attempts to limit their expansion. "I know. We're behind you as the only viable space program still in existence. You do have a pretty strong lobby with the power sector, and I hope you never need to use that lever. It would embitter a lot of the surface world, making them feel as if there's a gun to their head."

"The bitterness works both ways!" exclaimed Leticia. "We feel restrictions and costs on the continued supply of our materials are a yoke around our necks maintained by the surface people. Price increases have been applied every month for the last six months. We've had to increase the power rates we charge, and it's become a war."

"Leticia, we're with you."

"At some point we will be forced to make preparations for self-subsistence regardless of the UWG laws. This is our existence we're talking about."

"We're walking a very narrow path," said Martha. "We need each other, but a lot of jealously has arisen about your technology, and yes, still some fear."

"Sorry, Martha. I know you're with us but sometimes the pressure builds."

Martha put her hand on Leticia's shoulder. "We'll get through this, and I do understand about the need to unload sometimes."

"Thanks."

Chapter 42

Chen Xiao relayed the latest report to Robert Chaing. "We have been able to insert the Dragon Chip into all of the replacement computer boards we supplied for those damaged by the Foundation attack. Our stockpiles of those chips allowed us to meet accelerated deliveries and displace all our competitor's chips. Virtually all of the computers damaged and repaired have the Dragon Chip. We can monitor everything, and given the order, we will control those computers."

Robert glanced at the door to the Chairman's office. "The Chairman is watching the world situation closely. He will make small moves to eventually get control of the Orbiting Power System back. Most troubling is the control now held by the Homakuwa nation. At the Chairman's direction, we will take over that system again. You must be ready."

***

On January 31st, an alarm awakened Sylvix. Her monitoring function alerted her. "Power Satellite 24A has drifted and is beaming microwaves at Texas ranch land rather than the roof installed collectors. The energy density is not great enough to harm life on the surface." Why hadn't the system corrected itself? The redundancy built in to the computer systems made this nearly impossible. Sylvix quickly donned her EVA suit and mounted the sled. Of the group she had been assigned to watch over, satellite 24A was not the closest, but not the farthest away.

She approached the satellite forty minutes later. Sylvix coupled with the on-board systems and alerted Homakuwa–their attention became one with her. [The problem at Power Satellite 24A seems to be in the misalignment of the aiming system.] She felt several of the Collective minds link. [We need to confirm the coordinates of receptor target.]

Alan Brighton: [Our systems show it is properly aimed.] Alan Brighton was another Con directing operations from onboard the ISS.

Sylvix assessed: [The problem has to be the onboard computer. It's receiving correct targeting directions but has misread those coordinates.] She parked and entered. Alan notified his Surfacer supervisor of the problem.

Sylvix: [Homakuwa, we did an extensive board replacement to this onboard computer about a year ago. The pre-check of the boards indicated no problems. This was one I worked on myself.] She read her diagnostic system. As she looked at the readouts, Alan saw through her eyes. [Alan, I'm getting alarms from other satellites.]

Alan: [I know. We're seeing them here, and your sector isn't the only one. We've lost 20% in the last few minutes!] Alarms were going off all over the center. Empty monitor stations rapidly filled with personnel. [There's nothing showing up on the diagnostic.]

Sylvix confirmed: [Mine either. Leticia, we're getting a system wide crash of the Orbital Power System. [Nothing shows up immediately on the diagnostic readout. We're going to lose the whole system within an hour if we can't correct this.]

Leticia sent back: [I'm going to start a diagnostic from here.]

The Orbiting Power System crashed forty minutes later, essentially blacking out the world.

Chapter 43

In a joint Congressional hearing, the major power suppliers sat together at a table facing the panel of Senators and Congressmen posing for the cameras. The gavel struck. "This hearing will come to order," said Senator DiMaggio. "Let the record show …" and he went through the preliminaries of getting the meeting under way. The grilling started in earnest about an hour later.

The first witness was the Chairman of the Board for North American Power Consolidated. NAPC was the major supplier of power for the United States, Canada, and northern Mexico.

"Mr. Stevens, have you investigated the recent power outage which struck North America?"

"We have, Senator. We found improperly installed circuit boards caused the satellites to misread Earth coordinates and move off target. These boards replaced the ones damaged by the Foundation attack."

"Who installed these circuit boards?"

"The Homakuwa workforce under the maintenance contracts replaced the damaged boards."

"Were the Homakuwa teams experienced in this type of work?"

"This was their first contract for work in space."

Why was Homakuwa chosen when they had no record of experience in this industry?"

"Honestly, Senator, they bid the work at a fraction of the costs offered by the competing companies. The workforce was subjected to extensive training and testing, and all passed with high marks."

"Was a Homakuwa representative present at the time of the testing?"

"It was necessary in order to communicate with them."

Congressman Reynolds (D) CA spoke. "So all of the answers to the test questions passed through the representative."

"That is correct, Congressman."

A loud murmur swept through the gallery. This news of preliminary fault with Homakuwa had been leaked to the press a week before, but now that it was on the record it raised eyebrows.

Identical questioning continued with the other industry representatives. At last Leticia was called and sworn in.

"Ms. Gardner, you are the Homakuwa Space Initiative Director, are you not?"

"Yes Sir. Before you begin your questioning, I'd like to read a statement into the record, sir if I may."

"Go ahead, but please be brief."

"We initiated an investigation immediately into the cause of the outages. Our diagnostic equipment showed no abnormalities, yet they were in front of us. This led us to the conclusion that either there was a problem deep within the circuit boards we were supplied for replacements, or a problem existed with our diagnostic equipment. In the end both cases were present. The boards had an abnormal chip built into them." She held up a board. "The chips are so small as to be almost invisible to the naked eye. Here's a magnification of that chip." A hologram appeared and the small dot grew until the intricate circuitry could be seen. "This chip allows for external access from an unauthorized source to control this board. These chips were also found in our diagnostic equipment and skewed the readouts."

"An inspection of these boards showed they were from different suppliers. Further investigation revealed the components were supplied by different manufacturers, all of them in China."

The room erupted. The Speaker banged the gavel for many minutes before he was able to restore order. "Are you accusing China of supplying faulty equipment?"

Shouts and yells again exploded. Leticia had to wait for order to be restored before she could speak. "No, sir. I'm saying they sabotaged the efforts of Homakuwa to bring the whole satellite system back on line. I'm saying this was a conscious effort to discredit Homakuwa. We did some further investigation and found China to be the majority stockholder in all of the major power companies, and not just in the US. They actually hold the reins to the world's power. When they lost the repair and maintenance contracts, they lost control. This is their attempt to regain that control."

The noise in the room made it impossible to speak. The gavel pounded for several minutes before the Speaker roared. "This session will come to order, or I'll clear the gallery!" It quieted. "Ms. Gardner, these are grave accusations you are making. We'll appoint a committee to look into this. In the meantime, you will begin preparations to turn the system over to another agency which we will name. This session is over." Bang! The gavel came down again.

***

Ron had made one of his rare trips to accompany Leticia during the congressional hearing. Together they left through a back door. Leticia was so furious she was trembling. All of Homakuwa felt her rage at the unfairness of the system.

"We'll work through this, Leticia. Once they see the evidence we'll be cleared."

"In the meantime, Ron, we'll be out, and every problem they encounter will be blamed on us. I have no confidence the committee to be appointed will be fair. I have no confidence they'll even look at our evidence. We're going to be kicked out of space!"

Ron looked at her. Suddenly they both were laughing at the absurdity of that statement. "Kicked out of space!" He dropped her off at her hotel. In her room, Leticia tried to unwind, but the fury and frustration burned hotly.

Her distant memory of life with the government as a FBI agent surfaced. She had been railroaded out due to politics then also. She'd left the agency and joined Kahchk Kihhim, and it had turned out to be the best thing to ever happen to her. Perhaps the same applied here.

With her age and wisdom, she could now see the best course was to walk away. China would again gain control of the world's power system, and thus the surface world would come under their management. What a masterful ploy, and she had to admire how it had been pulled off. Still, she couldn't just let this go. Given an opportunity, she'd retaliate. In the back of her mind was the information they had gotten from the Foundation group. The makeup of that organization included more than the religious groups throughout the world. There had been several nations supporting that revolutionary effort.

If that information found its way to the public sector, what would happen? She'd have to think about how to handle this. Losing face was an important factor in Asian culture. Showing a betrayal of the UWG by a member would be critical. She'd have to play that card at the right time and in the right way–if she was going to.

What would be China's reaction? Denial, of course, but she would build the evidence until it was incontrovertible, or at least until the press made it seem so. Should she save Homakuwa's position with the OPS by discrediting China? Would China strike out or pull back? That was the crux of the matter. Certainly they would harbor animosity toward Homakuwa, but what could they do about it? An open attack was a remote possibility, but the UWG would protect them, wouldn't they?

An economic attack would occur, probably in the form of increased costs of lifting materials to orbit, but there remained competition with other countries not under Chinese control, at least overtly. She would have to research. It was something to look into. Who had control of the ESA and the Russians boost program? Other than the lift and launch systems, it would be hard to create economic hardship when Homakuwa had little to do with the world economy. They imported little and exported services.

No. The attack would have to be political. A campaign about the genetic technology seemed the most probable avenue for attack. How would a successful attack be measured? Homakuwa would never release that technology. It would be like giving a loaded gun to a three-year old. Tragedy lay down that path. Could China muster enough strength to withdraw membership? To what end?

In their mind it would be a loss of face, but Homakuwa would then expel the monitors in their sea habitats. Not a wise move. They would then be accused of all sorts of abuses. Best to keep the monitors or even increase the number.

China could build consensus to take away the International Fishing Industry Directorship. The industry would fail without Homakuwa's programs, and in essence they would hold the environment hostage to bend Homakuwa to their will. Their goal on controlling Homakuwa was certainly to gain control of the genetic technology. Homakuwa could strike back. They had done so in the past, but was that wise? She would have to have a full conference sometime soon, and that would include Ron and Kit. Their knowledge of the surface world politics was critical.

Chapter 44

The Collective made it possible to hold a conference with the participants scattered over the Earth and space, and it was proving invaluable. When minds were in the Collective, there was no time delay. Distance didn't matter.

Sylvix: [Leticia, I've been tracking the object we saw enter our solar system three months ago. It won't hit Saturn, but will pass through the rings. At a distance as close as that, Saturn's gravity may fragment the object, and the trajectory after impact with the rings is impossible to predict. The present trajectory will bring it close to Earth. Impacts with large objects, like ice blocks, in the rings will change the trajectory. I still don't think there's a danger to Earth, but the threat level has gone up.]

Leticia: [Thanks for the update, Sylvix. Keep watching. Chetnaz, you were with me at the hearing. We will be forced to leave the ISS. Where do we stand on our new habitats?]

Chetnaz: [We're actually pretty far along. The greenhouse construction is complete, but we need a way of getting the supplies to start up, and we need the materials to finish the internal furnishing to make it self sustaining.]

Leticia: [Instead of moving all of our gear back to Earth or parking it in orbit, do we have time to set up a habitat on the moon? Rich, are you with us?]

Rich: [Yeah, I'm following. You've presented an interesting idea. We could certainly park our gear in orbit around the moon and work from there. The moon would also act as the source of materials for habitat construction, and the lift penalty is low enough we could use our laser boosters to move materials. Usable quantities of water exist also. We'll have to dig it out, but we can do that.]

Leticia: [Jamie, you've been working on fast growing species for us to use in space habitats. Would they grow on the moon?]

Jamie: [They'd grow fine on the moon. The greenhouse construction may be the problem.]

Leticia: [Anybody, is the silica on the moon suitable to make solar tubes? Rich I'm assuming we would use the solar lasers to carve out underground habitats.]

Rich: [That's what I was thinking too. It would be the fastest way to get established. We could use the same mirror system we used at Kihhim to get light to the underground greenhouses. It would cut down on the need for glass.]

Katharine: [This plan may cause quite an uproar here on Earth. One faction will be glad to see us away from the OPS. We still earn enough with our enterprises here on Earth to send some supplies to low orbit. We'll need to find a way to boost from there, but it's probably doable.] Her presence stopped the communication momentarily. [There's the other faction on Earth that will consider this action as an invasion of Earth property. Unreasonable as that may seem, they will oppose us.]

Leticia snapped: [What can they do about it?]

Katharine: [Whether we like it or not, we're still dependent on Earth. The only control they have over us is supplying the materials we depend on, and they will not give that control up easily. In addition to the factions that want our genetic technology, there's also a faction that wants us destroyed. They will never give up on that. They refuse to acknowledge our right to exist.]

Leticia: [Okay, unless I hear objection we'll move our gear into Lunar orbit. We need them to get things moving. What is already here and ready to use, Chetnaz?]

Rich: [In addition to the small sails we used for the tugs, there are three large sails of 200 square miles each along with the tether systems. We can edge the nearly completed habitat out to high orbit, and then move it to Lunar orbit. We'll fill the habitat with everything we can. Once in Lunar orbit, perhaps we can start lifting water to get things started. We could at least live in parts of the habitat during Lunar construction.]

Leticia: [We need to move the solar laser from the ISS into high Earth orbit. We built it, and it belongs to us. Move all of the sleds out too. In fact, everything we've built needs to go with us.]

Sylvix broke in: [One other thing. Chetnaz and I and the rest of our teams have replaced the electronic computers with our organic ones. What do we do about those after the changeover?]

There was silence. [Let's leave them installed but hide them, and interface them so the next team uses the electronic system but ours is ready to take over.]

Katharine: [Leticia, what are you planning?]

Leticia: [At this stage I'm not planning anything, but I'm leaving options open. Somehow, I think we'll be back in near Earth orbit baling out the surface world's ass. Just a feeling.]

Leticia: [What's our schedule look like?]

Nothing, then Rich: [We'll be away from near Earth orbit in six months and have established habitats both on the moon and in orbit.]

Leticia: [Make it four months. I can stall Earth for that long. It'll take them longer than four months to train new crews, unless China already has them, and I don't put it past them.]

Chapter 45

In the Collective, Rich Lewis reported to Leticia and Katharine: [The move is going well. In the two months since we started, everything Homakuwa has developed and built is in route along with supplies enough for a crew to work on the Lunar habitat. The caves are carved out. Using the lasers worked well, because the fused lunar material forms glass, which effectively seals the tunnels. We are mining water and breaking it up into hydrogen and oxygen. The solar furnace is now in low Lunar orbit, and we're making clear glass to complete the greenhouses. Zygotes brought from Earth are ready to grow. With the habitat on the back side of the moon near the pole, we are out of sight from Earth. The solar collectors at the pole are able to supply power continuously. We are progressing well.]

Leticia reported: [I've been able to stall Earth from ousting us from the Orbiting Power System by maintaining the system while the transition teams from Earth are trained, and we keep supplying power. The new human teams are not ready, so we've seen no big push to get us out. They are starting to realize what a handicap they will be operating under. Most of the human support systems are in disarray due to disuse, and they will need to be refurbished. The OPS wishes to contract us to do that, but I've resisted. I do not want us to be blamed for problems, especially if a potential exists that will cost human lives.]

Sylvix: [Leticia, Katharine are you still there?]

Katharine: [Sure, Sylvix. What is it?]

Sylvix: [Two things. Another attempt to crash the system has been made. As we're operating with our organic computers, nothing happened, but I've documented everything and identified the sources. I'll get a report to you with the evidence.]

Leticia: [Great! I'm not sure what we're going to do. We'll need to think about that. We're committed to leaving the system in the care of Earth contractors.]

Sylvix: [The other thing may be more serious. The object which entered our solar system passed through Saturn's rings. It broke up, but was like a bowling ball going through pins. Stuff went everywhere. The ring was warped in places, disrupting things and sending things crashing about. The path was diverted too. The object is going to pass through the asteroid belt. The chances of another strike are slim, but the pieces of the object and a lot of chunks of ice are heading this way. I can't predict an exact trajectory yet, but meteors will reach the inner planets within nine months.]

Leticia: [Thanks, Sylvix. Keep me informed.] What did this mean? A worried Leticia called Martha at the Jet Propulsion Laboratory.

"Hey, Martha. It's Leticia. How are things?"

"Oh, Leticia I was going to call to let you know how sorry I was about how things turned out after the hearings. You know the committee did receive your evidence, but the chairman refused to allow it to be read into the record. He claimed it was hearsay. Bastard!"

"Thanks, Martha. Did you get the information from Sylvix on the object in the solar system?"

"It's coming in now. What's the deal?"

Leticia relayed the summary Sylvix had given her.

"Whoa! Let me review the hard data and get back to you. This could be serious."

"Call me when you've had a chance to look the report over and discuss it with your people."

"Thanks for the heads up, Leticia. If I can do anything for you, let me know."

Chapter 46

Chairman Hu was pissed. Robert Chaing tried to still the shaking of his knees as he faced the Chairman with the report on the latest attempt to further humiliate Homakuwa. "Our latest round of power outages failed. We tried to activate the Dragon chip and the viruses contained in the replacement boards, but there was no effect on the OPS computers. The control computers did not respond to our commands, and we were not able to read the data downloads. They have somehow negated our chips."

The Chairman shook his head. "Homakuwa crews will still be evicted and replaced by Chinese backed crews. The evidence that bitch Leticia Gardner presented has been suppressed from the committee and pooh poohed in the press as bogus. At least the money we spent supporting the committee members was well placed. We will need plans to remove all loose ends and anything that points to us. The press investigation into the ownership of the power conglomerate has forced us to divest ourselves of a number of those companies."

"Yes sir," said Robert, "but the corporate officers of those companies are still under our control. That is only a minor snag."

The Chairman nodded. "The issue now is raw materials to keep our industry rolling and people employed. Robert, past Chinese regimes have not lost power through wars. Unemployed peasants have overthrown them. UWG will not allow the necessary suppression, should an uprising take place. We must continue our vigilance and prevent any movement from growing."

They both knew deployed UWG forces could not stand up to Chinese military power. Holding this massive populace together depended on keeping them fed, housed and employed.

Robert had kept a close eye on the Chairman and seen the changes taking place as he aged. They seemed to accelerate lately. Hu was still in power, though he had to spend more time on give and take with his own people. Robert could see he was still vigorous at eighty-two, and with good care would last much longer. That also meant care in watching his back, which was Robert's job. Enemies existed both domestic and foreign. The Chairman had a long-term plan for China, and Robert was committed to that plan.

"Robert, once we regain control of the world power system, we will raise the prices, blaming the costs on the mess made by the Homakuwans. This money will go into monopolizing the raw materials markets, raising the prices and strangling any competition. Let the other nations deal with their unemployed. The key to control is the commodities, raw materials, power, and labor."

The Chairman also had another agenda. When a coalition formed to increase monitoring of Homakuwa, he would go after the genetic technology. With that technology in hand, he could extend his life like that traitor Ron Carson. The review of the Kahchk Kihhim history made it obvious Homakuwa was capable of controlling human aging. Katharine Levey, Leticia Gardner and Ron Carson were easily double the normal lifespan and showed no sign of getting older. He had to get that technology within the next two years, or he would lose power, and it would be forever beyond his grasp.

Chapter 47

The news was splashed across every internet news service and newspaper in the world:

"GIANT METEOROID HEADING FOR EARTH!"
"Scientists and astronomers sighted a large meteoroid that entered our Solar System several months ago. This object passed near Saturn, striking and disrupting the ring system. During this passage, it broke apart and now continues toward the inner planetary system. Parts of the object struck at least one asteroid in the asteroid belt and created a major disruption in the Solar System's orderly nature. The latest reports from the NEO (Near Earth Object) center show a string of at least six larger meteoroids and many smaller fragments heading toward the inner planets. Earth's orbit will intersect at least some of these objects. This meeting will take place 187 days from now.

"Orbiting telescopes trained on this swarm are assessing the size of the objects, their composition, and the danger they represent to Earth. Along with numerous smaller objects are those large enough to destroy life on Earth. The largest meteoroid is the size of a mountain, and if it strikes the Earth, the result will be the same as the strike

that wiped out the dinosaurs. All larger forms of life will become extinct."
London Daily Star

Another headline read:
"CRASH PROGRAMS UNDERWAY TO INTERCEPT AND DIVERT   KILLER METEORITES"
"Governments around the world are assuring people disaster will be averted. All nations with space launch capability are coordinating efforts to launch a fleet of interceptor ships to divert the killer swarm of meteorites."
New York Citizen

The article went on to assure the public that everything possible was being done to save the Earth and efforts would be successful.

While these statements were being issued, the leadership was preparing underground bunkers for themselves. Trajectory reports were coming daily.

***

Homakuwa was busy considering options, too. In a meeting of every citizen, the discussion was what could be done and what to do.

Rich: [We do have the capability of sending our laser platform to intercept. We would then push the objects out of an intersecting trajectory. Unfortunately, even if we were there right now, we could not move them all. Some are going to hit the Earth.]

Leticia: [What about the rest of the Earth's people. Can't they do something?]

Rich: [They're scrambling to build the vehicles and the launch platforms for interceptors. Even under a crash program, they can't move fast enough. At least the US, China, Russia, and ESA will get interceptor vehicles up within four months. By then the opportunity to intercept in time to move the objects enough to miss will be gone. Right now they're discussing what to do when they arrive at an intercept point. The present consensus is to use nukes to move them. Nukes might work or the objects might shatter, and we would end up with two to three times as many objects. It would be like switching from a rifle bullet to a shotgun. The real problem with the nukes is placing them.

[The objects are tumbling, some quite fast, so placing a thruster on them will be next to impossible. Landing and placing a nuke would be very difficult. They must fire a missile and do it from a distance, which will be of questionable effect. There isn't time to design and build anything else. We cannot count on any meaningful help from them.]

Leticia: [Let's rank the objects based on trajectory, size, and composition. We'll try to deflect the worst. It's the best we can do.]

Chetnaz: [Perhaps there is more. The objects are made up of water ice, methane ice, iron, and silica. These are the very things we are trying to mine and lift from the moon. What if we steered them into orbits and then mined them. If we're going to move them away, it takes little more effort to control where 'away' is.]

Rich: [Theoretically it is possible, given unlimited energy and time. We have neither. The control must be very fine because we have no way to slow them for orbit other than using the Earth's atmosphere. Slightly off, and the object hits the Earth.]

Katharine: [First priority is to prevent as much damage as possible to the Earth, which means moving the largest ones to miss. An inch is as good as a mile. How quickly can we put the laser at an interception point?]

Sylvix: [I ranked the objects according to size and danger. All objects under five hundred tons may cause damage, depending where they land, though they do not represent a major calamity to

Earth. If you're living in a city where one hits, you might disagree.

[The number of objects taken all together will change life on Earth. There are approximately twenty-three smaller objects that should be low on the priority list. The problem is the time. We could send the laser platform by fastest intercept, brake as we approached and fire at several as we pass. We then loop around Mars and catch up to them slowing to more closely match the velocity of the objects. We then fire on them continuously as we're heading back. If we put all our sails on the laser platform for maximum acceleration, we can intercept the first large object in one hundred and eighty-three days.] An image of a large irregularly shaped ice ball appeared.

Sylvix: [This object is a dirty snowball and is the fourth in line heading this way. It doesn't appear to be tumbling and is developing a comet-like tail. By hitting the side with the laser, the ice will vaporize, boring a cavity. Further laser blasts will create a jet to assist in pushing it to change the trajectory. My calculations show that sustained laser fire will move it out of Earth intersection trajectory after one hundred hours at the intercept distance. It will pass within two thousand miles of

Earth.] Another image appeared. It was a rocky chunk.

Sylvix: [The second large object is actually the eighth in line and is a displaced asteroid. It's not large as asteroids go, but at 12,000 tons of iron-nickel traveling at 22,000 miles per hour, it will cause major damage to the Earth. With sustained fire from our laser, we can move it from intersection trajectory after two hundred hours. We'll be moving so fast on the first pass we won't have that amount of time. We will zap it again when we come back.

[The third large object is also iron-nickel. Though smaller, it still represents a catastrophe if it strikes the Earth. The trajectory of this object appears less direct and may only strike a glancing blow, but we cannot take a chance. One hundred hours should ensure a miss.

[The fourth object is rock, mostly silica, and is the largest. Sustained laser fire of four hundred hours is needed to divert this object. We need to match its speed to have that much time.

[The fifth and sixth objects are close together and will strike the moon as it moves into the trajectory path. Yes, the strike will be on the dark side. Each is substantial in mass though one is ice and the other iron-nickel. I cannot say how close to the habitat the strike will be yet. We can move those to miss, but that means there will not be time for the final large object to be diverted before it hits the Earth. That object will certainly destroy civilization as it exists today. We do not have sufficient power or time to move the objects when they are less than fifteen days from Earth. This will be a very close call. Any delays and we will not have time to divert the last critical object.]

All over the Earth Homakuwa's minds were in turmoil, but no coherent thoughts came to attention.

Leticia: [Let's get the laser platform hitched and moving. We have one hundred and eighty-three days to decide what we're going to do and prepare.]

Rich: [We need to start preparing here on Earth also. Major changes will occur no matter what we do.]

Chapter 48

From Ocealla Leticia had taken charge of the intercept program, Katharine and Ron needed to deal with the surface world, and she stood before the assembled world leaders. The scientists raised the alarm with predictions of what could happen, but somehow the humans were incapable of understanding the immensity of the catastrophe. They were not preparing for potential disaster, but focused on mundane issues.

"Homakuwa launched an interceptor ten days ago. This interceptor has our solar laser platform to push the largest meteors out of the Earth intercept trajectory. We counted between thirty and forty objects of which six are capable of destroying life on Earth. We will not have time to prevent all the objects from hitting Earth, but will concentrate on the six largest. Some of the smaller objects will hit with the force of nuclear strikes equivalent to the Tunguska more than a century ago."

"That strike was in remote Siberia and flattened a huge portion of the surrounding forest. If such an object strikes a city, it will be destroyed. We'll be able to predict the impact sites more closely as the objects near. Those objects could be moved by the Earth launched interceptors in time to avoid strikes. The larger objects cannot be moved enough to miss by the time your crews arrive. Whatever you choose to do, we will be focused on those objects which will destroy us."

The assembly was numb for several minutes. The first question came from the US delegate. "First, I wish to thank Homakuwa for this quick reaction to the impending disaster. Being in orbit with the nature of the crew that on this platform, you certainly had the best opportunity for getting a vehicle there in time to avert the major hits. As you know, we are preparing to launch our interceptors within two months. Is there anything you can do to make them more effective?"

"I suggest you talk with our technical division. I'll put you in touch with Leticia Gardner." Leticia was listening, but Katharine didn't want to display the contact ability or relay the information. A face-to-face meeting would be better. Several other delegates expressed the same desire.

The Chinese delegate rose. "You say you have launched an interceptor to stop the large items but will let the smaller ones hit. Those will be enough to change civilization significantly from today. If the surface world were destroyed the world would be left to Homakuwa. Are you purposely allowing objects to strike the Earth?"

Leticia was furious at this innuendo. Before Katharine could stop her, she spoke through the communication system. "You dare accuse us of this! You, who actively supported the Foundation attack on the United World Government! You, who initiated the failure of the Orbiting Power System, blocked the introduction of evidence that points the finger at you, and then tried to attack it again! You, who are, even as we speak, trying to oust Homakuwa from directing the International Fishing Industry so you can take over and control the world's food supply! You, who supplied contaminated computer hardware to allow you to eavesdrop on conversations, monitor activity, and finally control those computers. So you know, I have released all the evidence of this malfeasance to the press. Homakuwa will not be idle while you accuse us."

There was stunned silence as the press releases appeared before the delegates. Several looked pointedly at the still standing delegate. He hastily sat and tried to make himself small. Heads would roll.

Chapter 49

Sylvix was on the laser platform speeding toward the meteor swarm heading toward Earth. More correctly, Sylvix was the laser platform. Soon after departing Earth orbit, Sylvix started integrating herself into the ship in a much more permanent way. No longer a separate being, she was the ship. The team had designed this to minimize the life support system requirements. During departure, Sylvix remained a Construct, but soon after departure, her body combined with the ship, and now the ship was the organism Sylvix. She was a true integration of machine and biology.

She could see in the visible spectrum but also from long radio waves through gamma. Her mind linked with the Collective, and though she could act independently, she had the thinking power of all of Homakuwa.

Days no longer had meaning. The passage of events marked time, and for now, nothing happened except she continued to accelerate with the solar sails and the laser reactor engine. Mars lay ahead, and she planned to intercept the swarm as close to Mars as possible. She would fire on the first large object, the ice ball, as she flew past. Sylvix would fire on the subsequent objects, but she was traveling very fast relative to them and would not be able to fire long enough to divert most of them. It would start the process. She had work to do before the intercept point, which approached quickly.

As though folding her arms, she drew the sails in and stowed them as bundles alongside herself. Sylvix reversed the platform and the mirrors, refocused them, and fired the laser reactor to begin braking. She sensed the change in acceleration.

Using radar vision, she saw the ice ball ahead. It was like a cloud, but the radar penetrated, and she could see the core. Heat from the sun had caused the ice to melt, evaporate, and create the cloud. The solar wind pushed it behind the head to form the tail. The density of the cloud around the head spelled trouble. If the laser couldn't penetrate the cloud to deliver enough energy to the ice ball, it would not push it. Unless she could come up with another plan quickly, there would not be time to deliver sufficient energy to divert it and the others to miss the Earth.

Sylvix focused her vision, adding the depth offered by the radar. Ahead of the ice ball were several other objects, some smaller pieces of ice, others of iron-nickel. These were objects that would not normally be of primary concern. An idea began to form. Whether it was hers or the Collective didn't matter, she was the Collective and the Collective was her.

From a distance, she started firing on one of the tumbling iron nickel meteors in an attempt to slow the spin. At first, not much happened, and then the rotation began to slow. Sylvix adjusted her course toward the object to have it between her and the ice ball. She picked another object and did the same. As she neared, the first object she fired. Material boiled off the meteor, and it began to move to intercept the ice ball. As she continued to fire, the vaporized metal jetted off, pushing the object. It picked up speed. She was able to direct the object to ensure a broadside hit on the ice ball. Once it was moving, she repeated the process with another meteor, until she had three moving.

Alone, none would have enough punch to make a difference, but the three along with Mars gravity should move the object. She was out of range and began firing on other objects as she flew past until it was time to begin the swing around Mars. Carefully, she maintained enough speed to escape Mars' gravity and catch up to the string of disasters heading toward Earth. While in the shadow of Mars, the sails were useless.

The gravity of Mars pulled her into an arc, and she rounded it, using the atmosphere to slow herself, yet keep enough speed to overtake the train of objects. Her speed had to allow her time to affect their trajectory with the laser.

She was moving too fast and redeployed the solar sails to act as brakes as she caught up to the meteors. She passed the trailing objects and fired on them. The diversion wasn't great enough to miss the moon, but it would start the process.

Perhaps Leticia would have another platform ready in time to intercept and further divert them, but she did not think so. As the next object came into range she began firing while adjusting her speed to allow the necessary time to move it. She passed and the next object came into range. She repeated the process.

There was a jolt. One of the smaller objects had struck one of her sails, passing through but leaving a gaping hole. Worse, with the loss of integrity, the sail began to flutter and collapse. She reeled it in. Sylvix could try to repair it but not now. The loss of braking power wasn't significant now. The problem would be when she returned to Earth. She would not be able to brake enough to go into orbit, and she would sail past toward Venus and the sun. They'd worry about that when she got there. In the meantime, a lot of work remained.

The ice ball had moved! It would still hit the Earth, but the movement was apparent. She needed to put more energy on it, but most of the energy was absorbed by the cloud before it struck the central mass. She searched for another smaller object that might be used to ram the ice ball. If she could only penetrate the cloud.

An idea came. She moved ahead of and closer to the ice ball until her sails were shading it. The cloud began to dissipate, but it was temporary as the solar wind was pushing her toward the ice ball. She fired the laser at her reaction mass to brake her movement toward the ice ball until she was actually moving away.

The cloud was dissipating and she saw the core. Sylvix reversed the laser and fired on one side of the ice ball and steam jetted out. She detected more movement, but the ice ball started spinning. She would have to reverse the laser and jet further away and start again. In the meantime, the cloud would reform.

The Earth interceptors might be able to move the last objects, but Homakuwa didn't paint a good picture of those chances. They wouldn't arrive until it was almost too late to make a difference.

Chapter 50

Katharine and Ron sat on a panel preparing Earth for the destruction heading their way. UWG President Heinz Schmidt spoke of the activity taking place. Few of the members were physically present, but attended as holographic projections. "The coastal cities are being evacuated to minimize the loss of life from sea impact driven tsunamis. Food is being stockpiled, and shelters are being built in refugee camps south of the 35th parallel and at least two hundred miles from the coast. It is a massive effort."

"The Foundation and other religious fundamentalists are pulling in huge membership as people return to basics in hope of salvation. For once, the churches are focused on giving comfort instead of intolerance toward all but their faithful."

Katharine was reminded of watching videos of New Orleans prepare for the arrival of hurricane Katrina. Buildings were boarded up, necessities were being hoarded, medical facilities were being beefed up. As the populations evacuated, eerie silence descended on the cities.

Homakuwa could do little to prepare. Their cities would be safe unless there was a hit within one hundred miles. Then nothing could save them. Katharine spoke for Homakuwa "We began a program modifying algae to grow in low light conditions, because an ice age is coming due to the dust, ash, and water that will be thrown into the upper atmosphere. The deep impact winter will last at least a year with little light, followed by two years of twilight. A massive die-off of all Earth species, including humans is coming. We are also working on species of fungus to grow in huge quantities because they grow without light. Somehow, we will have to produce food." It was so disheartening to know what was ahead and not be able to avoid disaster.

***

Leticia worked feverishly to try to protect the Lunar habitat: [Chetnaz, what's our status?]

Chetnaz: [We have reinforced the tunnels and the greenhouses. The orbiting habitats and greenhouses are not in danger as they can be moved once the final trajectories have been refined.

Materials from the moon are being used to expand the habitat structures though not enough time is left to outfit them. The priority is large orbiting greenhouses. The requirements of food, water, and air will be huge, especially if we're going to supply food to Earth.]

Homakuwa was in constant contact with Sylvix and knew what was being done to minimize the impacts and the destruction.

Chetnaz: [Leticia, is Sylvix going to be able return to Earth orbit?]

Leticia: [She will be traveling too fast to be captured and will fly past toward the sun. The only thing we've been able to do is get the ESA to launch a resupply rocket to dock with her. If she can successfully couple with it, she will have enough supplies to last more than a year, but she'll be out of contact. We won't know if she survived until we hear from her.

[She did her best and made progress though. Our calculations show that of the six largest and most destructive objects, only the ice ball remains the major threat to Earth. There are still the two threats to the Lunar habitat. Sylvix concentrated on the ice ball.]

Chetnaz: [Leticia, we're preparing as best we can. We're focusing on moving what we can and reinforcing the Lunar habitat, but I'm afraid we're still going to suffer losses, perhaps catastrophic.]

Leticia: [Chetnaz, everyone is going to suffer from this event, but I promise you and all of Homakuwa we will not ever have our survival threatened again.] It sounded good, and Leticia only hoped it was a promise she could keep.

Chapter 51

The first Earth interceptor arrived with twenty days remaining before impact. "Sylvix, this is Captain Chao Wong. We need to coordinate with you. Our intent is to hit the object with a fifty-megaton nuclear missile to move it out of the present trajectory. What do you advise?"

"I have been unable to move it far enough to miss the Earth. I suggest you detonate one thousand meters from the center of mass which means I need to move my ship away. If you impact the ice ball, it may fracture into parts, which we will have to deal with."

"Let us know when you are far enough away."

Sylvix changed the sail direction, moving away. After furling her sails, she shut down her systems except the heavily shaded visor and watched. Immediately after she radioed she was clear, she saw the missile leave the Chinese ship, streaking toward the ice ball.

The small sun erupted, obscuring the ice ball. The flash grew–expanding toward her–and she was afraid she had not moved far enough away. The energy dissipated as it approached. She felt the energy impact the ship, her skin stung as it burned her, and she was pushed by the wave front. When it had passed over her, the space where the ice ball had been was now occupied by several objects, two of which were large. They were moving in another trajectory, one that would carry them away from the Earth.

The Chinese ship was drifting, dead. As it tumbled, gas spewed out, and a scorched side became visible. The wave front had breached the hull. Sylvix radioed repeatedly, but got no response. Distressed, she moved toward it.

A weak radio transmission crackled. At first she couldn't understand the broken Chinese, but Homakuwa translated. "We have been destroyed. I am in a compartment with a handheld radio. I have no suit and suspect this is the only place with air remaining. Did we succeed?"

"You did. But I cannot help. I haven't a habitable place for you nor the ability for rescue."

"We did not plan to return. We only had fuel enough to get here. I am glad to know that we did not fail in our mission. I can hear air whistling now. Thank you for your help. Goodbye." The radio went silent.

Sylvix reassessed the new trajectories. Twelve objects of size floated before her though only three were dangerous. Of these, the large iron-nickel could strike the Earth. Two would miss, but one of those would hit the moon. She would work on the iron-nickel meteor until the US interceptor arrived in a day.

***

"Sylvix, come in. This is Captain Mortenson of the US interceptor. We are breaking hard and approaching your position. Please update us on the status of the objects."

"Captain Mortenson, this is interceptor Sylvix. My laser will not move the last object enough to miss the Earth, which will be catastrophic. I suggest you station yourself out of the blast radius and set your missile to detonate two thousand yards from the object."

"Roger. The Chinese craft arrived a day ago. Where is it?"

"They were not out of their blast radius, but they never intended to return."

Captain Mortenson paused. "I see. We do intend to return though we will be close on supplies."

"Good," responded Sylvix.

Sylvix moved away from the meteor, as the interceptor positioned and targeted. The white-hot streak flashed toward the chunk of iron-nickel. She shut down her sensors and waited. Again, she felt the flash on her skin and through shaded sensors saw the fireball engulf the space around it. As it spread and dissipated she observed a change. The object was tumbling more slowly. Her sensors showed it was moving, and calculations confirmed the object was no longer on a collision course with Earth.

"Good job, Captain Mortenson. You've been successful."

"Thank you, Sylvix. With us low on everything, we must leave. See you back on Earth." With that, the ship turned, its rockets leaving a streak. Wistfully, Sylvix watched it go. She knew she would probably never hear from Captain Mortenson again.

Chapter 52

The supply rocket approached Sylvix. Launched by the ESA before the meteoroids neared the Earth, it contained food, water, and oxygen to sustain her for more than a year, but only at minimal operation. She would have to conserve. As she neared the Earth system, she began the docking procedure. Once docked, the supply rocket would become part of her. Homakuwa watched and traveled with Sylvix as she passed outside of the moon's orbit on her way toward Venus and the sun.

[Sylvix, can you train your sensors on the meteor swarm?] As she followed the request, they saw a train from hell heading toward the Earth. Glinting objects struck the atmosphere, creating fiery trails. Mushrooming clouds of water vapor and dust rose, lit by red glowing light within as the Earth shook around them. The strikes were on the night side of the planet, but the chain was long enough that the rain of death traversed the entire circumference as the world rotated.

[Oh my!] Sylvix said as she and Homakuwa helplessly watched the spreading clouds cover the beautiful blue planet with a reflective cloud. She felt the tremors that those of Homakuwa who remained on Earth felt as well as the terror of those caught in the maelstrom of destruction. Civilization was being destroyed before her, and though she was not there, she was a part of it.

Sorrowful, she believed that if she could loop around the sun and repair the damaged sail, she could return after a year, but to what? Sadness filled her with the death of so many and the destruction of their home. She would remain with the Collective as long as she could, but she must set her course and shut down, hopefully to awake again.

Chapter 53

From the porch of his ranch in Idaho, Ron and Katharine watched the sky light up with blinding streaks of the incoming meteors. Many faded out, but some trailed orange balls of fire to the horizon. Occasionally, there were brilliant flashes as some exploded above the Earth's surface like nuclear blasts. Radio and television reception were merely a deafening static. In the eastern sky an orange glow spread while to the west clouds lit from within climbed into the sky. Wearing their collars, through Leticia's eyes in high orbit they saw a large strike in the heartland of America. Aghast, they observed a strike off the West Coast of Northern California and another mid Pacific.

From orbital view, they could see strikes in Northern Africa, France, South America, and the oceans. The rain of death marched toward Asia. The whole of the Homakuwa Collective was stunned when the individual lights that were the minds of Retseana and Zolynstra dimmed. They were destroyed in the mid-Atlantic and mid-Pacific strikes but remained in the Collective.

The shock wave from a near strike damaged Ajabada, but it survived. Through Leticia's eyes they watched as the clouds of climate change spread over the Earth. Ron was first to recover from the shock. "Katharine, we have to go south. An ice age is coming, and the north will be a frozen wasteland. Grab what you need, we'll stock the plane and head to Puerto Peñasco."

Two hours later they were in the air. The GPS and the autopilot normally used to fly the plane were inoperable. Ron trimmed for maximum range using a compass and Katharine's navigating to head south. A blood-red sun rose through murk that was now the Earth's atmosphere. To the west a black cloud soared above them, while the southwestern U.S. passed below them, showing no effects except the orange glow that passed for sunlight. With little fuel left, they landed at the Puerto Peñasco airport. Ron paid with gold coins to have the plane refueled and tied down. They took a cab to the Tres Palmas hotel, a small innocuous place two blocks from the beach that was clean and cheap. Mexican television showed only snow, but they found a radio station with an announcer reporting in English on conditions from the disaster.

"Coastal areas of Europe have been flooded by the tsunamis from sea strikes, some as far as 100 miles inland. Paris took a direct hit and is gone. The East Coast of the U.S. is also flooded, but the evacuations saved millions of lives. St Louis took a direct hit and disappeared in a cloud of vapor, but worse, the impact set off multiple earthquakes along the Mississippi Valley. Floods and destruction are wreaking havoc.

"Reports from the West Coast are not good. Multiple tsunamis have struck coastal areas from Los Angeles to Seattle, and Mt. St. Helens is rumbling and sending up ash clouds. Multiple earthquakes are reported along the fault lines from Washington through the Coachella Valley to the Sea of Cortez. There are indications that a fault might open up and the upper Sea of Cortez could carve through the land into Death Valley, flooding it."

As they listened, the floor began to shake. A picture crashed from the wall. Because the area sat on sand, the shaking from the earthquake was not dire. The Baja peninsula had protected the northwestern coast of Mexico from the tsunamis, but extreme tides damaged much of the coastal towns. Ron and Katharine listened until weariness overtook them.

***

The morning was indistinguishable from the night. Under a charcoal sky, Ron tried to call several numbers back in the US. but got nothing. The TV had several working channels, but all the U.S.-based news channels were off the air. His Spanish wasn't good enough to understand the staccato speech of the reporter, but the map behind him showed the extensive ruin that propagated across the world.

Large coastal areas were red where flooding and tsunamis had devastated the populations. Red circles were on the various continents indicating land strikes. China had received two strikes, but the circles were much smaller than those in France and the US. England was almost completely red. The coast of Brazil was red, along with the coast of Peru and Northern Chile. A huge red circle blotted out Mombasa and much of India. Africa sustained two land hits, and the eastern and western coasts were red. Siberia had been hit once with a large red circle in a remote area. Australia had no red circles though coastal areas were red as the tsunamis had caused devastating floods in the northwestern and eastern coastal regions.

The causality figures had to be in the billions. The pictures of the Earth from orbit showed a cloud shrouded ball while the pictures from the Earth showed an unending twilight.

Katharine awoke, at first sleepy, then her eyes flew open as she realized where she was, and when. "It's not good," said Ron. "I think we should find out what's happening with Homakuwa."

They donned their collars to enter the Collective. Through Leticia they saw the Lunar habitat. [As you can see, we didn't take a direct hit, but did have extensive damage. We've had some small hits on the lunar greenhouses but were able to circle the orbiting habitats behind the moon. That's the bad news. The good news is the large meteor that struck was water ice. The smaller one was iron-nickel. We have materials for rebuilding.]

Katharine: [That is good news.]

Leticia continued. [You know about Retseana and Zolynstra. They are total losses. Everyone is gone though we still have them in the Collective.

Earth is a disaster and going to get worse. Fires are ravaging all continents. The rainforests of South America are afire from the east coast to the Andes as is much of Africa. The forested areas of North America are burning along with the plains of the heartland. The particulate from the meteorites and the smoke from the fires will bring on unending night. With no sun, the base of the food chains will be destroyed, and starvation will move up the chain as mass extinction accelerates. The Orbiting Power System pulled through pretty well. We lost one concentrator completely and had two damaged. We can beam energy to Earth, and its frequency will penetrate the clouds, so if there are receivers, there will be power.]

[What about Sylvix?] queried Katharine.

[She received the supplies that were sent and is on her way toward the sun. There is a chance she'll circle and return next year. She really deserves a medal. Without her, the Earth would have been smashed beyond recognition.]

Ron: [You know as well as we do, Leticia, humanity cannot pull itself out of this disaster alone. Civilization is going to crumble without help. Katharine and I will attempt to get to

Sheppard Air Force Base for meetings with the UWG, and we'd like to have your voice heard.]

[Okay, Ron. Of course I'll be with Homakuwa, but I can also speak as a representative of the Homakuwa Lunar colony.]

"Let's take a walk and get something to eat," said Ron. They dressed and walked from the hotel toward town. From the rise at the foot of the mountain above Puerto Peñasco they saw that an extreme tide had flooded the harbor and boat building area. The Malecón was flooded, and many of the fish stalls destroyed. Past the harbor, the high-rise beachfront condos were also flooded, and there was massive erosion along the beach. At the Hotel Peñasco, they went to the restaurant, finding it deserted. A waitress took their order for huevos rancheros and coffee.

"It doesn't look like there was much loss of life here," said Katharine.

"No, but the fishing fleet and port facilities have been damaged. Luckily, much of their power is from the OPS, so they'll still have electricity. We need to get back to the U.S. and a meeting with the UWG. Once we know the extent of the damage, we can start making plans to save civilization."

Chapter 54

The final destination of their return flight to the United States was Sheppard Air Force Base. When the coastal areas had been evacuated, and the delegates moved inland, the UWG headquarters was relocated there in preparation for the disaster. There hadn't been time to set up the communication systems for contact with the representatives' home countries. Many of those had no one left in authority. A meeting was imperative to reestablish the UWG and begin gathering information and assets.

They left before dawn, flying into a starless inky sky. The sunrise seen from the air barely changed the sky from black to gray. Past computer projections predicted an impact winter that would take years or even decades to play out, but with the multiple hits over the Earth's surface, those predictions were worthless.

The countryside below them showed little change, but the horizon to the north and east was obscured. Devastated by the scene, Ron took to the radio.

"This is former president of the United World Government Ron Carson in UW Gov1 trying to reach anyone in the El Paso area. Come in, please."

"UW Gov 1, this is Ft. Bliss tower."

"I'm in route to the new UWG headquarters at Sheppard Air Force Base and need refueling. Any suggestions?"

"All civilian facilities are shut down at this time. Hold while I get my OIC." There was a pause of several minutes.

"This is Lieutenant Sandoval. As I understand, President Carson, you need to refuel to get to UWG headquarters at Sheppard AFB. Am I correct?"

"Yes, Lieutenant, and I'd like a briefing of the situation as you know it while we are there. Is that possible?"

"I'll pass this on to my CO, and we'll arrange what we can. Please lock onto this beacon, and it will guide you in."

Ron flipped a switch on the instrument panel and a red light came on. Within seconds it changed to green. "I'm locked on now."

"Sir, we read you west 270 degrees and two hundred seventy miles out. At present heading and speed, you should begin approach in forty-seven minutes. We will put you on automatic control."

***

It was an uneventful nighttime landing, but it wasn't night A young airman escorted them into General Emiley Picket's office a few minutes later. "Mr. President, it's a pleasure to meet you." Standing, the slender woman she reached out to shake his hand. A hint of a smile crossed her severe and lined face. "This must be the Ambassador from Homakuwa, Katharine Levey. I'm delighted to finally meet you." They shook hands. "The last word we had was that you two were in Idaho. How did you get here?"

With a sad look on his face, Ron related the story of their hurried departure from his ranch describing the rising clouds of destruction they had seen from the air. Their stay in Mexico was frustratingly short of information about the status of the rest of the world.

Grimly, the General advised them of conditions, "Mr. President, martial law has been enacted nation-wide. Due to the information we've received, we are preparing to deploy to the west coast. SEATAC is completely lost. San Francisco is reporting extensive flooding, with major quakes continually occurring. Much of the coast from San Diego to Los Angeles is under water from the massive tsunami of the Pacific strike. A rift is forming at the southern end of the San Andreas fault and the Gulf of California is moving north. Looks like Death Valley will flood, cutting off Southern California from Arizona. The base at Yuma has been evacuated along with much of southwestern Arizona and southeastern California.

"Military bases to the east are mobilizing to assist under U.S. command." Stopping to take a sip of water, the General sounded tired when she continued. "Unfortunately, we have little knowledge of conditions to the east. Communications are terrible. Civilian air travel is shut down, but I can route you through military installations to get you to Sheppard Air Force Base."

Ron turned to Katharine "Sheppard was chosen as the evacuation site for the UWG headquarters because of good logistics capability along with excellent security. As a training facility, it can accommodate the delegates. We hope that it is far enough from the natural disasters that are occurring, plus it has underground facilities for the tornadoes being predicted."

"When are you scheduled to deploy to the west coast?" asked Katharine.

"Our first convoy leaves by rail tonight. We're hoping to get past Yuma while the tracks and roads are still open. In three days, an additional unit will leave for the Los Angeles area."

Dismayed by the news, Katharine responded, "You know of the assistance Homakuwa offered during the disruptions caused by the Foundation. Would you be interested in having our residents assist in case communications are lost?"

Nodding in agreement, the General said, "Thank you. That might prove useful. How do you propose we meet up with them?"

"Let me talk this over with them. We can have our Altereds meet you. They can come in by sea, and since they are amphibious should prove helpful."

"Thank you, Madam Ambassador."

Leticia answered the inquiry. [I've been following the conversation, and we can dispatch Altereds on Travelers today, coordinating a meeting from here. Dahlfins could help in the totally submerged areas or any offshore assistance.]

Smiling with relief, Katharine said, "General, we will have Altereds and Dahlfins meet up with your troops on the coast. What frequency will your command be operating on?"

The General picked up her phone, spoke to someone, then relayed the information to Katharine.

[I've got it] said Leticia. [We'll be there in two days.]

Katharine advised the General.

Relief showed on the General's face, again thanking Katharine. Turning to Ron, she offered, "You should have food and rest before leaving for Sheppard. I'll arrange for rooms at the BOQ (Base Officer Quarters) for tonight and access to the Officer's Club. We'll have more information about conditions to the east in the morning. Lieutenant Nubaurer will be your escort while you're here. If you need anything, just let him know." Smiling, she added, "I need to get back to work."

Unsaid was the word 'dismissed,' but it was there. Grateful to have somewhere to rest, Katharine and Ron thanked her before leaving the room.

***

During breakfast in the morning, the Lieutenant approached, removed his cap from his close-cropped hair and asked if he could join them. They were given a short briefing. The news had changed little from yesterday. Communications were still spotty. The morning sky was darker than yesterday, and as the nose of the plane came up, a weak glow indicated east. The tower at Ft. Bliss had downloaded the flight plan and control into Ron's plane, and it climbed to the specified altitude.

Anxiously, Ron and Katharine looked below. The lights of towns passed indicating there was power. The glow in the east grew into a red circle as the sun rose. The land below was shrouded, impossible to make out. Three hours later, the radio crackled. "UW Gov 1, this is Sheppard tower. We have you on radar and will guide you in. Welcome to Sheppard AFB."

***

As a training facility, Sheppard Air Force Base had basic housing to accommodate the delegates. The Officers Club had been turned into the delegates' cafeteria. The worldwide communication system was made available for delegates to contact their home countries, though they had to rotate usage. Conditions were not perfect, but far better than a good part of the rest of the world.

Chapter 55

The logistics of a meeting of the UWG was difficult. Many delegates were the *de facto* new leaders of what remained of their countries. The large lecture hall had been converted to the UWG Assembly Hall. Although it not have individual microphones for each delegate, there were microphones at several locations throughout audience seating.

Ron and Katharine noticed the audio communications system was operating, but the holographic was not. They had power from the OPS which had withstood the ravages though much of the distribution systems had failed. The UWG president gave the opening remarks before introducing the chairman of his International Damage Assessment Committee, Olaf Stuvent. With his shaven head reflecting light like a beacon, he marched to the podium. Brushing his gray-streaked moustache, he cleared his throat and started.

"Ladies and gentlemen, I welcome you in these grave times. To those of you present and those of you listening, you are aware that the Earth has suffered a major calamity, with damage reports still coming in."

Behind him the large screen lit up with a map of the world. "In a quick summary of what we now know, fifty percent of our coastal cities suffered major damage." Red areas colored many of the coasts of the various continents. Only Australia and Antarctica were untouched by direct hits, but flooding had wiped out much of the coastal populations in Australia. "Several major cities have been utterly destroyed with the total loss of life." Red spots covered Paris, France and much of the United Kingdom.

"Other areas have been struck with major loss of life but not totally destroyed. Though the strikes in China were not on major cities, one caused a breach in the Three Gorges dam, and the Yangtze River flooded, destroying everything to Shanghai. Fires set off by the meteorites are ravaging the world's forests and grasslands. Skies are blackened by the detritus of this calamity." A view of the

Earth from space showed the cloud-enshrouded globe with occasional patches of blue. "Services are nonexistent."

With weariness in his voice, he continued, "We have very hard choices to make. Medical facilities are overwhelmed and stressed beyond limits. Industry is non-existent, the infrastructure has collapsed. Local governments have total authority where they exist at all. Martial law has been declared throughout most countries, but lawlessness is rampant." Pausing, he shrugged his shoulders, then continued, "I wish that was all the bad news."

"Things will not get better. The greatest peril for civilization is that the black skies will persist for several years. Without sunlight, we will lose the bottom of the food chain, which affects all species. We are facing starvation on a worldwide scale. In view of this projection, we propose a worldwide program to harvest all available crops immediately. Most herds of domesticated animals will perish, as will most wild species. To survive, we propose slaughter of all meat species.

"Preservation is the key to survival, so we must use every known method. That includes freezing, smoking, salting, canning, and irradiation. The grim reality is that even if we are able to harvest every scrap of food, we will lose at least fifty percent of the world's remaining population to starvation and disease."

Olaf took a deep breath and wiped at his eyes, distressed by the devastating information. "There is an ice age predicted. We expect to see frozen wasteland as far south as the 35th parallel in the northern hemisphere and as far north as the 40th parallel in the southern hemisphere. The ocean temperatures will drop. Without plankton and algae to maintain the animal species and oxygen levels, sea life populations will plummet.

"Rather than wait for them to die from inevitable starvation, we must harvest everything edible from the sea. Environmental laws have become meaningless. Man is now the endangered species. Scientists predict a dramatic swing from the ice age to extremely warm temperatures when the skies clear. The greenhouse gases released by the fires and the carbon dioxide liberated from the sea strikes will lead to global warming. This rapid swing in climates will lead to a mass extinction of most species left on the Earth. If we work hard, perhaps we will not be among them."

A hint of a smile crossed his face as Olaf continued. "But there is a bright side. The Orbital Power System suffered damage but still operates. The energy beams will be diminished as they penetrate the cloud layer, but usable power will be available. We will have fuels, wood from the dying forests, coal, and petroleum. Power for heat is available, enough to operate some greenhouses. It is imperative that we maintain plant species to re-seed the world. Sadly, the production from those greenhouses will only supply a fraction of the food needed.

"After a few years, we expect the skies to lighten enough to grow plants. Agriculture cannot begin until sufficient sunlight penetrates the cloud layer to sustain plants."

Raising the level of his voice, Olaf emphasized, "This is not a false doomsday prediction. This is the future, and we must prepare ourselves if we are to survive. A key to the survival of civilization is to maintain a strong United World Government presence. Without a government presence, the world will revert to warring tribes. I wish I could say we will not tolerate war, but the sad fact is starving people will do whatever it takes to survive.

Thank you for listening. For a report on the nation of Homakuwa, Katharine Levey will speak."

There was stunned silence as the image of a devastated world settled over the audience. Katharine brushed her hair from her eyes and adjusted the microphone when she took her place. "I'm Katharine Levey of Homakuwa. We too suffered destruction. Our city-states of Retseana and Zolynstra were destroyed. Several others suffered damage. The coming loss of the algae and plankton species will devastate our marine food system and may affect our oxygen supplies. The sea strikes liberated carbon dioxide and methane normally contained within the oceans which will further destroy the marine plant life. We hope the carbon dioxide release is not sufficient to smother low-lying lands, but we will have to wait to see. We believe these greenhouse gases will lead to a rise in the Earth's temperature. This is dire not only for Homakuwa, but for all of us. As to our Lunar Colony, I relay the status from Leticia Gardner." Katharine adjusted the microphone and Leticia's voice filled the room.

"First, I thank those nations who participated in the diversion of the major meteors from their destructive path. With your help we were able to prevent total destruction of life on the Earth. Sylvix, the ship we sent, was able to work with those who arrived in time to divert the largest objects.

"Our Lunar colony was damaged extensively, and the Orbiting Power System suffered damage, though we will be able to continue to beam power to earth. It is our intent to support that system and continue operation to the extent we can without Earth support. As you may know, the beam frequency will penetrate the water vapor clouds, but it will be scattered by the particulate. Still, enough power will reach Earth to help.

"Before the disaster, we began a program of building orbiting greenhouses in an effort to become as independent as possible. That program will be expanded to aid in maintaining species for the replanting of Earth. Because fungus is a species that does not require light, we will embark on a fungus development program. In addition, we plan to develop plants that thrive in low light conditions, so we can start replanting the Earth as soon as possible.

"Additionally, Homakuwa will assist in repairing the communication and Global Positioning System. We are in this together, and we will do what we can in this time of disaster. We will rebuild civilization, and this time it won't take 100,000 years." Katharine turned toward President Schmidt. "Thank you. Mr. President, I'll turn the dais over to you."

He rose to his full six foot height, brushed his gray moustache back and walked to the microphone. His angular face was somber. "I'm open to questions though I ask you to limit them to material we have not covered. If you wish to question the conclusions we reached or the details of how we arrived at this scenario, these subjects are addressed in our written report. Please don't ask me to justify these conclusions here; they were concluded as a result of logical deduction."

Chapter 56

After Sylvix had rounded the sun, she deployed her sails to carry her out to Earth orbit. [Homakuwa, this is Sylvix. I'm heading back with gifts.] Sylvix activated her sensors, so they could see the two large meteors accompanying her. One was water ice with methane, and the other was iron-nickel. Each had a sail attached.

[Will you need help parking them in orbit?] queried Leticia.

[I think not. I've had six months to aim and slow them. Just make sure Earth doesn't panic and shoot me down.]

With a smile in her voice, Leticia simply stated. [They haven't the capability anymore.]

Sylvix had been out of touch with Homakuwa for the entire trip, but upon reconnecting, she became aware that Earth existed in subsistence mode, barely able to maintain civilization.

Katharine spoke to her. [Sylvix, your return is being hailed by the survivors on Earth. You're being honored, and we're going to beam your arrival to the surface.]

Leticia added [It's also our opportunity to explain our plans, which aren't known outside of Homakuwa. Welcome back.]

The return was beamed to Earth from Sylvix's eyes. A hologram was projected to the assembled United World Government and around the world to all able to receive it. As Sylvix approached, the Earth grew larger, but it wasn't the beautiful blue ball of the past. Shrouded in clouds, only occasional patches of blue appeared. As she got closer, she saw the space around Earth was crowded. Hundreds of satellites orbited, mostly cylindrical and spinning slowly with large mirrors at the ends. The Orbital Power Satellites were also in place.

"As you can see," narrated Leticia to the world, "we've embarked on an extensive construction project. These orbiting habitats have been able to maintain flora and fauna species to repopulate Earth when it again is able to support them. Sylvix has returned with some of the meteors we redirected to miss Earth. We will use those to continue the habitat construction.

"I will take you through the construction process in time lapse." In the projection, a tug and several sleds neared an iron nickel meteor and started moving it toward a large mirror array. A laser lanced out and carved off a large chunk. The piece was moved into the middle of the mirror array, and the laser bored a hole through it. A tug started it spinning with the hole as an axis. The laser played over the wall of the hole, heating it.

The mirrors focused on the outside of the rotating chunk, and it began to heat. As the color of the spinning rock changed from gray to yellow to cherry in color, the force of the spinning caused it to expand, creating a cylindrical tube. When the diameter reached 500 meters, the mirrors were defocused as it continued to spin and cool. The rock formed into a long tube with a two-meter thick wall.

Another smaller chunk was carved from the meteor which was moved into the mirror array and spun. Again the mirrors were focused on it. This time, there was no hole, and the object flattened into a disc. When cooled, it was moved toward one end of the cylinder and pushed against it. Spinning together, the disc and the cylinder were fused together forming a cap. The process was repeated on the other end.

"There you have it, another habitat," said Leticia. Lasers cut doors in the ends and Constructs guided a glass tube made of moon silica down the center of the cylinder. As Earth watched, a parabolic mirror was attached to one end with another mirror at the focal point to beam the collected light down the glass tube to light the interior. The habitat began to spin slowly to give it a light gravity. "This habitat is now ready to be filled with everything necessary to sustain plant life. This process takes approximately four months and with several teams working, we have a shell from which to build a habitat.

"With the material Sylvix has brought back, we'll soon have more than fifty habitats. Most of those will remain in orbit here," stated Leticia. "The others will depart for Mars in about two months with a full contingent of Constructs. There will also be embryos and zygotes of many species. Sylvix will accompany the flotilla which will consist of the habitats, tugs, sleds and ships who are complete organisms like Sylvix.

"The transit time to Mars will be greater than three years. Once we enter orbit, we will use the two moons, Phobos and Deimos, as bases for larger habitats and begin to create species capable of living on Mars." Pausing for a second, she continued, "I can take a few questions."

The surface worlders had been so completely focused on their world they had no knowledge of any program by Homakuwa. They couldn't digest what had been presented. Finally there was one shaky voice. "You're going to Mars?"

Katharine answered. "Some of us are going to Mars, but we're staying here on Earth too. We are a part of Earth, and we belong here. If this disaster has taught us anything, it is that we cannot have our whole future in one place. For our civilization to survive, we must expand and grow."

"Are any humans going?"

"Humans were created by Earth and belong on Earth. To carry an Earth-like habitat for them to survive elsewhere is prohibitively difficult and can only be done on a small scale for explorative purposes. Homakuwa is going to Mars to live. We will, of course, share all that we learn with you."

Katharine sensed a spectrum of emotions ranging from betrayal to relief from the delegates which reflected those of Earth. There was envy and frustration at the inability of humans to embark on the program. Perhaps at some point the surface world could share in the Collective and experience Homakuwa, but that time was not now.

***

[You're going to be a mom, Leticia, along with all of us,] stated Sylvix.

[Yup! A lot of us are being inserted. Our mind will be imprinted, but the body will fit the environment, in this case the space habitat. Once we're ready to move into a new habitat, we'll do the same mix of new and old but with whatever physical body it takes to live there.]

Chapter 57

In what seemed an endless schedule of meetings, Ron and Katharine were again discussing the status of rebuild efforts throughout the world. A weary President Schmidt chaired the discussion.

"Since we ended our rescue program nine months ago, the expected explosion of deaths has occurred. The World Food Distribution Organization saved many lives, but seventy-five percent of the human population has perished. Many of those realized that the evacuation to refugee centers would merely prolong the inevitable. Instead of death by freezing or drowning, they would starve. They chose to remain in their homes.

"We are trying to stabilize the population with the resources we have. Our stockpiles of food are fully depleted, but our greenhouses, along with the edible fungus developed by Homakuwa, are able to keep up the supply. In addition, Homakuwa developed some new species based on those that inhabit the deep-sea volcanic vents. These species do not need light and form a basis for a new food chain.

"The Impact Winter still has us in a cycle of twilight and night. Finally, we are seeing indications the skies are lightening. The freeze and unending snowfalls left sheets of ice as far south as Tennessee in the U.S., southern France in Europe, and Wuhan in Asia, leaving large parts of the Earth frozen.. Entire countries no longer exist.

"Civilization will never be what it was before. Instead of the entire population being wiped out, we have the technology to adapt life to the Earthly conditions much faster than by the generational changes of natural selection. This is a new world. Katharine Levey of Homakuwa is here to speak about what's ahead."

Katharine pulled the microphone toward her. "In the midst of all the gloom we've been facing over the last year, I hope you see a ray of light. Yes, pun intended." There were a few low chuckles. Humor was so long forgotten it was foreign. "By maintaining the Orbiting Power System and using the extensive resources left to us, we managed to generate enough power to grow food to sustain small communities.

"The loss of the algae and plankton species of the sea resulted in a mass extinction of many marine species, but the loss of the oxygen production from the seas and the flora of the earth's surface had more dire circumstances. Fortunately, we have developed algae able to use the frequency of energy beamed from the OPS, and have started the process of building algae beds and collecting carbon dioxide from the atmosphere, hoping to head off the global warming cycle. We have an ongoing project to adapt algae to the conditions of Earth as they change to re-establish the base of the food chain. Plus we are developing grasses to distribute across the land as those areas become viable for life."

Looking around the room, Katharine continued, "We continue to create radically different greenhouse designs to re-establish farms. These communities will become the farms of the future, growing food and replenishing oxygen. Instead of being fast-growing, they are a direct food source with the essential nutrients for the human diet. Within a year, we anticipate supplying food to half of the human population."

Pausing to take a sip of water, Katharine smiled at the audience before continuing, "The meteorite strikes caused the ocean temperature to rise. Now the ice packs are shrinking. As the sky clears, Earth gradually warms, but we are in a race to balance the desired warming with the removal of greenhouse gases to prevent undesirable temperature rises.

"Plant species that adapt to the dim conditions are being developed which include rice, corn and wheat varieties. They are slow-growing due to the low light levels, but as the skies clear, their growth rates will increase. In addition, humans will be able to spread out as the world warms."

"We saved zygotes from many of the world's flora and fauna, and as conditions improve, we will release them or redesign them for the new conditions on Earth . We will re-seed the world, but it is up to us to grow in it wisely."

For the first time in months, there were smiles in the audience; a few people clapped their hands. Homakuwa had given them a glimmer of hope amidst the blackness.

What the human population was unaware of was that Homakuwa had participated in the destruction, suffering population losses due to the impacts and subsequent darkness and loss of food.

Those citizens not choosing to exist only in the Collective had been put into stasis until the environment could support them.

Chapter 58

"Greetings to both of you, and thank you for seeing me," the Prophet said when he arrived. His white robe whispered as he sat in the stiff-backed chair Ron led him to in the sitting room.

"Would you like tea?" Katharine asked. Knowing how rare tea was now, he smiled with pleasure. When Katharine returned with the steaming cup, they eagerly awaited his words.

"I'm sure you are wondering why I asked for this meeting. I know both of you will have presence on the upcoming trip away from Earth yet also remain here."

They glanced at each other. Outside of Homakuwa, nobody else knew of the ability of transference of those making up the group that had departed for Mars.

"You and Homakuwa need to understand the conditions that have transpired over the last year. Although you are keenly aware of the changes and destruction, there's something else you need to know that has to do with the people, the humans. Will you consent to this?" He waited for their reaction as he sipped his tea.

Not sure what he meant, Ron and Katharine glanced at each other before nodding their assent.

He put down his cup and pulled his chair close to them. "As you are aware, billions have died, and I have tried to ease that transition. I want you to understand what occurs during passage." Pausing, he said, "Perhaps you need your collars." They both donned them, and instantly the Homakuwa Collective was with them. The Prophet reached forward to take their hands in his. "Close your eyes."

At first they saw a grey fog. When it cleared, they were with the Prophet in a domed stadium, a monument to the days of large sporting events and audiences greater than 100,000. The area was dark, filled to overflowing with people, every available space packed. The cold seeped into them as they noticed the people were freezing. Everyone had the black of frostbite on their skin. The press of people around them was suffocating. Noticeably thin, Ron and Katharine realized they were starving. All hope was lost. In mute silence they stood, the only sound the hacking coughs of the ill. As they watched, suddenly, in the center of the dirt field below stood the Prophet. The people had drawn back, creating a clearing around him.

A soft glow enveloped the Prophet, and he rose above the floor of the huge arena. As the aura intensified it suffused through them like a warm current, bringing a sense of peace. When he raised his arms, the people in the arena started to whirl and rise. Clouds and grayness appeared over them, and below they could see heavy snow and endless ice in the city. Beyond the city, nothing but white showed.

They continued to rise, breaking through the clouds into a clear black sky, stars unblinking around them. Below, the cloud-enshrouded Earth shrank to a pinpoint and vanished. A smear of stars–the Milky Way–covered the blackness, and they started moving toward it. The stars whizzed past them as their speed increased until they became a blur. The galaxy brightened, the light intensifying as the stars around them became more dense and filled the blackness. In the center was a black spot, like an eye. On they went, the stars growing brighter until the light filled them. Their senses faded away, no sound, no touch, no sight, and the brightness faded into emptiness. Before them lay a concentration they could only sense as mind, and it opened and welcomed them in, gathering them as a loving parent gathers in children.

The feeling of peace and belonging was overpowering, and Ron and Katharine wanted to stay, but they were pulled back. Blinking, they opened their eyes. The Prophet sat before them. "This is why I am here–to show the way, to erase the fears. This is how I know mankind will change in the new Earth. You need to be aware of what has occurred at thousands of places across the Earth. Part of Homakuwa will stay, but it will also grow outward to other places. In part, I will be traveling with you, a presence you need only to call upon. But my main work is here with these children. Homakuwa must not forget that this is your origin and your home."

The shock of living through the mass deaths and the path the Prophet had guided them along had Ron and Katharine stunned. They could only nod as the Prophet rose to glide through the door. The Collective was silent, trying to absorb this, yet it would take decades before the true depth of the vision was understood.

Epilogue

Leticia, Kit, Ron, and Katharine looked through the ship's sensors as the Red Planet rotated beneath them. They opened their minds to project the vista to their Earth-bound selves through the Collective. Soon it would look like a home. The first fleet was in orbit with crews constructing habitats on Deimos and Phobos as well as mining materials to expand the orbital habitats. The first colonies would be on Mars within a year though subsurface until the greenhouses were operating.

The first lifeforms would resemble cockroaches more than any other Earth species. Cockroaches had survival capabilities that transcended eons. With the carbon dioxide rich atmosphere, Mars held much promise for thriving plant life. Jamie Wong was working on plants able to grow in ultra low pressure, low temperature with little water, and under harsh ultra violet light.

Mars was the immediate future, but they were looking beyond. Sylvix was again traveling, leading a group toward the asteroid belt to establish colonies there and bring back iron-nickel material for building. The Asteroid Belt was going to be populated, and a source of new space habitats.

Afterward, she would continue outward to Jupiter. The moons of the various outer planets and the dwarf planets would become habitats.

Kylex, a daughter of Sylvix, was leading a Venus mission to assess that planet and create an orbiting habitat around it. Mercury would be next for her. They were expanding into the Solar System. When time meant little because a lifespan was what one wanted, and the habitat was the ship, the Collective was moving out to meet the Solar System, and introduce the civilization of Homakuwa to it.

Though many of the species to inhabit the planets, moons, and asteroids of the Solar System would be too small to have the independent intelligence of Homakuwans, the Collective tied them together. The Collective was spreading throughout the Solar System, becoming an entity. The organism known as the star system of Sol was growing.

Beyond, the Galaxy awaited them, and they had forever to explore it.

ABOUT THE AUTHOR

ROBERT CLAYTON

After working as an engineer in mining and associated industries for almost thirty years, Bob Clayton moved into algae aquaculture and algae for biofuel. He designed, built and managed a small demonstration plant in Arizona for four years. Clayton continuously worked out of the norm leading to new and innovative designs for equipment and construction. This "Out of the box" thinking is apparent in his writing.

Having lived in Tucson, Arizona for more than fifty years, he's a true desert rat. Clayton's hobbies include cooking, reading, hiking, his 1929 Mercedes kit car, and old firearms. He and Linda have been married more than forty years and are going strong. His daughter and her family are the lights in his life.

NOTE FROM THE AUTHOR

On the following pages is an excerpt from *The Genesis,* the third volume in the *Evolution River Series.* Though *The Genesis* takes us eons into the future to the end of evolution, I have left room for a number of stories to take place. A whole series could be written around the life of the new species aboard Kahchk Kihhim. The Earth during the Catastrophe also is fertile ground for more tales. *The Genesis* has possibilities for more accounts of life on Earth as we try to recover and try to reestablish civilization after a devastation that scientists say is inevitable. Whether that occurs because of galactic events, biological events or due to our own destructive nature, changes in our environment beyond our ability to adapt will happen unless we take steps. It has happened numerous times in Earth's past. Earth's history is long, and ours is short. The lesson is that no species is permanent. The *Evolution River Series* opens our minds to one possibility of our distant future. As I wrote it, I came to see how possible it is, and how believable. It is a message I had to get out. Enjoy and open your minds to imagination.

The Genesis

The faint tickling within Sylvix's mind began to grow. It was alien. The Collective mind was curious, and she altered her course toward the nearest star system.

In the two hundred years since the Homakuwa species had expanded into the Sol star system from Earth, they sent out several star ships, all heading toward the center of the Milky Way galaxy. They had yet to encounter sentient beings.

Some of these starships were colonies–space nomads–while others were sole being star ships. Sylvix was an organism grown as a starship with the purpose of expanding Homakuwa and the Collective mind. Sylvix <u>was</u> the starship. She had left the Sol star system with the goal of reaching the center of the Milky Way galaxy more than a century before, though time measured in years ceased to have meaning.

Sylvix was part of the Collective mind and though her physical self was the starship, her mind was part of Homakuwa. As her species had grown throughout their home star system, their Collective mind allowed them to be part of a whole entity that was now made up of the Sol star system. It now consisted of more than the individual beings existing within the Solar system.

At her velocity of 0.5 light-speed, she must begin braking now in order to investigate. Sylvix deployed her sails and reoriented to begin braking. At her deceleration rate, it would take every bit of the distance to the star system to slow enough to orbit.

Most of the organisms of the Collective mind were light years away. Unlike the Collective mind, distance affected this "touch," and it became stronger as she neared the system. She mentally constructed a protective a shell around it, holding it apart to examine, like a specimen under a bell jar. It was small and seemed to writhe, making it difficult to study.

Leticia Gardner was "with" her today. Physically, Leticia was in the Sol star system on Earth, but through the Collective mind, they were linked.

Sylvix: [Leticia, what do you make of it?]

Leticia: [It's quite different from us. Our Collective mind is a conglomeration of individuals. This feels like a single presence. Can you feel anything?]

Sylvix: [Right now, it feels like an itch I can't scratch. I don't detect any sentience, just the presence. It is growing, though, and I'm not sure it's because I'm getting closer to the star system.]

Leticia: [Do you feel any menace?]

Sylvix: [All I feel is its existence. It just seems to be there, but it is definitely growing. I sense no thought within it. I will enlarge the shell around it, and then I need to focus on the maneuvering and braking.]

Leticia: [I'll keep watching it. You take us into the system.]

Through Sylvix's sensors, the Collective saw that the star system was a single Sol type sun with six planets and six planetoids. They did not detect a star system entity, but the presence emanated from the fourth planet, the one with an atmosphere.

Sylvix: [That's the one I'll orbit.]

Sylvix was totally focused on controlling the one thousand square miles of sails using the solar wind to slow herself. Leticia's warning came too late. The presence exploded through the shell, and a lance of pure pain shot into Sylvix's mind, searing her.

Leticia: [Pull out! Pull out! Pull out!] she heard through the blinding pain.

Sylvix: [Help me!] she sent, but there was no answer. For the first time in centuries, she was alone. The presence detonated within her mind, shattering her into small fragments. Frantically she tried to pull the pieces together. It didn't work. Sylvix the star ship ceased to exist.

Leticia: [NOOOOOO!] she screamed. Desperately, she tried to shut off the conduit from the Collective mind that had been linked to Sylvix. A squirming tendril tried to worm through. Leticia closed off her own mind, building a tight cocoon around herself. She had to isolate her mind from the Collective. The shield was tight, but she was trapped inside with the presence. Unlike Sylvix, she did sense something within the presence. Hunger.